MUSIC

AND

MALICE

IN

Hurricane

-Town-

For my parents,
for taking me to New Orleans
when I most needed to go.
I hope we find ourselves on
Bourbon Street again one day.

STRIPES PUBLISHING LIMITED
An imprint of the Little Tiger Group
1 Coda Studios, 189 Munster Road, London SW6 6AW

A paperback original
First published in Great Britain in 2019

ISBN: 978-1-84715-960-1

Text copyright © Alex Bell, 2019
Cover image © shutterstock.com

A CIP catalogue record for this book is available from the British Library.

Printed and bound in the UK.

10 9 8 7 6 5 4 3 2

MUSIC AND MALICE IN

Hurricane Town

ALEX BELL

Stripes

CHAPTER ONE

"Are you Jude Lomax?"

Jude spat a mouthful of blood on to the cobbles and squinted up at the scruffy boy standing over her. "Who's asking?" she grunted. She prodded cautiously at her tooth with her tongue, causing it to wobble in its socket.

"Benny sent me," the boy said, waving an envelope around. "Said to look for a red-headed girl. Said she'd probably be in a fight or in the gutter."

Jude scowled. She was in no mood for wise guys. "Just give me the message and clear off," she snapped.

The boy shrugged and dropped the envelope on the dirty cobbles in front of her before turning on his heel and leaving. Jude managed to sit up and prop herself against the nearby wall. It smelled like someone had taken a pee against it but she couldn't even be bothered to wrinkle her nose. Every part of her ached – her ribs, her head, her shoulders and her soul too, come to that. Blood dripped into her eye from a cut on her forehead, it hurt to breathe and nausea churned in her stomach. What a shit of a morning it had been. What a shit of a life, really.

She glanced around the street to make sure Sidney Blues Sampson had gone and wasn't about to come out and take his boot to her again. There was no sign of him. It appeared her landlord had finally left, now that he'd delivered his threats and his kicking.

The night before, Jude had gone to play at Moonfleet Manor as usual but when she turned up at the front door, her trumpet case beneath her arm, she'd been turned away. The master was not having a good day, Paris had said, a familiar sneer on her perfect lips.

Jude's heart had sunk straight into her boots, she'd been relying on that money, but there was nothing to be done except try to find work at short notice elsewhere. So she made her way to every jazz club and honkytonk in the Hurricane Quarter, every goodtime house and creep joint in the meatpacking district, every midnight supper club and gambling den in the vampire's Ruby Quarter, and every steamship and pleasure boat moored at Paradise Pier. But nobody wanted a trumpet player.

Walking back through Cadence Square that night

she'd noticed a plate of congri, black-eyed peas with rice, placed beneath the sycamore trees, surrounded by a circle of silver coins. Her stomach had rumbled at the sight of the food and her fingers itched at the sight of the money, but she'd walked right on past and left it there, just like every other sensible person in Baton Noir. They all knew it had been placed there by someone who practised cajou – that strange, dark, powerful magic no ordinary person dared mess with. To take that money, or food, would be to invite disaster into your life.

She had arrived home in the morning only to find her landlord waiting for her. And he'd been in no mood to listen to explanations about the late rent. No mood at all.

Once Jude's head finally stopped spinning, she picked up the envelope the boy had dropped, tore it open and pulled out the letter. As she skimmed its contents her heart lifted. There was to be a jazz funeral, and the Done and Dusted Brass Band had been asked to play in it. That meant work, a pay cheque and not getting the living crap beaten out of you because you were behind on bills. But then Jude scanned down the letter for the details and her elation quickly vanished. The funeral was now, today. There were no canals in that part of town so she couldn't even take the swamp boat. She'd have to run halfway across Baton Noir to have any hope of making it, and right now she felt as if she could barely manage to hobble back to her own front door.

She groaned and gritted her teeth. There was no choice. She couldn't afford to miss this. Jazz funerals were only for Baton Noir's more important and distinguished citizens, and who knew how much longer it might be until another one of them snuffed it?

She dragged herself to her feet and hurried back up the stairs to the tiny apartment. To her relief, her pa still hadn't emerged from his bedroom and she was able to get changed, snatch up her trumpet and get out of the door in record time. Before she left the house, though, she scrubbed their front step with brick dust from the bucket kept by the door for that sole purpose. Such a practice was said to ward off any hexes or curses put on the home by an enemy. Jude didn't know whether she completely believed it, but she scrubbed their porch each morning just the same. Even on a day like today, when every second counted.

And then it was simply a question of running as fast as she could. It was blisteringly hot and she could feel sweat trickling down the back of her shirt between her shoulder blades. The blue brass band uniform she wore was sticky and uncomfortable in the scorching heat. The military-style peaked black cap kept sliding into her eyes and her bow tie hung crooked, the lace-up St Jacques flats on her feet vigorously rubbing away the skin of her right ankle.

But if she let herself slow down or rest then she'd miss the funeral. She would just have to fight through the pain, that was all. She would damn well make that funeral, even if it killed her to get there. She let herself think of all the things she was so furious about, and the anger was like a flame that fuelled her determination and made her run faster.

"Girl, you gotta find some way of letting go of all that anger you carry around," her best friend Sharkey kept saying to her. "It's gonna get mighty heavy otherwise. Even going to get you killed, maybe."

Jude knew that the anger was destructive but sometimes it felt like a wild beast she couldn't control no matter how hard she tried, and other times it almost felt like a friend that helped her struggle past the point where she wouldn't have been able to struggle any further otherwise. So her feet pounded along the ground, the sweat ran down her back and she was glad of the pain and the chance to burn.

She knew she'd reached the Hurricane Quarter by the music. Jazz lived in this part of the city day and night, spilling out from the doorway of every club and honkytonk. It played on juke boxes and phonographs, and scratched and crackled from radios in the barber shops and shoeshine stands. The air smelled of stale rum, the onions that were already sizzling on the greasy griddles of the hot-dog carts, cheap perfume and sweating oyster barrels that had been left out for too long in the smouldering sun.

Jude loved it all. She loved every cobble, every weathered plank of wood, every iron balcony and crooked street, every hot-dog stand and flower box, every neon sign and lamp post. For all that cajou had warped and corrupted Baton Noir, it was still the most wonderful city in the world, as far as Jude was concerned.

Finally she skidded round the corner to the Done and Dusted Brass Band headquarters. She was starving and had been hoping there might be a few spare minutes to scoot into the kitchen and grab a steaming cup of chicory coffee and a sugary beignet, but the funeral was ready to begin. Everyone was getting into position in lines before the coffin, which rested in a shiny black carriage. Like all of the carriages in Baton Noir, this one was horseless

6

and had a long rope attached to the front for four strong human bearers to pull along.

Jude noticed that she didn't seem to be the only one who was late. There were quite a few members of the band missing. Sharkey was there, however, dripping in cajou charms from head to toe, as usual. They hung from chains around his neck, were pinned to the front of his band jacket and dangled from bracelets on his skinny wrists. His skin was coal-black and his cheekbones were so striking that he normally had at least three girls lusting after him at any one time. Jude wasn't one of them (despite what her ex-boyfriend had thought). She'd known Sharkey, or Kerwin as he'd been back then, since she was five and he was seven. He was like an annoying older brother to her.

Despite the fact that he was every bit as poor as she was, he had a distinguished way of carrying himself, soulful brown eyes and a straight patrician nose. His family had lived in Baton Noir for so long that even Sharkey's accent was gumbo-flavoured. He played the saxophone in the row behind her, and Jude raised her hand in greeting as she took her place and gasped for air.

"Cutting it a bit close, darlin'?" Sharkey remarked,

raising an eyebrow. Then he took in her appearance, frowned and added, "Barely even midday. Bit early for scrapping, ain't it?"

"I wasn't scrapping," Jude replied, breathless. "This time."

Sharkey gave her a doubtful look and Jude could hardly blame him. She got into fights a lot, and normally because she had sought them out herself. It wasn't difficult to find a fight in Baton Noir. And a lot of the time, punching something seemed to be the only way to blank out the thoughts and worries inside her own mind, even if just temporarily.

"Honestly," Jude said. "It wasn't my fault. My landlord beat me up."

Sharkey's eyes narrowed. "You all right?"

She shrugged. "I've been better. Where is everyone anyway?"

"Some turned it down. Said it weren't worth the risk, even with the danger pay thrown in."

Jude frowned. "Danger pay?" she repeated, wiping sweat from her forehead. "But whose funeral is this?"

Sharkey looked startled. "Don't you know?"

Jude shook her head. She hadn't read the message properly in her haste.

Her friend leaned forward, causing his charms to

jingle together. "It's the cajou queen," he said in a low tone.

"Ivory Monette?"

Sharkey nodded. "Went and got herself murdered last night."

Jude was astonished. Ivory Monette was one of the city's most powerful players and wielders of magic. Untouchable, or so she'd thought. She had seen her at Moonfleet Manor on more than one occasion.

"Where did it happen?" she asked.

"At the Blue Lady."

The Blue Lady was a jazz club on Moonshine Boulevard where, by all accounts, the cocktails were strong, the clientele were dangerous and the jazz was hot.

"People are saying she won't go to her grave quietly," Sharkey went on. "That's why half the band ain't here."

Jude snorted. "Cowards."

A live cajou queen might be a force to be reckoned with, but a dead one was just a lump of meat like everyone else in Jude's opinion. When she said as much to Sharkey he shook his head and said, "I wouldn't be so sure."

Like most people in Baton Noir he was a great believer in cajou. Two years ago he'd pawned the beloved diamond sock suspenders he'd inherited from his uncle in order to buy a powerful charm to make him into a better musician. After that, he was the only person in the band skilled enough to play the fiendishly difficult jazz piece, *Sharkbite Sally* – hence his nickname.

Unfortunately, Jude's ex-boyfriend Leeroy Lamar was one of the band members who had decided to show up. A smug-faced and handsome drummer with pale skin and cruel eyes, Leeroy was the one and only boyfriend Jude had ever had. The relationship had been toxic and unhealthy from the start, a disaster, enough to make Jude feel that she never wanted to date anyone else ever again. She could still hear his voice inside her head sometimes, those words that had wormed their way beneath her skin and bitten down deep into her bones. The dawning realization that what she had first taken for love and concern was in fact nothing more than a determination to control every aspect of her life.

"*Where the hell were you?*" he'd hissed that final evening, stale beer strong on his breath, his fingers clamped too hard on her skin.

She felt a little bit sick every time she saw him now but there was no avoiding him unless she quit the band, which she absolutely refused to do. She would die before she gave him that satisfaction.

When Leeroy saw her, he leaned over to his friend Ollie and whispered something. The two of them worked together as clerks at the same fancy hospital in the Fountain District. They both laughed at Leeroy's comment and then turned to look at Jude, smirking. She glared back, hating him, hating the way he was somehow able to make her feel so worthless and small, hating how he had scraped out her soul with his cruelty and chipped away at the self-confidence she'd always been able to rely on before.

Leeroy turned and whispered something else to Ollie and they both burst out laughing. Jude felt her ears burning, certain that Leeroy had probably just made some crass, lewd comment about her. Why the hell had she ever let him see her naked? What had she ever seen in him in the first place? How could she have been so unbelievably *dumb*?

Sharkey leaned forward from the row behind and said in his lazy drawl, "Say, fellas, I know you ain't got no more class between you than a can of beans, but if you don't stop that giggling you're gonna feel the blunt end of my boot up your ass."

Leeroy and Ollie stopped sniggering abruptly. Everyone knew that Sharkey boxed when he wasn't in the band and that he somehow seemed to win every fight in the ring, despite his lanky frame and gentle nature. Perhaps he had a cajou charm for that too but either way no one really wanted to cross him in a fight. Leeroy and Ollie scowled but turned back round in their positions without saying anything more.

Jude threw Sharkey a grateful look and seconds later the bandmaster gave the signal and they were off. Although the band was reduced in numbers, the remaining musicians did their best to make up for it and the jazz funeral proceeded through the Hurricane Quarter in a noisy, boisterous group. First there was the brass band, then the coffin and then the mourners following on behind. As usual, there were plenty of bystanders lining the sidewalks to watch the procession pass by, but something felt a little different this time.

Normally the spectators would be dancing and singing and calling out to one another. Jazz funerals were a lively, vibrant, joyous affair after all. But today the people were mostly just standing in silence, staring with sullen eyes at the coffin as it passed by.

There was a taut, expectant feeling in the air, as if a violin string had been wound too tight. You could almost hear it whining and straining to snap. Jude supposed Ivory Monette had had her share of enemies.

She'd been murdered after all. And it was well known that she dealt in hexes and curses just as much as love potions and good luck charms.

Some of the bystanders wore the red crown charm marking them out as members of the so-called magical Royalty. It was hard to tell what they were just by looking, except for the vampires who gave themselves away by lurking in the shade beneath the wrought-iron balconies. Other than that, they could be anything: witch doctors, cajou priests, conjurers, even descendants – people with the legba blood of cajou spirits in them somewhere.

Jude recognized some of the spectators. There was Doctor Herman, a renowned witch doctor, with his long hair in elaborate knots on top of his head. Within these he carried his various *gris-gris* – tiny bags filled with powders – as well as dried lizards, animal bones and even a small owl's head. He was known to throw the owl's head at people who displeased him, so Jude was glad to walk on past as quickly as possible.

As they marched on down the street, Jude began to find it more and more of an effort to lift her knees up high. It was terribly hot – the collar of her shirt seemed as if it was throttling her. Her stomach grumbled and she felt faded and thin, like a pencil drawing that was being slowly erased. The feeling only got worse when they marched past Cadence Square, where the food market was. The humid air was full of the smell of pecan pies and sticky, nutty, golden, delicious pralines filled with coconut or caramel popcorn.

Jude's anger had fuelled her before but now it was like a firework that'd had its burst of colours and sparks and was fizzling away into thin trails of smoke. Sweat dripped into her eyes and she couldn't clear her vision. The ground wobbled beneath her and all the strength ran out of her legs like water. Everything went slow and stretched as melting tar, and Jude sank forward on to her knees.

Sharkey was immediately beside her, gripping her by the collar and hauling her to her feet. He pulled her back into his row and gave her his arm to lean on.

"When did you last eat, girl?" he said, leaning close to Jude's ear to be heard above the band.

Jude shook her head. She couldn't remember. She couldn't think straight.

Sharkey huffed at her. "You should've asked me for help. Now, listen, do you think you can make it through to the cemetery? If you can just keep up with everyone then you'll still get paid. It ain't that far."

Jude nodded. She had to get paid. She just had to.

She seemed to have lost the power of speech and her trumpet hung loosely from her hand. She was dangling right at the end of her rope, running on empty.

It seemed to take an age to reach the St Clémence Cemetery, where Ivory Monette was to be laid to rest in her family crypt. But finally the charm gates marking the entrance came into view. The twin iron gates were ten feet tall and completely covered in mojo hands, amulets and cajou poppets. Some were designed to ward off evil or silence the dead, while others were offerings to gain favour with the spirits. They were all different shapes and sizes and colours. An eclectic assortment of witchcraft and cajou. Jude breathed a sigh of relief because they were almost there, it was almost over.

But the moment the bandmaster passed through the charm gates at the front of the procession, a rotten and appalling scream started up. It cut through the band like a knife, silencing the music as the musicians all faltered to a stop, leaving only that blistering shriek filling the air. It was an insane sound, consumed with torment and rage, a scorching inferno of hatred and bile.

"Good gods, where is it coming from?" somebody gasped.

Everyone stared around, looking for the culprit. Most people immediately turned to the coffin itself, as if they thought perhaps Ivory Monette wasn't dead at all and had suddenly woken to find herself entombed in a velvet-lined prison. But the scream wasn't coming from the coffin. It was coming from the charm gates.

"There!" Sharkey cried, pointing.

They all followed the direction of his finger to a poppet that had been tied to one of the gate's iron poles. It was, unmistakeably, supposed to represent Ivory Monette herself. The little doll was about the size of Jude's palm and made from a sewn cloth bag adorned with colourful beads and buttons. It had many bright turbans wound around its head, long flowing skirts and big hoops in its ears. Cajou poppets usually had shapeless lumps for hands, but this one had actual fingers, with dozens of tiny rings sparkling from them. But what really identified the poppet as Ivory Monette was the big white snake on its shoulders.

The Monette women had been cajou queens of Baton Noir for generations. Every year, on the sacred evening, Cajou Night, a queen would be picked from the city's inhabitants by a magical pair of cajou snakes – creatures from the spirit world who were said to represent Daa, the Snake-God himself, the sky father and original creator of the universe. Although Daa had long since left their world to be run by the legba, he still picked the one human on the planet who would be crowned and allowed to see and speak to the legba directly.

It was common for queens to rule for the duration of their lives, and this had been the case with Ivory. The Cajou Night ceremonies had mainly been a formality. She had owned the pair of snakes, until the black one mysteriously disappeared some twenty years ago. For the whole of Jude's lifetime, Ivory had only appeared with one snake, a twelve-foot-long albino python named Beau. And this was the one draped around the poppet's shoulders.

Cajou dolls were inanimate objects. Everyone knew that. They had no actual life of their own. And yet there the Ivory Monette poppet was, with its eyes bulging and its sack mouth open wide and the loudest scream in the world coming from its throat.

People were muttering and moving away from the cemetery, eager to put some distance between themselves and whatever dark magic this was.

"What do we do?" one of the band members asked.

"Keep going!" Benny, the bandmaster, called from the front.

He turned and marched through the charm gates, straight past the screaming poppet. After a moment's hesitation, the rest of the band resumed playing and followed him. The music helped to drown out the scream to some extent, but you could still hear it.

When it was Jude and Sharkey's turn to walk through, Jude saw that the poppet had bright green buttons sewn on to its face for eyes. As she met the doll's gaze, those eyes seemed to get bigger and bigger until they filled Jude's vision entirely. Everything else fell away – the cemetery, the band, the poppet, the gates. The entire world, in fact. Just melted away like fog, leaving only Jude and the poppet. Staring at each other.

Finally the poppet's mouth snapped shut and the scream abruptly stopped.

CHAPTER TWO

Jude found herself sprawled on the dry, crumbly earth beneath one of the drooping ancient trees that filled the graveyard. Baton Noir preferred to bury its dead above ground and the space was filled with stone crypts and marble tombs. The air beneath the shade of the branches felt cooler and easier to breathe. She found herself sucking it in in big gulps.

"That's it," Sharkey said and Jude realized he was kneeling beside her. "You just take nice deep breaths."

He helped her sit up and the tree trunk felt reassuringly solid behind her back.

"What happened?" Jude asked. "Where's everyone else?"

"You keeled over, that's what," Sharkey replied. "As for everyone else, they're off putting madam in her crypt before she can climb out of her coffin and start hexing everyone. Here, take this."

He passed her his flask, which was full of sweet iced tea. Jude sipped it gratefully, feeling the cool, sugary liquid glide down her throat

"Did that poppet really start screaming?" Jude asked, lowering the flask. "Or did I dream it?"

"It happened, all right," Sharkey replied. "Creepiest damned thing I ever saw."

"What does it mean?" Jude asked.

Sharkey waved the question away. "Beats me," he said. "And who cares anyhow? I'm more interested in you at the moment. Feelin' any better?"

Jude nodded. She *was* feeling better, actually. The shade and the sweet tea and the rest had taken the edge off, even if she still felt like she was recovering from the flu.

"Got you a present yesterday," Sharkey said, drawing a small pouch from his pocket and handing it to her.

"That better not be what I think it is," Jude said, eyeing it with distaste.

Sharkey didn't say anything so she opened the strings at the neck of the pouch and shook out the small object inside. It was a delicate silver bracelet with a single charm in the shape of a snowflake.

"It's a cool-headed charm," Sharkey said, an obstinate edge to his voice. "Meant for hotheads like you who can't control their anger."

Jude rolled her eyes. "I know what it is." She thrust the bracelet back towards her friend. "I don't wear cajou charms. You know that."

In fact, she was the only person in the Done and Dusted Brass Band who didn't own a single musical charm. From time to time she'd hear one of the others muttering that it was all an act and that she must keep her charms hidden, sewed into the lining of her jacket, filling her pockets or tucked into her panties. But Jude didn't care what anyone else thought. *She* knew that her musical ability came from her and her alone, and that was enough.

"You're your own worst enemy, you know," Sharkey said.

"Yeah."

"I'm not an idiot," he said. "I know this little charm probably ain't enough by itself. But it can't hurt, can it?"

Jude said nothing. The simmering anger she'd carried around for the last eight years had recently got worse and worse, almost without her even noticing. All her grievances bubbled up to the surface and she wasn't able to control them. She picked fights she couldn't win. She got hurt and she bled and she didn't care.

Sharkey peered into her face. "I could just murder that Leeroy Lamar."

"Don't do that," Jude said wearily. "I was angry long before he came along. He's not responsible."

And he's not all bad, some small, treacherous part of her wanted to say. *He made me feel special once.*

That was the worst thing about it all, really. The fact that sometimes she still had confused feelings of affection for Leeroy mixed in with the dull ache of humiliation. It was still hard, even now, to accept that she could have got him so wrong.

"Didn't help none, though, did he?" Sharkey grunted. "What with being a good-for-nothin' asswipe."

That boy'll break your heart if you let him, Sharkey had warned Jude when she'd first started seeing Leeroy. And he'd been right.

"I wish you'd let me buy a conjure ball to roll across his yard," Sharkey went on.

"No," Jude said with a small smile. "No conjure balls."

Sharkey returned her smile. Then he put his hand on her shoulder and squeezed.

"Something has to change, beautiful one," he said. "You're getting dragged down to a no-good place. You gotta stop all this fighting and raging at the world."

"I know," Jude replied. "I want to change. It's just

that it's harder … much harder than I ever expected it to be." She saw herself through Sharkey's eyes and it made her feel all used up and spat out. All of a sudden it was difficult to meet his gaze but Sharkey moved his hand to her chin and wouldn't let her look away.

"No need for shame, darlin'," he said softly. "Not with me. I can be every bit as much of a stubborn son-of-a-bitch as you can. And I ain't letting you go down like this, you hear me? I ain't."

"I am trying," Jude said, her voice barely more than a whisper. "Sofia has been teaching me some exercises—"

"And that's great," Sharkey replied. "But it ain't enough. You know it ain't. Jude Lomax, you need all the help you can get, so you're goddamn gonna let me help you any way I can."

He pressed the snowflake charm back into her trembling palm. "Look at me," he said, his dark brown eyes gazing into hers. "I'm on my knees begging you to wear it. Do it for me, even if you don't wanna do it for yourself right now."

Jude found herself taking the charm. Actually taking it. Something she never ever thought she'd do. But then, lots of things hadn't gone to plan.

She put the bracelet in her pocket. "I'll think about it," she said.

Sharkey nodded. "That'll have to do for now I guess."

There was movement on the other side of the cemetery and they looked up to see that the mourners seemed to be dissipating. The funeral was over. Sharkey jogged over to get their pay packets from Benny and then returned to Jude. Her entire body still throbbed from the beating she'd taken earlier and she felt absolutely awful, but she was back on her feet, and that was a start.

"Late lunch?" Sharkey asked, tilting his head to indicate the Dead Duck café just over the road.

As they made their way back through the charm gates, Jude looked for the cajou queen poppet, but it had vanished. When she asked Sharkey what had happened to it, he shrugged.

"Probably got swiped by some ghoul," he said. "Or one of the family. Perhaps they'll keep it on the mantelpiece to remember her by."

Jude didn't know much about Ivory Monette's family, apart from the fact that she'd had a daughter who'd rejected cajou and left Baton Noir, but Ivory's granddaughter, Charity Monette, was still here.

They walked over to the Dead Duck, took a table by the window and ordered coffee and beignets.

"Looks like you took quite a battering," Sharkey

remarked, eyeing Jude across the table.

Jude shrugged and prodded her tooth with her tongue, hoping it might have magically re-rooted itself. Unfortunately it still wobbled in her gum, and stung like anything.

"No worse than I've had before," she replied.

"Your landlord is a no-good piece of shit," Sharkey said.

"Yeah."

"Weren't you supposed to be playing for the Monster of Moonfleet last night?"

Jude rolled her eyes. "I wish you wouldn't call him that."

"Well, that's what he is, ain't he?"

Moonfleet Manor had a dire reputation in Baton Noir. Everyone knew that the Majstro family who owned the house were all mad. The blood of a cool legba flowed through their veins, and not just any cool legba, but Krag himself.

It would have been over-simplifying it to say that warm legba were good and cool legba were evil, but it was a pretty good starting point for people who were new to Baton Noir. Some people said that the legba were cajou spirits, while others claimed that warm legba had started off as angels and the cool legba had once been devils, before the world became godless.

Krag ruled over the cool legba and people were wary of his descendants because of the prophecy that, one day, one of them would unleash the chaos horses of the apocalypse and bring about the end of the world.

There was no denying that the Majstros were a warped and wicked family. Fifty years earlier, a police raid had uncovered a nightmarish scene. Terribly mutilated people tortured in the attic – several of them still alive, still breathing, although some had had limbs removed, while others had had additional limbs sewn on, the subjects of ghoulish experiments. Violetta Majstro was hanged for these crimes but there had been other Majstros living in the house at the time and, because of the strange way descendants aged, it was difficult to know whether any of them were still alive.

It wasn't just that descendants had a longer potential lifespan, sometimes the aging process seemed to pause too. This could happen when they were anything from five years old to ninety, and could last for many years. It was therefore almost impossible to know exactly how old a descendant actually was.

André Majstro, otherwise known as the Phantom of Moonfleet, seemed to be the only one now left at the house. Everyone said he was disfigured and deformed, and he was rarely seen in public, hence his unfortunate nickname. Even Jude had never laid eyes on him, though she'd been working at Moonfleet for a month now.

Her pa had been livid when she'd received the offer. "Don't you even *think* of going to that wretched place," he'd said. "They're devil people! He'll want something from you. And how did he even find out where you live, eh?"

"He says he heard the Done and Dusted Brass Band play and he asked Benny for my address," Jude had replied.

"You will not go to that place, Jude," her pa had said. "Not while you live under this roof."

So Jude had meekly agreed that of course she wouldn't go, and then had lied about getting a job elsewhere and gone straight to Moonfleet anyway. She'd made many mistakes in her life, but she'd never been dumb enough to turn down paid work.

"This'll tide us over for a while anyway," Jude said now, pulling her pay packet from her pocket.

In her head she was already doing the mental calculations for how much money they needed to keep them going until Cajou Night in a few days' time. She knew that she, and every other musician in the city, would have work then.

"How much is this danger pay anyway?" she asked. The envelope definitely looked fatter than usual.

"About half again," Sharkey replied. He took a nail file from his pocket and began filing his already perfectly shaped nails. "Ivory Monette requested us special."

"She did?"

Jude was surprised. They were a decent enough band, sure, but they couldn't compete with the likes of the Ruby Red Brass Band, the Okey Poke Marching Band or the Drunken Devil.

"Perhaps she realized the fellas would be antsy about playing?" Sharkey suggested. "Worried about being cursed or hexed or the like. A poorer band like us is more likely to be swayed by the danger pay."

"I guess that must be it."

Jude looked down at the envelope in her hand. Having seen the way that poppet had come to life, she was starting to think that perhaps she shouldn't have scoffed at the idea of being hexed from beyond the grave after all.

"I'm going to give Sidney the rent straight away," she said, stuffing the envelope back in her pocket. "He'll only demand more interest otherwise."

"I'll come with you," Sharkey said, standing up.

"You don't need to do that," Jude replied.

"I ain't got a thing to do for the rest of the day," Sharkey said firmly. "I'm comin' with you."

So they made their way to the Fountain District, with its rows of elegant white-columned houses and manicured gardens. Sharkey waited on the sidewalk with his hands in his pockets while Jude delivered the money to Sidney's unsmiling butler.

When she rejoined her friend she immediately noticed a man standing a few yards away, leaning on a lamp post. It was the middle of the afternoon but he wore formal black evening wear, a silk top hat and a pair of smoked dark glasses. A watch chain hung from his pocket; he carried a jackal-topped cane in one hand and a cigarette in the other. It was hard to tell with the dark glasses but it very much looked as if he was watching them through the haze of his cigarette smoke. The moment Jude's gaze fixed on his face, his mouth slowly stretched into a lazy grin.

Jude felt the skin at the back of her neck prickle.

"How long has he been there?" she asked.

"Who?" Sharkey replied.

"That man dressed up like—" Jude broke off. He had suddenly disappeared, leaving only cigarette smoke behind. "Oh. He's gone." She looked up and down the street but could see no sign of him. "There was a man there, dressed up like Baron Lukah."

Sharkey pulled a face. "Why would anyone dress up like Baron Lukah?"

Baron Lukah was perhaps the most famous cool legba of them all, the legba of death. He was always depicted in evening wear with a top hat and smoked glasses. He loved cigarettes and swamp whisky and carried a pocket watch to keep track of when people's time was up.

Ever since the Snake-God left, the world had been ruled over by identical twin brothers, Ollin and Krag. Ollin was the prince of the warm legba and controlled all the spirits of the day, and Krag commanded the cool legba, the spirits of the night. Known as the evil master of the crossroads, he was responsible for allowing the crossing of all bad luck, misfortune, destruction, injustice and suffering into the world.

The brothers were always depicted as two old black men, wearing suits that had seen better days and wide-brimmed straw hats. They both carried smoking pipes that they puffed on lazily. In paintings, they usually appeared on opposite sides of the spiritual crossroads.

One of the only noticeable differences between them was that Ollin was often accompanied by a faithful, grey-muzzled elderly dog, for dogs were sacred to Ollin. Krag had an owl on his shoulder and sometimes carried a horsewhip, with which to command the chaos horses of the apocalypse. The horses that would one day devour the world.

Jude was amazed that anyone in Baton Noir would have the nerve to dress as Baron Lukah. She shook her head and tried to dismiss the unease that still prickled over her skin as they walked back to the streetcar. As usual the Citizen section of the car was packed, forcing them to squash tightly in with all the other passengers. Jude ended up with her face practically buried in a large man's armpit and couldn't help casting resentful looks beyond the velvet rope to the Royalty section, which had actual seats and was half empty.

How many times had she witnessed a doddery old lady clutching one of the poles and trembling as she tried to stay upright, while perfectly strong and healthy vampires, witches or descendants sprawled comfortably on their chairs not giving a damn?

"It's just the way things is," Sharkey would say, whenever she brought it up. "And there ain't a bit of use stressin' and frettin' about the way things is."

When they returned to the Hurricane Quarter, Jude left her friend at the station.

"See you at HQ tomorrow," he said, giving her a hug. Benny had called off their band practice tonight on account of the jazz funeral but from tomorrow, they would be practising at headquarters every night once again in preparation for Cajou Night. "Look after yourself, yeah?" Sharkey added.

Jude waved him goodbye and then walked down Moonshine Boulevard. It was permanently party central here, but especially busy in the run up to Cajou Night. People travelled from all over to join the city for the celebrations and they'd already started to arrive.

Locals and tourists alike danced in the street to the music of a brass band playing on a nearby corner, revellers sang heartily along from the wrought-iron balconies of the bars lining the streets and hundreds of multi-coloured plastic beads rolled around in the gaps between the cobbles, clogged up the gutters or hung in rainbow strings from the black lamp posts and bronze statues of jazz players. It seemed there was nothing a drunk enjoyed more than to hang their beads off something.

Jude walked on to her local grocery store, pausing to pick up the ingredients to make her pa's favourite gumbo before heading home. Their tiny apartment was perched atop a gumbo store in a row of two-storey houses, all weathered with age and run down with neglect. The window shutters were rotting; the front porches were worn from the tread of feet; the beads hanging above the lintels were faded and grey. The apartment itself was cramped and muggy and the little wrought-iron balcony clinging to the side was rusted and probably unsafe. But it was a place to call home and as she climbed the rickety staircase Jude felt a great swell of satisfaction that she'd managed to keep a roof over their heads for another month.

When she reached the front door, she saw a box of food had been left on the doorstep again. There'd be no note with it. There never was. It was from her guardian angel – the mysterious benefactor who had helped on and off for the last eight years, ever since her pa's accident. At least, that's what her pa insisted on calling it even though it had, in fact, been an attack.

At first it was just food, always seeming to arrive at the time when they needed it most. But as the years passed, other things began to appear in the packages too: sheet music, books and little plastic trumpets dangling from orange cajou beads. It was as if the angel somehow knew Jude's tastes and tried to provide her with the things she would most like.

Whoever this person was, Jude had never seen him or her. The parcels always appeared when she wasn't in or during the night. But sometimes, when she sat out on her balcony playing her trumpet in the evening, she felt sure there was someone there, just out of sight on the street below, watching her…

She picked up the box and shouldered her way inside. "Guess what we're having for dinner?" she called.

Then she froze in the doorway, staring into the room. Suddenly her heart was beating too hard against her bruised ribs and a familiar dread crept its long fingers right down her spine, making her shudder.

Was it going to be today?

Was this the day it finally happened?

The kitchen had been left in a mess and there was a broken mug with a bloody handle on the floor, a dark brown coffee stain soaking into the peeling lino. The bin hadn't been emptied and a couple of bloated flies buzzed around it lethargically. The house was silent. And too still. Like the flies were the only living thing in the place, coming to feast on the death that Jude was so afraid she would find inside. Part of her wanted to turn and flee. To run straight back down the steps and never have to face it.

Instead she forced herself to step further into the

kitchen. "Pa?" she shouted.

But still there was nothing except the deafening silence and the dull droning of the flies. Jude put down the box of food and her bag of groceries and then forced herself to take the short yet impossibly long walk down the corridor.

Finally she entered the living room where she found her pa slumped in his chair. There was blood on his clothes and a white-hot jolt of shock flooded through her. For a moment she was sure he was dead, that he'd actually done it. But then she realized he was breathing and staring at the wall, his one remaining hand held loosely in his lap, smearing blood on to his tattered robe. Not dead yet, for what that was worth. It was her greatest fear that one day he would take it upon himself to end it all but it seemed she could breathe easy for one more day at least.

His hair was unbrushed and too long and he hadn't shaved. He was still a large man but he tended to curl in on himself these days. When he had leaped into the swamp eight years ago, the gator had taken off his right arm at the elbow, as well as a big chunk from his right thigh. By the time he was pulled from the water, two of the fingers on his left hand had gone and a slash ran from behind his left ear right down to his collarbone.

"Never run near the water," he'd always warned Jude and her little brother Daryl, when they lived at the edge of the Firefly Swamps. *"You might fall in. Them gators are beautiful creatures but they're also wild beasts who'll tear you limb from limb."*

Jude and Daryl had always been careful around the swamp and there had never been any incidents. Until the day of Jude's ninth birthday party, when the stranger came to their home. Jude could still hear his voice sometimes, inside her head.

"Well, well. Is it somebody's birthday?"

All she had to do was close her eyes and she was back there. She could feel the moss on the trunk of the ancient tree she leaned against. See the fireflies winking and blinking their soft golden glow over the murky water, smell the shrimp grilling on the barbecue. Hear Daryl calling her name from the pier behind her…

Jude shook her head and tried to banish the memory as she turned her attention back to her pa. A gator man all his life, he'd once seemed big and strong and invincible. Now his body was a ravaged mess of scars, his hair had turned prematurely grey and he was constantly hounded by pain that only the green fairy could soothe. But they both knew it could have been worse. Daryl had not been so lucky. Whatever remained of him had long ago rotted into the swamp.

"Pa?" Jude said from the doorway. "Can I—"

"Don't need your help," he grunted. "Leave me in peace."

She took a tentative step into the room and tried to keep her voice steady. "At least let me bandage your—"

"I said I DON'T NEED YOUR HELP!" he roared, grabbing a nearby glass and throwing it at Jude so hard and fast that she instinctively ducked.

Her ribs screamed in protest and she gasped at the pain that spread up her right-hand side. She was only dimly aware of the glass shattering against the doorframe above her. Her right hand went on the wooden floorboards to steady herself. She tried to straighten up but the attempt made it feel like a rib was about to burst right through her skin. Her insides felt all torn up. Her heart felt that way too, whenever Pa turned on her like this. Before the attack he'd barely ever so much as raised his voice.

"What are you carrying on for?" Pa grunted from his chair. "Glass didn't even hit you."

Jude gritted her teeth and tried to stand again. This time, to her relief, her ribs allowed her to. She still felt wary of making any sudden movements, though, and leaned against the door for a moment to catch her breath. She could feel her pa watching her from across the room, taking in her split lip.

"Fighting again," he grunted. "It's no good, Jude. You should cut it out."

"What do you care anyway?" she replied.

She turned and limped back to the kitchen. Ignoring all the aches and pains in her shoulder and side, she emptied the bin, shooed away the flies and opened the windows. Then she struggled back down to the floor and cleaned up the broken mug. It left a stain on the floor, but it was so stained and dirty already that it hardly seemed to matter. She made the gumbo, and she and her pa ate at the kitchen table in silence.

Once they'd finished, Jude cleaned up and then walked into the corridor. She'd almost reached her bedroom when her pa spoke from the kitchen doorway.

"I do," he said hoarsely, then cleared his throat and added, "Care, that is."

Jude looked back and saw that he was staring at the floor rather than her.

"I do care," he said again.

"I know," Jude replied. "It's OK."

It wasn't OK at all, but sometimes you just had to pretend. Lately it had seemed to her that her pa's eventual self-destruction was no longer a possibility but a probability, a certainty in fact. Like a steam train racing straight towards her, only she couldn't get out of its way, no matter what she did. She could hear it coming for her, feel it in her bones. No one could go on in that state forever and the new medicine she'd been getting from Sofia wasn't enough. One day it would happen. The only thing she didn't know was how. Would he hang himself? Drown himself in absinthe? Obtain a shotgun from somewhere? She was so terrified that one day he'd be gone and it would be Jude's fault for not being able to help him. And she would be alone. That thought scared her most of all.

She slipped into her bedroom, glad to get away from everyone and everything for a little while. Her room was barely more than a cupboard, with just enough space for a narrow single bed, a stack of drawers and a mirror.

Before going to sleep, she took her most treasured photograph from its place beneath her pillow and spent some time looking at it. The picture was faded now, but it was the only one she had left of her brother – back when they had all been happy. It was such a distant and impossible memory that Jude sometimes had to look at the photo to accept it had ever happened at all.

She then fell into bed and slept like the dead until the sun woke her up, streaming in through her window. Her eyes seemed glued together and she had to prise them open with a groan. Her whole body was just one big ache from the beating she'd taken the day before. Everything seemed to have got worse during the night and she had to sit up slowly and get out of bed carefully, like a person made of glass.

Dressing was even more difficult and ten minutes had gone by before she finally managed to struggle into her dungarees. But as her trembling hands did up the buckles, her pocket moved. She looked down and saw a turbaned head nestled in there.

With a cry, she dragged out the cajou queen poppet and flung it across the room on to the bed.

CHAPTER THREE

The poppet remained motionless on the sheets. When several minutes had passed and it had made no move to attack her, Jude crept closer and stared down at the horrid thing.

It was just as she remembered from the charm gates, except for the fact that it was no longer screaming its head off. Carefully, she picked it up. Her first instinct was to throw it out of the window, burn it or stick it straight in the trash. But even ordinary poppets could be powerful magical objects, let alone screaming ones, and the last thing Jude wanted was to bring a curse upon herself. Her thoughts immediately went to her witch doctor friend, Sofia. If anyone would know what to do about this, it would be her.

Jude picked up the poppet. And an explosion went off inside her head.

She dropped the doll and reeled back, gasping.

Her bedroom spun away from her and she was suddenly at her old home in the Firefly Swamps. The evening air was sticky and there was blood all over the wooden walkway, and she couldn't stop staring at the disembodied arm lying limp and loose on the planks – the largest piece of Daryl they'd been able to find.

"*Come on,*" Mr Treventi, her music teacher, was saying, tugging at her hand. His voice shook and there were tears on his cheeks. "*Come away from there.*"

The swamp vanished to be replaced by her pa's ruined face as he told her she could no longer take up the scholarship at the music academy. Then she was ten years old, playing the trumpet on the street corner for pennies. Then she was eleven and cleaning up her pa after he'd got drunk and pissed himself, the heavy, stinking wetness of his trousers in her hands…

Then she was seventeen and Leeroy was glaring at her, his eyes glittering in the dark, his body too close to hers on the tiny balcony outside her bedroom. "*You ungrateful bitch…*"

Jude groaned and screwed her eyes up tight. It felt like the memories were being dragged from her, like there were fingers, flicking and rifling through her mind, lingering over the memories that were the most painful and awful. Those unbearable ones that Jude tried to keep buried deep down.

Anger and resentment bubbled up inside her and she pushed back against the unseen presence, reaching out with her own mind to poke and probe at this alien thing that had somehow insinuated its way inside her. She felt a shock of surprise that wasn't hers, and then a confusing flash of images and sensations: a diamond ring clasped between long white fingers; a sweet stolen kiss in a smoky room; an explosion of jazz; indigo petals; the exquisite agony of a blade slicing through flesh.

Then there was a hard mental shove, as if two hands had pushed her firmly away. Jude was back in her bedroom and she could feel the juddering *bam-bam* of a heart beating inside her chest that was not her own, rocking her where she stood. And there were eyes staring out from behind hers.

She looked in the mirror above her dressing table and saw an old, pale woman looking back at her. She was dressed in a blue bloodstained evening gown, with an elaborate cloth turban wound about her head and big gold hoops in her ears. Her long white gloves were sticky with blood, her face was wrinkled with age, her mouth pursed into a thin line.

"*You...*"

The old woman's voice rasped in her throat and she broke off coughing, before starting again. "You will ... help me ... Jude Lomax."

"Oh my gods, what the hell do you want?" Jude could feel the colour draining from her face. "How ... how did you get here?"

"Murdered," the cajou queen replied, blood dribbling between her lips. "Must find out ... who did it..."

Jude grabbed the poppet and fled from the room, pausing just long enough to pull on her swamp boots. She tore from the apartment and away down the street, straight to Mojo Alley – a crooked, narrow, winding place where all the best witch doctors and cajou people traded their wares. Jude had avoided Mojo Alley her whole life until recently, when she'd ventured there out of desperation for her pa. Traditional painkillers and medicines didn't seem to help him much and Jude couldn't bear to see him writhing in such agony, so she'd finally been driven to seek magical help. And that was how she'd first met Sofia.

She sprinted down the street as fast as her aching ribs would allow and burst into Madam Zombie's House of Herbs, the bell above the door clanging in protest.

The small dark room within had a sloping wooden floor and smelled strongly of the herbs, powders and ointments that lined its walls. Sofia's familiar, a glossy black raven named Benedict, was perched on a skull on top of a bookcase in the corner, peering down at the store with bright beady eyes. Sofia herself was behind the counter and thankfully there were no customers.

Sofia Moreau was a stunning witch. Not only was she extremely tall, but her black and gold hair was arranged into hundreds of micro-braids that hung all the way down to the small of her back, even when they were swept up into a high ponytail. She had flawless chocolate-coloured skin, laughing brown eyes and a curvy figure that Jude could have happily killed someone for. Of course, she also had half a dozen beauty charms in the form of earrings dangling from her right ear. Jude had never seen her without them and had no idea what she looked like naturally.

Today Sofia wore a black corset that showed off her big bust and small waist rather spectacularly, along with black leather trousers that looked like they'd been spray-painted on, and towering stiletto boots that added several more inches to her already imposing height. A collection of magical amulets hung from chains around her neck and her Royalty cajou charm dangled from a cuff that she wore at the top of her right ear. She was only a year older than Jude at eighteen and as a witch and a member of the Royalty Jude had been determined to dislike her at first. She wanted to hate all Royals because it was easier that way, but the more she got to know Sofia the more she realized that not all Royals were evil and dangerous. Not like the stranger who'd come to her home eight years ago, his crown charm glowing a bloody red in the dusk.

"I'm a friend of your father's," he'd said, only Jude knew he was lying because her pa's friends were the animals that lived in the swamp or other gator men. He'd never be friends with a member of the Royalty. And he'd be furious if he ever found out that Jude was friends with Sofia. If he knew that his medicine came from a witch, he'd refuse to take it ever again.

"Hi, Jude," Sofia said. "What's—"

"I need you to help me!" Jude cut her off.

She pulled the cajou queen poppet from her pocket and threw it on the counter between them. Sofia took one look at it before hurrying to flip the door sign over to say that the store was closed. Then she turned the key in the lock and came back to the counter.

"What the hell," she said, "are you doing walking around with a poppet of the murdered cajou queen in your pocket?"

"I think she's haunting me," Jude said. She explained about the jazz funeral, the charm gates and glimpsing the queen in the mirror back in her apartment. "She says she wants to find out who murdered her."

Sofia looked aghast. "Are you freakin' kidding me? Jude, this is bad. Really bad. This is a leapfrog poppet."

"What does that mean?"

"It's a powerful black magic charm," Sofia replied. "The magic is triggered when the corpse of the person it represents gets close and then it leaps into the soul of someone living." She looked at Jude. "Why did it pick you? Did you signal it in some way?"

Jude gaped at her. "*Signal* it?" she said. "Why the heck would I do that?"

"All right, cool it," Sofia said. "It's just that normally I'd expect there to be some sort of connection between you. A link of some kind."

"Well, I *looked* at it, I suppose, but so did everyone else."

Sofia shrugged. "I guess you were just unlucky then."

"How do I get rid of her?"

"You can't."

"There's got to be some way! Look, can't you just burn the poppet or something?"

"It wouldn't do any good," Sofia said. "There's no magic left inside it now that it's performed its function. It's just an ordinary doll. Do you mind if I keep it? I'd love to examine it properly."

"Well, I certainly don't want the horrible thing."

"I'm sorry I can't be more help." She slipped the poppet into her pocket. "But Ivory Monette will go when she wants to, and not a moment before."

CHAPTER FOUR

Jude left Mojo Alley and quickened her pace towards home, as if this possession was something that could be outrun. She'd been sure that Sofia would have some simple answer for her. A potion she could drink, or a spell she could perform that would undo whatever the heck had happened here.

She was almost home when, to her dismay, Ivory's rasping old voice echoed inside her mind:

Your friend was quite right, you know. I'm not leaving. Not until I've got what I want.

There was no way to shut Ivory out, no way to escape from her.

I've given you time to get used to the idea, Ivory went on. *But now I'm afraid we really must get down to business.*

Jude ignored her and ran up the steps to the apartment. She burst into the kitchen, hurried down the corridor to her bedroom and slammed the door behind her. And immediately saw the twelve-foot-long albino python coiled up on her bed.

For a long while, Jude and the python simply stared at one another. The snake's pink eyes were unblinking in its broad, flat white head, and it gazed at her quite calmly while Jude's heart seemed to beat at a hundred miles an hour. Her eyes went to the open window and the balcony outside. Could the snake have come up through the drainpipe? Or perhaps it had simply materialized in the room? This was a magical cajou snake after all, the servant of the Snake-God himself and the source of all the queen's Power.

That's Beau, Ivory said.

"I know what it is," Jude snapped.

The snake was famous all over Baton Noir. It seemed to sense the cajou queen's presence somehow because the next moment it was uncoiling itself, slithering down to the floor and making its way over to Jude. She remained absolutely still, half convinced that the snake would strike her at any moment. But instead it wrapped its long body round her leg, climbed up to her arm and then settled its great weight across her shoulders. Jude could barely breathe. Inside her mind, Ivory was crooning happily to the snake.

There he is, she rasped. *There's my beautiful boy.*

Jude carefully unwound the python from her shoulders and hastily placed him on the bed.

"I'm sorry," she said, a little breathless. "But even if I wanted to, I can't help you. You both need to go."

Suddenly there was a rap on the door and her pa called out. "Jude? Everything all right in there?"

"Yes, Pa, everything's fine."

"Can you open the door?"

Jude looked down at the giant python on her bed and silently panicked. Usually she and her father were quite content to shout at each other through closed doors so why the heck he wanted her to open it now, she had no idea. She quickly slid the snake under her bed and pulled her bedsheets down to cover it, praying that it stayed put for five minutes. Her pa wasn't the most observant of men these days, but even he would notice a massive great cajou python. Then she hurried over to the door and yanked it open.

Her pa was standing on the other side. In his hand he held a plate with a sandwich on it. Jude was amazed when he thrust the plate towards her and said, "Here."

He hadn't prepared food for her since the accident. Not so much as a single slice of toast. His grip on the plate was awkward due to his missing fingers and Jude saw that his hand was shaking slightly.

She felt a flare of hope deep in her soul, from a flame she'd thought long extinguished, as she reached out for the plate.

But the next second an iron grip squeezed her wrist and a cold force took hold of her tongue. Jude knocked the plate from her pa's awkward grip. The sandwich fell to the floor and Jude heard herself snarling words she had no wish to say.

"You think a sandwich can fix everything that went wrong in the last eight years, you deluded old fool? It won't bring Daryl back. It won't change the fact that he'd still be alive if it weren't for you." She spat on the ground at his feet. "Screw you."

There followed an awful silence as Jude raged inside her own mind, desperately fighting to win back control. At last she managed to mentally shake off the cajou queen but it was too late. She stared at her pa, feeling sick. Those words were things she'd thought sometimes in the guilty secret spaces of her own mind, but she would never have dreamed of saying them out loud.

She thought perhaps her pa might fly into one of his hopeless rages, screaming at her and throwing things, but he took a deep breath and then turned and walked down the hallway to his bedroom without a word, shutting the door quietly behind him.

Jude slammed the door to her room and groaned in disbelief.

"You *bitch*!" she exclaimed. "Do you know how long I've waited for that? Do you realize what you've just done?"

You will help me, whether you want to or not, Ivory whispered back.

"How did you even know those things?"

I'm inside your head, Ivory replied. *I know everything you know. I've seen everything you've seen. Your own thoughts have told me exactly how to strike and where. You think that was bad? You haven't seen anything yet, girl. You're strong all right, I'll give you that, but you can't fight me all the time. It'd only take a moment of lapsed concentration and I'd have you putting rat poison in your pa's tea rather than milk. Do you understand?*

Jude slammed her fist against the wall, hard enough to knock out a piece of loose plaster.

"I can't do what you're asking!" she said. "Even if I

wanted to, I can't hunt down a killer. I'm just a trumpet player."

You've got me and all my magic to help you, Ivory said. *I will protect you and keep you safe. Use your head, girl. There could be something in this for you. I'm prepared to make a bargain.*

"You've got nothing I want."

I can help your father, Ivory whispered.

Jude felt a deep, hopeless longing at the idea but forced the feeling away.

"Can you give him back his missing hand?" she demanded. "Or his house? Or his dead son?"

No. But I can help ease his pain.

Jude stilled, unable to keep the hope from bubbling back up. Could it possibly be true?

"No power can cheat fate," she said. The anger suddenly went out of her, leaving her feeling tired. She lowered herself to sit cross-legged on the floor and leaned her head back against the wall.

Cajou can, Ivory said. *Cajou is more powerful than anything in this world. Even fate. Let me show you what it can do.*

She began to hum inside Jude's head. A dizzying, disorientating tune that seemed to charm Beau into uncoiling himself and coming over. Despite herself,

Jude couldn't help being fascinated. She had always liked snakes and this one was remarkable. He slithered round her waist, wrapping his long body round and round her. Jude immediately felt a strange warmth seeping through her skin and then the ache in her ribs began to ease. Rapidly it got less and less until it was no longer there at all. Her tooth didn't wobble in its socket and the absence of pain was an indescribable relief. Jude felt lighter, as if a big black weight that had been holding her down had suddenly been removed and now she might float away altogether.

Feels good, doesn't it? Ivory breathed. *And you've lived with your pain for less than twenty-four hours. The hurt your father feels is infinitely greater than yours and it's a burden he's carried for eight years. Just think of the gift you could give him.*

Jude's breath caught in her throat as she felt a bone-deep tremor of joy at the prospect of being able to help her pa in some kind of meaningful way. Here at last might be a chance to get out of the path of that speeding train. And Ivory was surely right that if anything was powerful enough to change the course of fate itself, then it was cajou. Having lived in Baton Noir all her life, Jude was well aware that it could do wondrous and unspeakable things if wielded by a talented practitioner. And who could possibly be more talented than the cajou queen herself?

What Ivory was suggesting was unspeakably dangerous, but if there was anything in this world that would persuade Jude to go over to the other side and make a deal with the cajou devils then it was a chance to save her pa's life, and she felt her resolve harden.

"All right," she said carefully. "I'm listening."

Oh. Ivory seemed taken aback, uncertain for the first time. *That's not what I expected you to... I thought I'd at least have to hex one of your friends or something first in order to demonstrate my power.*

"You don't know me," Jude replied. "So you've got no idea what I'll do or say."

Well, aren't you scared? Ivory demanded. She sounded mildly offended. *I'm pretty powerful, you know, and—*"

"Of course I'm scared," Jude snapped. "But that doesn't matter. I've been scared before. So just tell me what it is you're proposing."

I've already told you, I want to find out who murdered me.

"Yes, but what do you expect me to *do* if we find the murderer? Because if it's going to be hexes and curses and chopping up bodies into little bits then you can count me out. I'm no killer."

Don't be ridiculous, Ivory said. *When you find out who did it, you'll report them to the authorities.*

Jude chewed her lip. "Even if by some miracle I manage to do that, how do I know you'll keep to your end of the bargain?"

Ivory Monette laughed, a low, throaty sound that tickled the back of Jude's throat.

But you don't, she said. *You can't. We're just going to have to trust one another.*

Jude rolled her eyes. "I thought you'd say that."

Her mind raced as she tried to work out what to do. Could she possibly trust the cajou queen to keep her word? Even if Sofia hadn't had any ideas, that didn't mean to say that someone else in Baton Noir may not know how to banish Ivory's spirit.

You know I can hear your thoughts, don't you? Ivory said with a sigh. *Trust me, my dear, no one in the whole world would be able to help you get rid of me. I'm wedged in here deep. There'll be no dragging me out unless I'm willing to go.*

Jude ignored her and continued to think it through. There was no denying that the cajou queen *did* have power of the type Jude could only dream of. She felt a twinge of greedy desire for it, right down deep in her soul. She knew this chance would never come again.

And if there was any possibility at all of saving her father, of maybe even getting some semblance of normality back, then it was a chance Jude knew she would have to take.

"All right," she said, hoping she was making the right decision. "You have a bargain. I'll help you and in return you'll help my father. So, where do you want to start? Do you have some idea about who might've been responsible for your death?"

My dear, I've been the cajou queen of Baton Noir for fifty years. My list of suspects is as long as your arm. I always thought this might happen one day. Why do you think I put the leapfrog poppet on the gates in the first place? I want to go back to where it happened. To the Blue Lady.

"But I can't go in there," Jude replied. "It's Royals only."

Well, that doesn't matter, Ivory replied. *You can wear a crown charm now too. It will react to me and glow as if you were a Royal. No one else will know the difference. You can go anywhere I could go.*

Jude wrinkled her nose. In her mind she saw the man who had ruined her life, calmly walking away into the dusk that was falling over the Firefly Swamps, his crown charm glowing a bloody red. Jude may not have hated every individual member of the magical elite but she still loathed what they stood for, and the thought of having to wear a crown cajou charm was abhorrent to her.

"I don't want to be one of you," she said.

Well, that's too bad, Ivory replied, *because right now you've got more black magic swirling around inside you than anyone else in Baton Noir.*

"Perfect," Jude muttered.

But if joining forces with devils was what it took to save her pa then Jude would damn well march straight into the fiery hells in her swamp boots.

She left Beau sleeping on her bed, closing the door firmly behind her. Then she cleaned up the sandwich and went down the corridor to her pa's bedroom door.

"Pa?" she said softly.

There was no answer but she hadn't expected one. She wanted to say she hadn't meant the things she'd said to him earlier, that she didn't blame him. But that wasn't completely true. Some small part of her *did* blame him. If he hadn't made an enemy of a warlock then Daryl would still be alive. The man had only thrown him into the swamp to punish her father for his unpaid debt. They both knew that. It would ring hollow and unconvincing if Jude tried to claim otherwise. To make things even worse, the warlock had skipped town immediately afterwards and had never been punished for what he'd done.

"I'm sorry," Jude said through the door. "And I love you."

More than you know, she added inside her head.

Nothing came back to her but silence. Jude turned away. The best chance she had of helping him was to help Ivory, and to do that she needed a crown charm, so she made her way back to Sofia's store.

When she turned into Mojo Alley she passed a destitute woman selling buckets of brick dust on the kerb outside a love potion store. The entire window was filled with neat rows of beef hearts decorated with toad's feet and scorpion legs, spritzed with perfume and tied up with ribbons. Jude shuddered to think what they might be used for.

The next store had window boxes overflowing with bottles of cajou acid, as well as several baskets of conjure balls, big lumps of black wax the size of a fist, fashioned into balls and stuck all over with pins. They were said to contain a piece of human flesh and were intended to be rolled across the front lawn or back yard of an enemy's house at midnight in order to bring misfortune into their home. It wasn't uncommon to see them left on doorsteps either.

The store even had a sign in the window advertising that they could perform fright hexes, one of the most terrifying and vicious hexes in existence. The victim would wake one morning to find a black heart mark like a tattoo on their body somewhere, meaning that one day they would be doomed to experience their worst fear. They never knew when or how this might happen. But there would always be that black heart there, beating away, a reminder of the horror that was waiting for them.

Jude hurried past to Sofia's store, remembering how she'd first chosen it because of the tatty model of a zombie standing outside the door. He was a ghoulish-looking thing, but he wore a top hat and a bow tie with little bats printed on it, and if a zombie in a bow tie wasn't enough to coax you into a store then Jude didn't know what was.

She pushed open the door and went straight to the counter.

"Back so soon?" Sofia said, looking concerned. "Has something else happened?"

"No, but Ivory and I have … well, we've made a bargain."

The witch raised an eyebrow. "And you think you can trust her?"

"I don't trust her," Jude replied. "But it's a risk worth taking. She says she can help my pa."

"Well," Sofia finally said. "It's not like you can get rid of her anyway, so something good may as well come of it. What do you need?"

"A crown charm," Jude replied. "To get me into the Blue Lady."

Sofia drew out a tray and set it down on the counter between them. They were all extremely expensive but to Jude's relief Sofia gave her one free of charge.

"You can give it back to me once all this is over," she said.

As soon as Jude clipped it on to her bracelet, it glowed red. She was quite sure she would never get used to seeing it. It was like waking up in the middle of a battle to find that you were suddenly wearing the other side's uniform.

"I'll come with you to the Blue Lady," Sofia offered. "They know me there, it's one of Belle's favourites."

Belle was Sofia's girlfriend, a petite, pretty witch, with creamy skin and very blond hair that reached halfway down her back. She had a white cat familiar named Dazzle and her particular gift was divination.

Girls went to her to find out the name of their soulmate or how old they would be when they married. She'd offered to read Jude's cards for free more than once but Jude had always declined. The idea that the future was some inescapable fate already set in stone gave her the creeps.

But even though she'd always turned Belle down, sometimes Jude felt like the witch looked at her in a strange sort of way, as if she could sense something about her future even without the aid of the cards. It wasn't a pleasant thought and had always made Jude a little uncomfortable around Belle. That and the fact that she knew that all of the witch's favourite jazz bars and clubs were Royals-only.

"But who'll mind the store?" Jude asked Sofia.

"Belle will be here for the afternoon shift soon," her friend replied. "She has her own key. The store can stay shut until then."

So she locked up and the two of them made their way to the Blue Lady. It started to rain as they reached Moonshine Boulevard and the neon lights shone through the drizzle, flashing in the puddles that formed on the uneven cobbles, flickering between blue and pink and green and orange. The bar's sign depicted an elegant lady in a tasteful blue bonnet, with a parasol slung casually over her shoulder. A velvet rope guarded the entrance, along with a large man with a Subject charm dangling from his wrist. If an ordinary Citizen – or Scrap, as they were more commonly known – was able to ingratiate themselves with a Royal somehow then they would be awarded Subject status, which generally came with various perks and better treatment. Pretty much any ordinary human of any importance was a Subject, and that included the Mayor, the police and all the politicians. The city was corrupt down to its bones.

The doorman glared at Jude the moment he saw her and said, "Royals only."

Sofia looked every inch the witch with her amulets, corset, divine hair and the magical daggers tucked into the waistband of her black leather trousers. Jude, on the other hand, wore her usual dungarees over a tatty old vest, along with a pair of swamp boots that needed cleaning. Her red hair was cropped short in a boyish style, exposing the musical notes tattooed behind her right ear and all the way down her neck. And of course she had too many freckles on her fair skin and did not look the part of cajou Royalty one bit. She therefore very much enjoyed holding up her bracelet to dangle her crown charm in the man's face.

He gave her a startled look and quickly apologized, his entire demeanour changing instantly.

"My apologies, ma'am," he said. "No offence meant."

It was dark and smoky inside the club, with a long bar taking up most of one wall and a raised stage at the other end. In the middle there were tables and navy velvet booths, each with its own small beaded lamp that gave off a cool blue light. A row of stuffed alligator heads adorned the wall behind the bar, and strings of Cajou Night plastic beads hung from the ceiling, the light fittings and the paintings. They were all different shades of blue, the colour of the witches, from bright teal to dusky indigo. There were a few guests sitting nursing their drinks with their crown charms glowing in the low light.

Where did it happen? Jude silently asked Ivory.

The bathroom, the cajou queen replied. *I think.*

You think?

I can't remember properly. It's all a bit of a fog. Take me back there. I want to look around.

Jude sighed. "Where's the bathroom?" she asked Sofia.

"Over there," the witch replied, indicating a door on the other side of the room.

They went through to the corridor at the back of the

club, only to find that the women's toilets had an *Out of Order* sign taped to the door, along with a couple of lines of police tape. Ignoring this, Jude pushed open the door and ducked under the tape. She switched on the light and both girls instantly gasped.

The bathroom, like the rest of the club, was lavish and luxurious. A huge floor-to-ceiling fish tank shaped like a pillar stood in the far corner, filled with blue seahorses. The sinks took the form of giant blue shells, held up by savage-looking mermaids. The mirrors hung in gold frames. The walls and the floor were pearly white. Or at least they had been.

Someone had clearly *attempted* to clean up, but the bloodstain in the centre of the room was still there, shocking and surreal in its faded scarlet gore. Jude felt something then that she hadn't felt since that day eight years ago when the swamp had churned pink and her brother was torn apart in the water – a desperate sense of horror and revulsion that made her want to crawl right out of her skin if that was what it took to get away.

Closer, Ivory rasped inside her head.

"Isn't this close enough?" Jude groaned.

The cajou queen didn't bother to reply but took control of Jude's body and walked her over until her swamp boots were in the very centre of the bloodstain. Then Ivory jerked Jude's head up towards the mirror, forcing her to look at a reflection that wasn't hers. The cajou queen stared out of the glass, her mouth twisted in some unspeakable torment as the memories of that evening came rushing in.

Before Jude's eyes, the reflection morphed. Sofia disappeared and the room was empty but for Ivory. The bloodstain was gone. The sound of jazz, hot and smoky, came muffled through the door. Jude stared out from behind Ivory's eyes as the cajou queen moved over to the sink and washed her hands before putting her white evening gloves back on.

There was the sound of the door closing and the soft click of a key turning in the lock. Ivory turned round, only to find that the room was empty. Frowning, she walked over to the door and tried to push it open, then raised her hand to rap her knuckles on the wood.

"Excuse me!" she called sharply. "I'm still in here!"

There was no reply. And then a small object rolled through the crack in the door. Ivory glanced down and saw that it was a coin, a large gold one, dull and tarnished with age. She felt a flare of dread deep in her gut and then there was something warm running down her face. When she put a hand to her hairline, her gloved fingers came away sticky with blood.

Jude couldn't quite tell where her own thoughts and emotions ended and Ivory's began. Perhaps they were all tangled up together in one big messy knot. She looked slowly over to the mirror and saw that several more lines of blood were snaking their way down the cajou queen's face from small cuts that were appearing all by themselves. Ivory's skin was old and paper-thin and Jude saw another piece split before her eyes, like the skin of a grape.

Ivory stared into the mirror and the next moment something slashed right through her throat. She never saw any weapon but she felt the skin tear and the rip of soft flesh as her vocal cords were severed. There was a moment of complete rage, followed by fear and agony as the pain of the injury suddenly burst into her awareness in a blinding-white star that felt as if it would take the top of her head off.

Blood poured down Ivory's front, splattering down her blue dress and over her white gloves as she lifted her hands to her neck in a hopeless attempt to keep her throat together, staggering to stay on her feet as all the strength drained from her legs.

The cut to her throat was too wide and deep and her fingers snagged in the tattered flesh. The room spun about her and there was nothing she could do to prevent herself falling on to the marbled white floor, feeling her life drain away with her blood.

Her arms fell out to her sides and she could no longer move at all – was powerless to do anything other than lie there, trying to call for help through a ruined throat that only gurgled wetly. Ivory's eyes darted about but there still didn't appear to be anyone else in the room, just that gold coin, gleaming across the floor at her like a serpent's eye…

Ivory didn't want to go. Old as she was, she didn't want to die yet, but her heartbeat slowed and then stopped, before she fell into the deep, dark blackness of a never-ending night.

CHAPTER FIVE

Jude staggered back with a yell, straight into Sofia who put her hands on her shoulders to steady her.

"Hey, are you OK? You've gone white."

Jude shook her head. "I just … I was back there," she gasped. "When Ivory was murdered."

Without waiting for her friend to reply, Jude turned and hurried back to the main room. She went straight to the bar with Sofia on her heels, pulled up a stool and leaned across it to the barman, a small, squirrelly man with a Subject charm hanging from his wrist.

Jude looked right at him. "Give me the strongest drink you've got," she said.

The barman frowned at her, then his eyes dropped to her hands, spread on the bar, and the crown charm she wore.

"Comin' right up," he said.

He poured a strong stiff drink into a glass but because this was the Blue Lady and not a rough-and-ready bar, he started fussing around with diamond swizzle sticks.

"Never mind all that," Jude said. She leaned across the bar, snatched the drink from him and downed it in one, relishing the burn as it slid down her throat. She slammed the empty glass back on the bar. "Again," she said.

How exactly is this helping? Ivory asked inside her head.

"It's helping me plenty," Jude snapped.

The barman looked up. "I'm sorry?"

"Just pour the drink."

Sofia hopped up on to the stool next to Jude.

"Anything for you, Sofia?" the barman asked as he set Jude's drink down.

"I'll have a Steamboat Slaughter," Sofia replied. "On the rocks."

Jude felt like she could still taste murder at the back of her throat, could feel death reaching for her with greedy, clutching fingers. She felt skin tear and blood pour down her front again, and shuddered, knowing that she would relive that moment over and over again in her dreams.

It wasn't pleasant for me either, you know, Ivory said. *I can't think what you're carrying on for anyway. I'm the one who was murdered – not you.*

Jude ignored her. She sipped her drink, slower this time, and tried to concentrate on breathing. She couldn't shake the feeling that there was something wrong about what she'd just seen, something that didn't quite make sense. The thought niggled at her but when she tried to reach for it, it scattered like smoke.

What happened? she asked Ivory. *There was nobody there! How were you killed?*

I remember it now, Ivory replied. *That was a devil's coin that rolled through the door.*

Jude had heard of devil's coins but had never seen one. Everyone knew that devils lived in the swamps and that if you wanted to make a pact with one then you didn't go to the crossroads any more – you went to the Black Bayou and sought out the devil's wishing well, where the price would be a piece of your soul. In return the devil would give you a devil's coin, which would allow you to do wondrous and unspeakable things. You could only spend it once and after that it lost most of its power. But it was still an extremely valuable item, not least because it could be used as an aid to hexes and curses.

"So, Harry," Sofia said, as she stirred the ice in her drink. "Were you working the night Ivory Monette was killed?"

The barman shook his head. "No, but I heard all about it from Frank," he said, eager to share gossip. "The cajou queen went to the bathroom and she didn't come back. Her granddaughter got worried and went after her but the door was locked. They had to get some vampire to break it down and then they found her, lying there in all that blood."

Who else was here? Jude asked Ivory, picking up her drink. *Who were you with? Did you see anyone in the room you weren't expecting to see?*

Turn round, Ivory replied. *Let me try to remember.*

Jude shuffled in her seat until she was facing the room. She felt the cajou queen's mind casting back and suddenly the scene shifted and changed, just like it had in the bathroom, and Jude was looking at the Blue Lady as it had been on the night of the murder.

She was no longer sitting at the bar, but at one of the tables near the stage, clasping a long cigarette holder between her gloved fingers. Wisps of blue smoke curled in the air from the many cigarettes and cigars. A jazz band played on stage and the room was bustling with people. A girl sat across from her, wearing a peach beaded tea dress that matched her skin colour, and looking rather bored by the proceedings. She was extremely petite with a tumble of blond hair piled up on top of her head, threaded with cajou charms.

My granddaughter, Ivory whispered inside Jude's head. *Charity. And the drip next to her is her boyfriend, Wade.*

The young man sitting beside Charity had light brown hair, pale eyes and a vacant expression. There was a thin, sickly look about him and a greyish tinge to his already ghostly pale skin. He did not look at all well.

Consumption, Ivory said, hearing Jude's thoughts. *Not long for this world, if I'm any judge. I took them out for Charity's birthday. She turned sixteen last week.*

It was hard to hear much over the sound of the jazz but Jude watched carefully from behind Ivory's eyes as she gazed around the room. Suddenly the cajou queen noticed someone and gasped. Jude felt the swell of her heartbreak, an emotion so intense that it took her breath away. It was a feeling she recognized, her pa had broken her heart several times over since Daryl died, but she was amazed that anyone had ever managed to make the cajou queen feel that way.

Yes, Ivory whispered to herself. *Yes, he was here that night. I remember now.*

Who? Jude asked.

Etienne Malloy.

Jude saw the man Ivory was focusing on – tall, with ice-blond hair slicked back from his face, high cheekbones and blue eyes. He wore a dark suit that was probably worth more than Jude made in a year. He didn't look like he could be older than thirty but that didn't necessarily mean anything in Baton Noir. He was one of the most handsome men in the room.

Who is he? Jude asked.

He's the love of my life, Ivory replied.

Her agony was an awful thing. Jude could feel it clawing away at her guts, like it was desperate to get out.

But if he's the love of your life then surely you don't think— she began.

Look at him! Ivory snapped. *He's a vampire. I'm a human. I aged. He didn't. He dropped me when I stopped being young and beautiful and I … I did not take it well. He broke my heart, you see. So I broke his right back.* She sighed. *No, Etienne Malloy has every reason to hate me. More reason than most, in fact.*

He stood at the edge of the room, gazing around as if looking for someone. Then he saw Ivory and his eyes, if possible, seemed to turn even colder. Jude flinched.

The next moment, the vampire had turned away and disappeared from the room. Ivory's memories faded and the present-day half-empty Blue Lady returned.

Did you see him again that evening? Jude asked, shifting back round in her bar seat. *Did he approach you? Speak to you?*

No, Ivory said in a flat voice. *But he hated me enough to do it. I know he did.*

They left the club and Jude filled Sofia in. When she got to the part about Etienne Malloy, the witch stopped in her tracks.

"Etienne Malloy?" she repeated.

"You've heard of him?" Jude asked.

"He's one of the most dangerous vampires in Baton Noir," Sofia replied.

"Well, most vampires are dangerous."

"Etienne doesn't wear a humanity charm any more."

"Oh."

When vampires turned, they lost most of their humanity in the process of dying and coming back to life and became cold, heartless versions of themselves;

76

retaining their memories, their likes and dislikes, but losing some vital part of their soul, including the crucial bit that allowed them to love.

Then cajou practitioners created humanity charms, which could restore some of the vampire's humanity or at least magnify whatever shred of it they had left. Many vampires chose to wear them, claiming life was more interesting and exciting when you could burn with passion, but there was the occasional vampire who chose to damp down their emotions, who preferred to be cold and a little dead inside, for whatever reason.

It was my fault, Ivory said softly in Jude's head. *He took off his humanity charm because of me.*

You'd better tell me the whole story, Jude said silently to the cajou queen. *But not right now. I'm expected at Moonfleet Manor this afternoon.*

Moonfleet! Ivory exclaimed. *I could tell you stories about that place which would make you sick! Why on earth would you want to go to that cursed house?*

I work there, Jude replied. *I play the trumpet for André Majstro twice a week.*

Do you now? Ivory replied. *Well, well. I never saw you.*

I saw you, Jude replied. *From the Owlery. That's where he likes me to play.*

The Phantom doesn't want you in the house, I suppose.

What did you go there for? Jude wondered. She had always been curious.

But Ivory clammed up immediately. *That's none of your concern, my girl,* she said.

Well, I've got to go, Jude said. *I suppose you won't like it but I can't afford to give up paid work, cajou queen or not.*

She expected Ivory to raise a ruckus but to her surprise she agreed readily enough.

It'll give me time to work out what to do about Etienne, she said. *If you could get a lock of his hair then I could perform a spell that would compel him to confess, but he spends most of the time at his club, and that's invitation only.*

Jude didn't think she'd stand much chance of getting a lock of the vampire's hair even if she did have an invitation to his club.

Let me worry about that, said Ivory.

Jude shrugged and said goodbye to Sofia. She then went home to collect her trumpet before going straight to Moonfleet Manor.

CHAPTER SIX

Moonfleet Manor had stood in the Fountain District for the last three hundred years – a strange, beautiful abomination of a house, designed and built by madmen. It was undoubtedly one of the finest homes in Baton Noir. It was also the most infamous and indeed worthless, since no one but a Majstro would live in the place after the things that had happened there. It even had its own graveyard in the garden, filled with the skeletons of past Majstros from days gone by.

The edge of the swamp lapped at the graveyard and Jude could just make out the swamp boat moored there, as well as the old paddle steamer, slowly rusting away into ruins. The mansion sat in the middle of the extensive grounds, hulking down like a spider amid the outbuildings, of which there were several, including the conservatory, the gazebo and the Owlery – a magnificent red-brick tower several storeys high. Alcoves lined the walls all the way up, with perches for the various owls.

They were not popular creatures in Baton Noir. Their association with Krag meant it wasn't unusual for citizens to maim any that they came across. Even people who disliked the cruelty were not prepared to bring the owls into their own homes, so they would leave them at the gates of Moonfleet for the Phantom instead.

Jude didn't mind the owls but couldn't help resenting the fact that they lived in far greater comfort than the vast majority of ordinary people in Baton Noir. But then the Majstros had always been a fabulously wealthy family and the Phantom seemed to be the only one left. Having grown up in splendour and plenty, he probably had no notion of poverty, no concept or understanding of want at all. And Jude couldn't help hating him a little for that, even if his employment was the reason she and her pa still had a roof over their heads.

Today she pushed open the door of the Owlery, relieved to find that Paris wasn't waiting to turn her away like last time. The ground floor consisted of a small, circular room with a red rug on the stone slabs and a single stool placed in the middle. Glossy wooden candlestick holders stood around the rug, the candles sending out flickering light that scattered dancing shadows all the way up the stone walls into the darkness above.

Jude could hear the soft shuffling of the owls on their perches but couldn't see them except for the occasional flash of light reflected in a pair of big round eyes. A decorative screen divided the room – a beautiful thing stitched with an image of Papa Louis, the legba of music. One of the most beloved legbas, he was depicted as a beaming, happy man, despite the fact that his fingertips had been worn down to the bone from the many hours he spent playing the piano. Papa Louis could play any instrument in existence, but there was none he loved more than the piano. And so he beamed his musician's joyful smile, even as the bones poked through his fingers and the blood ran down his wrists.

The Phantom always took his seat behind the screen to hear her play. Jude supposed there must be another entrance to the building on the other side. Either that or he made sure to always be there before her, for she never saw him walk in. Around the image of Papa Louis there were meshed panels in the screen which, Jude supposed, allowed him to see her to some extent, although she never managed to catch more than a shadowy glimpse of him. She simply came in at their agreed time and began to play. The Phantom didn't require, or want, small talk. Which suited Jude perfectly.

Her eyes flicked to the screen and as usual, she couldn't make out anyone beyond it but she *knew* the Phantom was there somehow. She could feel his eyes watching her, could sense his presence in the room as clearly as if he'd greeted her out loud, as any ordinary person would have done. As usual, she took her trumpet from its case, sat on the stool and started to play. The smooth, smoky jazz notes filled the room, soaring all the way to the top of the tower.

Much as Jude had dreaded coming here initially, these evenings at Moonfleet had come to be the most enjoyable of her week and she found she actually looked forward to them, as long as she didn't allow herself to think about the unseen man on the other side of the screen. It was hard not to be nervous at the thought of being so close to any descendant, let alone one who was related to the prince of the cool legba himself.

Jude had been playing for fifteen minutes or so

when the Phantom spoke for the first time since she'd arrived.

"Stop."

Jude lowered her trumpet into her lap and waited. He did this sometimes – he'd interrupt her playing to request a different song or offer some instruction that might improve her technique. Jude expected him to do one of these things now, but instead he said quietly, "What happened to your face?"

Jude had no idea what he was talking about for a moment and then recalled the split lip she'd received from Sidney Blues Sampson. Beau's healing hadn't quite extended to the ugly scab there.

"Oh. I … I had a disagreement with my landlord," she said. "About rent."

"You are in arrears?" came that quiet voice through the dark.

"Temporarily."

"Could it be that you have been spending your money on unwise things, Jude?"

He did this sometimes too – asked her personal questions about matters that were none of his business. One day, just after she'd first started, he'd asked her, "Does scrapping in bars make life any easier to bear?"

She *had* lost her temper and been involved in a bit of a scuffle before she'd arrived, but it was the other person's fault for shouting out a lewd comment at her. Unfortunately, when she'd punched him on the jaw it had bruised one of her fingers, which affected her trumpet playing – the only reason the Phantom noticed, or cared, in the first place. When she tried to explain, the Phantom had cut her off. "I pay you to play the trumpet and I expect you to be in a fit state to do so. What you do after you leave is your own affair, but do not fight before you come here in future."

Those words still stung whenever Jude thought of them and caused a flush of resentment to creep over her face. Who did he think he was anyway, interfering in her life like that?

"It's a bit hard to spend money at all," she said now, more sharply than she'd intended to, "when you're sent away without any payment."

For a moment there was absolute silence, broken only by the owls rustling their wings on their perches above. Then the Phantom spoke so softly that Jude had to strain to hear him.

"I beg your pardon?"

Silently, she cursed herself and her big mouth. What

if she'd offended him? What if he sent her away and told her never to come back? This was the easiest money and the best paid job she'd ever had.

"I'm sorry," she said. "Of … of course, I'm happy to come and go as you want me to. It's only that last night I was sort of relying on the money for the rent, that's all…" She trailed off uncertainly.

There was another silence that stretched on for slightly too long. Jude was about to ask whether she should go on playing when the Phantom spoke again.

"You are telling me," he said, "that Paris sent you away last night *without* giving you the money?"

Jude felt a small flicker of guilt at the thought that she might be getting the other girl in trouble, but that soon vanished when she recalled the sneer Paris had had on her face when she'd spoken to her, as well as the feel of Sidney's boot as it smashed into her ribs.

"I never saw any money," she said with a shrug.

"I see." The chair beyond the screen creaked as if the Phantom had just leaned back in it. "Please continue with the music."

Jude raised the trumpet and began to play a ragtime song but the Phantom's soft voice interrupted her.

"Play 'Blue Bianca'."

Jude wondered whether a "please" would kill him but switched straight over to the requested piece. She'd barely played two bars, however, before he said, "No. Not like that. Play it like this."

Jude felt a flare of excitement in the pit of her stomach. Every nerve stood on edge, waiting for what was about to come.

And then there it was, the violin music. It was glorious, and perfect, and it made Jude's soul sing to hear it. It wasn't just that the Phantom was a master musician, it was also that he owned an ebony violin. Said to be the favoured instrument of Krag himself, they could only be played by people with cool legba blood in them and they were black as night except for their extra string. Where a normal violin had four strings, an ebony violin had a fifth that shone star-white – the infamous ghost string.

"That was wonderful," Jude said, once he'd finished. "But I can't replicate it."

"Why not?" the Phantom asked coldly. Sometimes the way he spoke to her made Jude wonder if he hated her, but then why on earth would he have asked her to play at his home in the first place? Perhaps he simply hated everybody.

"Well, I … I don't have a ghost string for a start,"

Jude said. "So I can't—"

"Think like a musician, if that's what you are," the Phantom cut her off. "And work out how it can be done."

Jude frowned as she searched her mind for a way to compensate for the lack of a ghost string. The idea came to her after a moment or two and she played a few notes on the trumpet to try it out.

"Not bad," the Phantom said. "Now slow down the tempo. Just a little."

Jude did as he'd said and gradually, with a tweak here and an alteration there, the piece was transformed and she was playing it better than she'd ever played it before. And that was the other benefit of coming to Moonfleet. When the Phantom tutored Jude in this way, she knew that she was improving as a musician as well.

At the end of the allotted hour, the Phantom said, "Thank you, Jude. That will do."

She began to put her trumpet away in its case. Normally at this point she would say goodbye to the Phantom, take her money – which he always left in an envelope for her by the door – and leave him in the Owlery. This time, however, he wanted a different arrangement.

"Your payment is there," he said, but then added, "Allow me five minutes. Then come to the front door of the house and wait."

Before she could reply, she heard the sound of a door beyond the screen opening and closing and assumed that the Phantom must have slipped out through the other entrance. Frowning, she stood and waited for the requested five minutes before walking out into the grounds, the marshy grass spongy beneath her swamp boots. She didn't technically need to wear them now that they were no longer able to live in the Firefly Swamps but Jude loved how chunky and reliable they were, and something about them reminded her of when times were better. Before the stranger came, Daryl died and her pa was ravaged by the gators he loved so dearly.

As always, Jude took the long way back to the house in order to avoid coming too close to the cajou tree. Some people called it the Hanging Tree because when people finally discovered what Violetta Majstro had been doing in the attic, she had been dragged from the house by an angry mob and then strung up on that very same tree. Her body had been cut down the next day and she'd been buried in the family's private cemetery, but some people still claimed that a hanging body appeared on the tree from time to time and that if you listened closely enough, you could hear the rope creaking in the breeze.

Jude had never seen anything of the kind and she knew that Moonfleet was the sort of place that was always going to attract wild speculation. Some people even said that one last prisoner remained in the attic at Moonfleet, a forgotten lunatic who raved there still. But the police had done a thorough search at the time and had been quite confident that everyone had been freed. Or buried.

Even so, Jude avoided the tree. Not only was it a sprawling, tangled black octopus of a thing, covered in rusty pins, bent needles and strange black feathers, but there was also the cajou ivy to consider. If you got too close, it would whip straight towards you, reaching out like fingers, trying to grab whatever came within reach.

So Jude took the long way, around the back of the house. It was an imposing, unwelcoming building. The ground floor rooms had its drapes firmly drawn across the windows, all except for one, which was always left bare. Jude had peeked inside on a couple of occasions and was always met by the same sight, a small, wood-panelled parlour with a table in the middle of the room.

It was covered in a tablecloth and there was a single tall-backed chair placed at it. The table was always set for dinner for one. A knife and fork lay on either side of a plate of long-cold congri and a wine glass stood at the side of the plate, filled with a deep red wine.

Jude had seen the same thing every time she'd glanced into the room, although there never seemed to be anyone actually seated at the table.

The Ghost Room, Ivory remarked inside Jude's mind, causing her to jump. She'd almost forgotten the cajou queen was there.

"What do you mean?" she said back.

The Phantom has to keep a place set at that table, Ivory said. *It's for one of the Majstros, I forget which. Perhaps old Julian Majstro – he liked his food, as I recall.*

"What happens if the table isn't set?" Jude asked, in spite of herself.

Julian goes berserk, from what I hear, Ivory replied. *Starts destroying things within the house. But give him a place at the dinner table and he's perfectly happy. That's why the curtains are tied back too, you see. He likes to look out on the grounds.*

Jude's eyes went to the empty chair and, for just a moment, she almost thought she saw a shape there, a glimpse of one bony ankle crossed over the other, a confused impression of a burgundy robe abruptly yanked aside to cover them.

She blinked hard and when she opened her eyes, there was nothing looking back at her but an empty chair. She shook her head and continued on to the front of the house.

This was the closest she'd ever been to it. Marble columns flanked the front door, which was made of solid black wood, smooth and shiny as oil. Jude set down her trumpet case on the doorstep, not knowing what to do next.

How long are we going to have to wait here for? Ivory complained.

"I have no idea," Jude replied. "He didn't say."

Try knocking on the door, Ivory said.

"I think I'd better just wait," Jude replied.

And so they waited, but the wait stretched on from five minutes, to ten, and then twenty.

He's probably got caught up in something and forgotten about you altogether, Ivory said.

Jude frowned and gazed around, as if hoping the Phantom might suddenly materialize out of nowhere. He *had* asked her to wait but perhaps there had been some misunderstanding? She didn't want to just leave without trying to find out first, so finally she gripped the heavy metal knocker and brought it down on the polished surface of the wood. She could hear the knock echoing within the house, but no one came in response.

Why don't you go in and look for him? Ivory suggested.

"I don't think he'd like that," Jude replied. "He's never allowed me into the house before. Besides, the door's locked—"

Easily rectified, Ivory replied.

Then before Jude could think of stopping her, the cajou queen took over her tongue, jerked her head down to the keyhole and whispered a single word: "*Skelekey.*"

There was a thunk as the lock clicked back and the door swung slowly open. Magic seemed to sizzle right down to the ends of Jude's fingertips. There was no denying that it was a pleasurable feeling, sweet and seductive as a first kiss. It didn't feel like a bad, evil thing at all. It felt like something special and wonderful.

It's the Power, Ivory whispered inside Jude's mind. *All cajou people tap into it to some degree but a queen has more of it flowing through her veins than anyone else can imagine.*

"I don't care!" Jude replied, wrestling back control of

her tongue. "You shouldn't have done that!"

She stepped forward with the intention of gripping the door handle and drawing it closed, but she couldn't prevent her eyes from taking in the hallway. Part of her had always longed to catch a proper glimpse of the inside of Moonfleet Manor, even as the more sensible part dreaded the possibility.

Before her was an ornate dark hallway, with absinthe-green-coloured tiles on the floor gleaming dully in the candlelight cast from the lit sconces on the walls. A massive chandelier hung from the ceiling, but it was unlit and so covered in spiders' webs that it looked more like a cocoon of some kind than a light fixture. The room was dominated by an imposing double staircase, carved from black wood that twisted up to the floor above. And from the gloom, quite clearly came the sound of a child – a girl – crying. The soft sobs seemed close, as if perhaps the girl was sitting in the shadows at the top of the staircase.

Jude couldn't have explained to anyone why the noise appalled her so, or why goose bumps appeared on her skin or little prickles of horror crawled along her scalp. She only felt some strong conviction that there was something *more* to the sound somehow, that it wasn't just a little girl crying in the dark, it was something *else*, something she should make every attempt to avoid.

Do you hear that? she thought at Ivory.

I do.

Is there a child living here?

Of course not, Ivory replied. *Moonfleet is no place for children.*

Jude cleared her throat. This was ridiculous – ludicrous to be afraid of a child who was clearly upset. She should call out and ask if the girl was all right. And yet although she cleared her throat a second time, she found she simply couldn't bear to utter a single word.

Don't call to the girl, Ivory said, reading her mind. *Don't try to speak to her.*

Why not? Jude thought back.

Just take my word for it, Ivory replied. *There are some things in this house you don't wish to know about.*

But … what if she's hurt? Or needs help?

You can't help her, Ivory whispered. *Nobody can.*

We shouldn't be here anyway, Jude replied, trying to convince herself. She felt a painful twinge of guilt about not even trying to help the girl, but she had her own problems to deal with after all. And coward that she was, she was afraid to peer too closely at the shadows in Moonfleet Manor.

Jude's eyes swept the room one final time and she was just about to retreat to the front porch when Ivory cried out inside her head.

Wait! That letter on the table there. It has the Fang symbol.

What the heck are you talking about? Jude thought back.

The Fang! Ivory replied impatiently. *Etienne's jazz club.*

Jude looked down and saw that there was a small table with elegant curved legs set by the front door. A stack of mail sat there and one of the letters peeking out from the bottom of the pile did indeed have a red symbol stamped on it.

Why would Etienne Malloy be writing to the Phantom? Jude asked.

Oh, the two of them go way back. They're good friends. Or at least they were.

How old is the Phantom anyway? Jude asked, wondering if Ivory knew the answer. He sounded like a young man but that didn't necessarily mean anything when it came to descendants. He could have been anything from twenty to two hundred.

No idea, the cajou queen replied. *But I first met him fifty years ago, so he's seventy-five at least. Probably more like a hundred. Take the letter. Perhaps it says something about me in it.*

Jude rolled her eyes. *I don't think he's likely to have written out a confession for you to—*

But that was as far as she got before Ivory seized control of her wrist, snatched the letter and thrust it into Jude's pocket.

Would you stop doing that! Jude exclaimed.

She was about to replace the letter on the table when a door opened down a nearby hallway and there was the sound of footsteps striding along the tiles towards them. Hastily, Jude hurried back out on to the porch, drawing the door closed behind her and not resisting as Ivory took over her tongue to whisper the magic word to lock the door behind them.

Jude's eyes remained fixed on the dark wood, convinced for a moment that the Phantom himself was going to appear and that he would be able to somehow tell, just by looking at her, that she'd been inside the house and taken something.

Her breath caught in her throat and her heart hammered in her chest as the lock clicked and the door swung open.

But it was not André Majstro who stood there. It was Paris Wing.

CHAPTER SEVEN

Jude had been quite mesmerized the first time she'd laid eyes on Paris, enchanted even. The girl was a Pearl and Jude had never seen one up close before. In a city flooded with beauty cajou charms, pretty women were common enough in Baton Noir, but there were some girls who were so exceptionally gorgeous that they didn't need to wear any beauty charms at all.

Since such women were highly sought after, it became common for girls to try to hide beauty charms in the lining of their clothes to pretend that their beauty was natural. To counteract this, a special cajou ceremony was devised that involved summoning Amelia, the legba of beauty herself, to judge whether a girl met the beauty standard to be awarded a cajou pearl. If Amelia deemed her lovely enough, then the girl would be given a charm in the form of a pearl. Like the cajou crowns, it glowed with a light of its own, this one sparkly and white, perfect and pure. If you saw someone wearing a pearl, you knew their looks were given by the gods, and that awarded them a special status in Baton Noir.

But, like everything else in the city, Pearls had been turned into something darker. The Pearl House on Moonshine Boulevard advertised itself as an upper-class establishment for the entertainment of its gentlemen members, but everyone knew the club was in fact a whorehouse. The Pearls who worked there were just another thing to be owned.

Some men visited the Pearls at the Pearl House while others, if they were particularly wealthy, preferred the Pearls to come to them. Some even had them live in, as if they were wives. Jude wasn't quite sure what the nature of the Phantom's arrangement with Paris was. Sometimes she was there and sometimes she wasn't, as far as Jude could tell. Still, the very fact that she was there at all made whatever respect Jude may have had for the Phantom vanish. By paying her to be here, he was part of the problem, after all. Part of the reason why pretty girls could be treated so horrifically in Baton Noir.

Unfortunately, though, Paris clearly had no warm feelings towards Jude. She'd made it quite clear that she disliked her the first time they had met at the front gates. Jude had tried to establish a friendliness between them by complimenting Paris on her dress. The other girl had turned such a withering look of contempt on her that Jude had actually flinched.

"Nice dungarees," Paris had said with a sneer. "My five-year-old brother has a pair just like them."

Today Paris wore her cajou pearl on a delicate silver chain, the sparkling sphere resting in the hollow of her throat. Her honey-blond hair was pulled back in a complicated plait that ran down to her shoulder blades. Her skin was the colour of cream, her complexion flawless and her eyes were a deep, dark green, the shade of goblins and sorcery. She was a rare butterfly of a girl and it seemed almost impossible that anyone could be that stunning without magical assistance, yet there the cajou pearl was.

She wore a pair of black jeans with a white sleeveless shirt, and the simplicity of her clothes only seemed to make her even more beautiful. A stack of pearl bracelets adorned one wrist and more pearls were threaded through her plait. Her eyes, as she looked at Jude, were full of resentment.

"Well," she said in an icy voice. "I hope you're pleased with yourself. He's furious."

"That's on you," Jude replied. "Not me. It's *my* money. You had no right to take it. And I need it more than you do."

Paris's eyes flicked to Jude's split lip and a sneer came over her pretty face. "Don't be so sure!" Her eyes moved to the front gates at the end of the driveway. "You're out there. And I'm in here. With *him*."

She shuddered, as if the mere thought of the Phantom was disgusting to her. Of course, Paris would be one of the few people who had actually seen him properly. Jude's curiosity got the better of her and she couldn't prevent herself from asking, "Is it … as bad as they say?"

"Worse!" Paris snapped. "Now, take your money and get out!"

She took a bundle of bills from her pocket and threw them at Jude, scattering them over the front porch.

"He insisted on giving you double. It might interest you to know that the extra money comes out of *my* wages. Count it if you like. It's all there."

And then she turned on her heel and walked back into the house, slamming the front door behind her.

Jude sighed, then got down on her hands and knees and gathered up the money.

Well, well. Ivory laughed softly inside Jude's head. *Paris really hates you, doesn't she?*

Goodness knows why, Jude replied, stuffing the bills into her pocket. *I've never done anything to her.*

She wasn't too keen on me either, if it makes you feel any better, Ivory said.

I don't care if people like me or not, Jude said.

She grabbed the last bill and straightened up. She could feel the crumpled letter in her pocket and thought about shoving it back through the letter box.

Don't even think about it, Ivory warned. *Not unless you want to be coughing up toads for the next hour.*

You can't do that! Jude exclaimed.

Don't test me.

Jude sighed. She turned away from the house and walked down the driveway. As she went, she couldn't shake the conviction that there were eyes on her, and when she glanced back at the house she could have sworn a curtain twitched aside in one of the upstairs windows, as if someone had suddenly stepped back. She shook her head and stepped out on to the street, glad to leave Moonfleet Manor brooding behind her.

The whole way back home she felt the letter burning inside her pocket. She couldn't shake the thought that the Phantom would know she'd taken it.

Don't be such a fool, Ivory said, reading her mind. *How could he know? He's not a magician, despite what everyone says.*

Descendants have powers that manifest in strange ways, Jude replied. *Everyone knows that. I just hope this letter is something worth stealing. I'm going to be pretty mad if it turns out to be a birthday card, or something.*

I don't think vampires send birthday cards, Ivory said.

In fact, it was an invitation. Jude tore the envelope open as soon as she was back in the privacy of her bedroom and a thick card slid out.

ETIENNE MALLOY
REQUESTS THE PLEASURE OF YOUR
COMPANY THIS EVENING AT A PRIVATE
UNVEILING OF A RARE ITEM SOON TO
BE AUCTIONED AT THE FANG.

STRICTLY INVITATION ONLY.

BLACK TIE
BLOOD AND CANAPÉS
7PM TO MIDNIGHT

Jude felt Ivory shift inside her mind.

This is perfect, she breathed. *There's no name on the invitation and the event is this evening.*

"You're not seriously expecting me to go there, are you?" Jude replied.

Why not? You have an invitation. I'd stake my life on the fact that that 'rare item' is the devil's coin. The brazenness of it!

"Look, I can't go tonight because I've got band practice. Cajou Night is coming up and we've got to—"

I don't care about your band practice! Ivory snarled inside her head. *You can do that any time, but this is your one and only chance to go to the Fang and we can't waste it. I need a lock of Etienne's hair in order to conduct a truth spell.*

"There is no *way* I can possibly get a lock of hair from—"

I'm not expecting you to pluck it from his head, Ivory snapped. *He has a private dressing room at the Fang. You can take it from his hairbrush. It'll be simple.*

Jude sighed. "Fine. I'll send a telegram to Sharkey to tell him I don't feel well and can't make practice. And I'll just have to hope my bandmaster is cool with it."

Good, Ivory replied. *We need to get you ready, but first I'd better explain what exactly you'll be walking into.*

♛

You might find it hard to imagine now but I was very beautiful when I was a young woman. I had some natural beauty of my own but I'd worked on that with cajou, used my own body to hone my craft until I was one of the most stunning women in all of Baton Noir. I wanted to be the greatest cajou queen who ever lived, more powerful than even my mother before me. And so I worked on my Power, nurturing it and feeding it, right from the beginning. My mother died young and I was crowned cajou queen at the age of nineteen.

I met Etienne Malloy at a jazz evening in one of the Fountain District's most musical mansions. He sought me out and we became lovers and soulmates for a time. I loved him more than I had thought it possible to love anything. It was a love that burned and blazed like a star. I thought that soulmates were forever – that they had to be.

But the years passed, as they must. Etienne is immortal, of course, and so he remained unchanged, as handsome and perfect as ever. But try as I might, I could not keep up. Cajou magic is strong and powerful but there's only so much it can do. I danced through my twenties, turned thirty and then forty. Cracks began to appear in the façade and I couldn't keep them at bay forever. Wrinkles would no longer be banished. Hairs turned grey and my body, which had once been so flawless, began to wither and sag.

Etienne said that he didn't care. That I was his great love and we would remain together. And idiot that I was, I believed him. Until I returned to our home on Song Square one day and found him in bed with that slut, Delilah. She wasn't even Royalty. Just a society girl who had wormed her way into Etienne's affections. But she was young and beautiful, both things that I no longer was. And I saw how foolish I'd been to expect Etienne to remain content with our arrangement when he still looked the way he did while I grew old.

I moved my things out that same day and Etienne didn't try to stop me. I put a sickening hex on Delilah so that all her hair fell out. Oh, I wasn't trying to hurt her, really. I only wanted to make Etienne suffer. But she was nothing to him and I had to wait another ten years before he met Jackie Jevais.

Jackie was a beautiful dark-haired vampire and the first time I saw them together, I could tell. I could see she was different, that Etienne cared for her, might even grow to love her. And being a vampire she would stay young and beautiful forever. I longed to strike there and then but I was disciplined. I bided my time and allowed their love to grow and grow. To flourish. Finally, when it was at its fullest bloom, I bribed one of their servants to steal a lock of her hair for me.

Back then I had two cajou pythons. Beau had a sister, you see. A black snake named Betty. She was my favourite. My darling. But magic like that requires sacrifice and so it was my favourite snake I had to kill. I knew that having only one cajou snake rather than two would reduce my Power, but I would have done anything. So I poisoned my snake and once she was dead I ate her brain, sobbing with every bite, then peeled off her skin and used it to perform my darkest spell yet.

It took several attempts and a great deal of energy and commitment, but eventually I was able to conjure up a living snake inside Jackie, born of black magic. She would have felt it inside her, wriggling around beneath her skin, coiled within her belly, growing fat on the food she ate, while Jackie herself became shrivelled and starved and skeletal.

But that wasn't the extent of it. The snake grew stronger and stronger and then it reached right into her soul and ripped away her name. People don't realize the importance of names but we all have one, even unnamed babies carry their true name with them inside their soul. It's what grounds us to the world and without it we don't know who we are or what our place is supposed to be. Within a week of the spell, Jackie went insane. She even turned on Etienne. Attempted to murder him with a stake. In the end, he had no choice but to send her away to an asylum. I believe she raves there still, tormented and wretched.

Etienne shut up his mansion and withdrew into its mirrored rooms for a while. No one saw him for several months. I began to worry. Began to fear that I had injured him too greatly. I regretted my actions but it was too late to take it back, although I did try, oh, how I tried. Once someone's sanity has been broken apart, it can't be put back together again. The cracks will always be there.

Eventually Etienne opened his doors and returned to society, but without his humanity charm. He'd removed it during his confinement and has never put it on since.

He knew I was to blame, although he couldn't prove it, but he must have known who was responsible. I could see the accusation in his eyes whenever we found ourselves in the same room at some social engagement. I expected him to strike back. Day by day, and month by month, and year by year, I waited for a blow that never came. Twenty years passed and I came to believe that he held off in order to torture and torment me.

I turned seventy this year. I suppose he decided now was the time to strike, before old age and natural causes could *do the job for him. So, there you have it. I loved him and I destroyed his life and took away whatever humanity he had left. Now he's had his revenge at last.*

The cajou queen stopped speaking. They were in the bedroom and Jude was sitting cross-legged on her bed, with Beau coiled up in her lap. There was a long moment of silence.

Then finally Jude said, "Ivory Monette, you are a stupid, stupid woman."

The cajou queen bristled inside Jude's mind.

Stupid?

"Naïve too."

I may be wicked and evil, but I am not stupid or naïve, you grubby Scrap!

Jude shook her head. "You destroyed three lives, including your own, from the sound of it. All because some guy jilted you."

She couldn't help thinking that it made her own spate of self-pity after Leeroy seem nowhere near as bad. But Ivory didn't agree. The cajou queen's anger simmered through Jude's body, fizzed through her veins and fluttered in her stomach.

You speak of things you do not understand. You do not know what it is to have a soulmate. Everyone has that one person who they would burn down the world for.

"Just because you love someone doesn't give you the right to take over their life," Jude replied. "Love isn't supposed to be selfish."

My dear, ignorant, naïve girl, love is the most selfish thing there is. Perhaps you will find that out for yourself one day.

Jude shook her head. She was perfectly content with her music and her father and the dark city. She didn't need anyone or anything else. More importantly, she didn't *want* anything else. Certainly not after the anguish of her failed relationship with Leeroy.

"Seems like an awful lot of hassle and unnecessary bother if you ask me," she said.

I didn't ask you, Ivory snapped. *Now look, you need an outfit. You can't go to the Fang in swamp boots. Don't you have anything else to wear?*

"Afraid not."

Then you'll have to purchase something, Ivory said. *There'll be no getting into the Fang dressed like that. I know a place.*

For a moment, Jude felt tempted to refuse outright. The story Ivory had told her about Etienne and Jackie had filled her with revulsion and reminded her that the cajou queen was without scruples. She didn't want anything to do with the woman and her black magic.

She didn't want to sneak into a dangerous vampire's club and attempt to steal his hair.

But then she thought of her father, rotting away with pain and regret and heartbreak in the next room, and how Ivory had offered her a way of helping him when nothing else had worked, and she knew then that she would walk into the Ruby Quarter, right into the vampire club and steal Etienne's hair. She'd even wear a goddamn dress if that was what it took.

"Fine." She sighed. "Just tell me where I need to go."

CHAPTER EIGHT

Ivory sent Jude to a witch on Goblin Street, where all the fanciest boutiques and stores were located.

Take Beau, she said. *It'll help her believe that I'm really here. If you'd stolen him, he would have swallowed you whole long ago.*

"How comforting," Jude replied.

She draped the huge snake over her shoulders and set off, drawing more than a few startled glances from passers-by.

"I hope this witch owes you a big favour," she muttered under her breath. "Because my budget won't stretch to buying so much as a button from any store on Goblin Street."

Don't worry about that, Ivory replied.

When they reached the store, its window was full of glass baubles. Inside each one there was trapped a small sad swamp fairy, with wilting wings and a dying firefly glow. Jude figured they were supposed to be pretty and entice people in but she just found them depressing. Like Scraps, fairies weren't worth much to cajou Royalty, and no one was going to stop anyone from imprisoning them on a whim if they felt like it, even if it was for a reason as stupid as making their overpriced boutique look attractive.

Jude pushed open the front door and stepped inside, her swamp boots seeming big and clunky on the marble floor. She'd barely had time to close the door behind her before the witch behind the counter let out a shriek of alarm.

"I'd know that snake anywhere – that's Beau! What the hell are you doing with the cajou queen's snake?"

Jude was about to reply, but the cajou queen took over her tongue and this time it was Ivory's voice that came out of her head, the old lady's rasping croak like sandpaper against Jude's throat.

"Hello, Marietta. Yes, it's me. I'm afraid I'm not quite done calling in favours. I need you to dress this girl and make her presentable enough to get into the Fang tonight."

Marietta was middle-aged, her dark hair scraped back into a severe bun. She wore a red skirt and jacket two-piece, with scarlet lipstick to match. She couldn't have looked more appalled if a zombie had just walked in. Tight-lipped, she said, "I'll close the store. You can come through to the back."

She locked the door and showed Jude to a fitting room. Her Royalty charm, like Ivory's, was extremely ornate, dangling from the end of a chain that sparkled with rubies. Jude saw that her hands trembled slightly.

"How have you done this, Ivory?" she asked. "What devilry is this?"

"None of your concern," the cajou queen snapped. "And you'd better not whisper a word of it to anyone either. I'll come back for you if you do, I swear it."

Marietta raised her hand. She'd gone white to the lips. "Please," she said. "There's no need for threats. I won't tell a soul." She looked Jude up and down and her mouth twisted in obvious displeasure. "The girl will wear a beauty charm, of course," she said.

"The girl will not," Jude replied, pushing the cajou queen aside before she could speak for her.

Let me choose what I wear, she warned Ivory inside her head. *Or I'm not going.*

Very well, she replied. *Although you'd be a fool not to take a beauty charm from Marietta. She has some that are extremely powerful.*

I don't care.

Leeroy had tried to persuade Jude to wear a beauty charm several times while they'd been dating.

"All women wear some kind of beauty charm in Baton Noir," he'd said one day in Jude's bedroom. "It's like wearing make-up."

"I don't wear make-up either," Jude had replied.

Then he'd produced a beauty charm from his pocket and clipped it to the brace of Jude's dungarees before she could stop him.

"There," he'd said, looking delighted. "Isn't that better?"

Jude's eyes went to the mirror on the opposite wall and she saw how the charm had smoothed away her freckles, evened her pale skin tone, brightened her eyes, concealed several little blemishes and immediately made her look far more attractive. But it wasn't real. It wasn't her. She tore it off and thrust it back at Leeroy.

"I don't want it," she'd said. "I … you know how I feel about cajou."

His eyes narrowed and his expression went suddenly cold. "Well, that's a nice thank you. This cost a week's wages."

"I'm sorry, Leeroy, but I really don't want it.

114

Perhaps they'll give you a refund if you take it back to the store?"

Leeroy stared at her for a moment, then slowly shook his head and gave a harsh laugh. "I never met a girl who thought she was above a beauty charm before. I hate to break it to you, Jude, but you're not the looker you obviously think you are."

How that comment had shrivelled her heart in her chest! The frustration of being so profoundly misunderstood. Jude didn't think herself above beauty charms, it was simply that she was quite happy being plain. She had never wanted to be beautiful.

"I'll wear a dress if I have to," she said to Ivory. "But that's it."

"At least let me do something about your figure," Marietta said. She flapped her hands at Jude and said, "Look at you. You're all straight edges. Like a boy. Most of my gowns won't fit you."

Do you really think you can do better than me? Leeroy's voice whispered, incredulous, inside her mind. *Gods, Jude! My little brother's got bigger tits than you.*

Jude forced the memory away. Crossed her arms and lifted her chin. "That's your problem," she said. "I'd be quite happy going in dungarees."

After a bit of fussing around, Marietta produced a

long grey dress with a sweeping skirt and an open back that had a timeless look of elegance about it, especially when they added a pair of long white gloves. Once the dress had been sorted out, Marietta produced a pair of silver high heels but Jude shook her head.

"No can do," she said. "Couldn't walk in 'em, even if I wanted to. Which I don't."

Marietta sighed. "I suppose we could find you some flat satin slippers, as long as they're strappy and sparkly—"

"I'm keeping my boots," Jude cut her off.

The witch looked at her, aghast. Ivory sighed inside her head.

"You can't!" Marietta said.

"Why not?" Jude replied. "The dress is so long that it hides my feet anyway, so what does it matter?"

"It … it just does!"

"Too bad," Jude said. "I'm walking into a vampire's lair. I'm wearing shoes I can rely on if I suddenly need to run away."

She picked up Beau from his snoozing spot by the mirror and draped him over her shoulders before going to the counter and taking the bag from Marietta. She was almost out of the door when she paused, looked back and said, "Oh, and one other thing." She gestured at the window. "Ivory wants you to release all these fairies. Immediately."

Marietta scowled but gave a curt nod. Jude disappeared out of the door before Ivory could correct her. Fortunately, the cajou queen didn't seem to care much what happened to the fairies either way and so as Jude walked away from Goblin Street, she was pleased that at least she'd been able to do some good with her shopping trip.

The shopping isn't done yet, Ivory piped up inside her mind. *We need to get the ingredients for a gris-gris bag.*

I'm not doing any black magic, Jude protested.

You certainly are, Ivory replied. *Only a fool would go walking into a vampire's lair without magical protection. You need a concealment charm. Vampires have heightened senses. There's always a chance he might sense me, somehow.*

Sofia—

Sofia might be able to do a spell on your behalf but it will be more powerful if it comes from you. Ask her if you don't believe me.

Jude went straight to Sofia's store and asked the question.

"She's right," her friend said. "The spell will be more powerful if you do it yourself."

Jude sighed. "I was afraid you were going to say that."

She left Sofia at the counter and walked around the store, picking out all the items Ivory wanted her to get – nails, herbs, salt, roots, crystal and the hottest red pepper they had.

You must always put an odd number of objects in a gris-gris bag, Ivory said. *No more than thirteen and no less than three—*

I don't care, Jude replied. *Spare me the lesson. Just tell me what I need to do.*

That's everything apart from the graveyard dirt and the chicken, the cajou queen replied.

Chicken? What the hell do I need a goddamn chicken for?

Ivory sighed. *After you've assembled the bag you need to cut out the chicken's heart and—*

No, Jude said.

The cajou queen paused. *What do you mean, no?*

I'm not killing a chicken.

A goat then.

No.

Why not?

I won't do blood magic.

The thought of it disgusted Jude. She knew that it happened, of course. Sometimes it seemed it was impossible to walk through Cadence Square without seeing the evidence of some gruesome cajou rite that had been carried out the night before – a half-dead rooster, still tied to a tree, with nine silver pins sticking from its chest, or a skinned chicken weeping its guts out into the dirt. She had seen hundreds of gentle goats plodding placidly through the Hurricane Quarter alongside their handlers, en route to their doom. Animals had no say in the matter, no defence against cajou evil at all. And it wasn't right. Jude felt her resolve hardening into a solid core of anger within her.

Ivory sighed. *Most cajou magic is blood magic, girl. And you eat meat, don't you? What's the difference?*

I'm not killing any animal for cajou spells, Jude said. *There must be another way.*

The gris-gris bag needs some kind of sacrifice, Ivory said. *An animal sacrifice is the most powerful kind.*

But not the only kind? Jude pushed.

No, Ivory admitted. *There's another method you can use to seal the gris-gris, but I expect you won't like that either.*

Tell me anyway.

You have to lie to a friend, Ivory said. *Or break a promise. The bigger the lie, or the betrayal, the more powerful the spell.*

Jude decided that was preferable to chicken-killing,

so when Sofia asked her what she needed the ingredients for and whether there was anything she could do to help, Jude told her that she was performing a spell to aid Ivory's memory of that night and they still had no idea what their next move should be.

Is that it? hissed Ivory. *Such a feeble lie is next to useless.*

It isn't feeble to me, Jude replied. *The invitation says you can bring a guest. I was thinking of asking Sofia to come with me tonight and now I can't. I'll have to go by myself.*

I suppose it'll have to do, Ivory sighed.

Jude said goodbye to Sofia and then went to the nearest cemetery, St Jacqueline's, to gather some graveyard dirt. She filled the jar she'd brought from the store and then straightened up. Her eye fell immediately on a man a few feet away from her. He was tall and lanky, all knobbly elbows and strange angles. He wasn't moving, just leaning against a shovel, staring at a nearby crypt.

Jude felt Ivory's flash of alarm at the sight of him.

What is it?

That's the Gravedigger, Ivory replied. *One of the cool legba. Just back away from him slowly. Don't touch him.*

The Gravedigger tilted his head, as if he'd heard Ivory's words somehow. He had bushy white hair that puffed out from a large bald spot on top of his head. It blew about in the warm breeze, although the man himself still didn't move.

What happens if I touch— Jude began.

Girl, you don't want to know.

Clutching the jar, Jude took a few slow steps back until her nerve broke and she turned and fled from the cemetery.

Back away SLOWLY, I said! Ivory hissed.

Behind her Jude could hear an odd high-pitched laugh that sounded as if it should come from a woman, but when she glanced behind her, she saw only the Gravedigger. To her relief, he was still bent over his shovel, staring at the crypt, although his shoulders shook with mirth.

You better not do that if we ever come across Garrow, Ivory scolded as Jude left the cemetery. *If you ever turn your back on Garrow he'll—*

"I don't want to know what he'd do!" Jude exclaimed. "I don't want to know who he is. How can I even see them anyway?"

You can see them because I can, Ivory replied. *And we're both looking through the same pair of eyes at the moment.*

"So that was really Baron Lukah I saw outside Sidney's house yesterday?" Jude asked. She paused at a street corner to catch her breath. "The legba of death himself right there on the street, smoking a pipe?"

Baron Lukah is very fond of smoking, dear, Ivory replied. *And he's got to smoke somewhere after all.*

Jude recalled those blank, smoked glasses and couldn't help shuddering at the thought that she really had been that close to the legba of death. She'd felt his shadow looming over their home many times, but to actually look at his face was another matter altogether.

You'd better get on home, Ivory prompted her. *There are things we must do to prepare.*

Jude tried to push all thoughts of Baron Lukah from her mind as she headed for home.

CHAPTER NINE

As Jude walked, the laughter of the Gravedigger rang in her ears the entire way. When she arrived home, she made straight for her room before her pa could see her and start asking questions about the twelve-foot cajou python round her neck, the jar of graveyard dirt in her hand or the contents of any of the odd-smelling bags she carried. She closed her bedroom door, locking it behind her, and deposited Beau on her bed, where he promptly curled into a coil on her pillow.

"Right," she said to Ivory. "You'd better tell me what to do."

You need to set up the altar first, Ivory said. *Can't perform any spells or rituals without an altar.*

Jude sighed. As someone who hated magic and cajou with a passion, the last thing she wanted in her bedroom was a black magic altar, but she proceeded to follow Ivory's instructions.

You need to include the four elements, the cajou queen said. *A bowl of water for water, a stick of incense for air, a black candle for fire and a jar of graveyard dirt for earth. Arrange them in a cross shape, with the incense at the top and the dirt at the bottom. The candle is in the east and the water in the west. I don't suppose you care but the cross shape is very powerful in cajou. We used to make all our deals with devils at a cross in the road, after all. Before the swamp devils arrived and pushed the old devils out. Now you just need a grugii.*

"A what?"

A grugii. It's like a kind of guide to direct the magic. Beau will have been working on one for you. It's probably ready by now.

Jude looked over at her bed, and the snake was already gliding down towards her. He stopped beside her knee and then opened his mouth wide and started to make a gurgling noise. Jude recoiled.

"Oh no, he's not going to be sick, is he?" she asked. She dreaded to think what kind of things the python might puke up on her bedroom floor. "What does he eat anyway? Should I be feeding him?"

Don't worry about that, the cajou queen replied. *He gets his sustenance from the spirit world. And he isn't going to be sick. He's giving you your grugii.*

The next second, an object slid from Beau's jaws, landing on the floorboards with a clatter. Jude grabbed a handkerchief to wipe off the snake saliva before holding it up to examine it properly, and gasped.

When Jude was at her lowest, when her pa was being particularly difficult and she felt wrung out with the effort of trying to keep them going, she had often imagined her despair as a sort of octopus. A tentacled thing that clung to her back and refused to let go. And now here was another octopus in her hand – only it wasn't dreadful and debilitating, it was weird and beautiful and lovely.

Despite herself, Jude was a little bewitched.

"She's glorious," she breathed.

The object in her hand was about the size of her palm and made from delicate china. Half girl, half octopus, she lay on her front, propped up on her elbows, gazing dreamily at something only she could see. Her top half was human, with red hair tied up on her head and red freckles dusting her pale face and shoulders. Her bottom half was a mass of octopus tentacles, black as night, shiny as oil. They looked as if they'd suddenly frozen mid-writhe. It was a peculiar, dark thing, but Jude loved it immediately.

Place it on the altar, Ivory said. *Then you light the candle and the incense and put the gris-gris bag in the centre of the cross.*

Jude did as she'd said. The gris-gris bag was a small velvet drawstring pouch, red for protection, with magic words inked on to the lining. Ivory had Jude bless each of the items she'd bought at Sofia's store and put them into the bag one by one. Then she had to pick up the bag in both hands, raise it to her lips and breathe into it.

Now draw the cords tightly, Ivory said. *At this point we would normally soak the bag in chicken blood but you'll just have to hope that your lie does the trick instead. And pray that nothing untoward happens tonight.*

♛

Jude prepared a simple supper for her pa and then told him she was going to band practice. He didn't think anything of it, and why should he? Musicians all across the city would be practising every evening in the days leading up to Cajou Night.

Jude couldn't exactly walk out of the house in her evening gown, so she stuffed it into a bag and then went down to the wooden pier at the back of the house where she hopped on to the swamp boat. It was a relic from their life before, when her pa had still been able to work as a gator man and swamp guide. He never set foot in the boat now, of course, but Jude still loved it.

She had decorated it with the orange cajou beads and plastic trumpets her guardian angel had sent her over the last couple of years, and the necklaces clicked together as she got on board. The propellers started up their usual roar and Jude eased the stick forward to set off carefully down the swampy canal.

It was wide enough for a couple of boats to pass each other in opposite directions, but nowhere near large enough to be able to put the accelerator down full throttle and tear around, skimming over the water, as she had loved to do when they still lived in the Firefly Swamps.

There were no fireflies here but there were ancient, knotted trees that lined the banks, leaning their crooked trunks out over the water, with long tendrils of swamp moss and cajou ivy hanging down in thick curtains from their branches. You had to keep watch for the cajou ivy because it seemed to have a mind of its own and would move around in the shadows, reaching for you with its hairy branches.

The trees were thought to absorb evil and negativity so if a hex or a jinx was placed at their base, the tree was supposed to neutralize its power. This explained the dolls. There were hundreds and hundreds of them, resting against the base of every tree, their misshapen heads lolling on their shoulders, their bright button eyes staring without seeing.

Jude figured they were dolls that people had found hidden under their front porches or buried in their backyards. Not all cajou dolls were supposed to cause harm. Some, like Ivory Monette's leapfrog poppet, were protective in nature. But the dolls here all seemed to have malicious intent behind them, as evidenced by their sewn-together lips or scorched hands, the nails driven into their stomachs or the needles in their eyes. After discovering these mutilated versions of themselves, people would offer them to the swamp trees in the hope that they would be able to absorb the evil from the dolls.

Leaving the poppets behind, Jude found a deserted side river to get changed in, then navigated the boat straight down Squid Ink Canal towards the Gargoyle Bridge. The old stone structure was hung with dozens of glass zombie bottles decorated with feathers and beads, with misshapen clay heads for corks. Most of the heads had lopsided eyes and lips that had been sewn shut. Zombie bottles were dark magic that had been illegal before the war but now hung here in plain sight, brazen and bold. People paid a great deal of money to cajou priestesses and conjurers to obtain these items, in the hope of turning the object of the spell into a zombie who would lose their free will entirely and do only the bottle owner's bidding.

It was dark by the time Jude arrived at the Railway Pier but the moon was full and shed plenty of silvery light over the dark jagged outline of the Smoky Mountains, as well as the Ghost Station at their base. It loomed before her in all its ruined, faded glory, the moonlight reflecting off its hundreds of dirty and broken windows.

Fifty years ago, it had been the largest, grandest railway station in the world. But then the war broke out and changed everything and Baton Noir became a corrupt place, a hotbed for cajou Royalty, and no one wanted to visit any more. The funding dried up and the railway fell into disrepair.

Cajou had always been part of Baton Noir but the city had historically belonged to Ollin. The two brothers always allowed the people to decide which one they wanted. When Ollin ruled, there was order and there were rules. Some of the most evil types of cajou were banned, like the zombie bottles. But when

Krag ruled, there was power, corruption and a certain amount of chaos. And that suited some people better.

Such as the young Ivory Monette, who didn't want to do things the same way her mother had done them. On her mother's death, there was still almost a year to go until Cajou Night, meaning that the country would have to go without a cajou queen until then. Ivory used the time to campaign relentlessly in favour of Krag.

Many people agreed that it was time for a change, but others dreaded the idea. The city – in fact, the entire country – seemed to be split right down the middle. And so fighting broke out, starting in Baton Noir before eventually spilling into the surrounding provinces that lined the Razzmatazz River and together made up Burnt Bones Country. (So named for the scorch marks left by the fire devils that had once roamed there, before the swamp devils chased them all away.) Baton Noir was the country's capital but all provinces got a vote as to which of the legba brothers sat on the throne.

And so the civil war raged on, becoming bloodier and bloodier with every passing day. By the time Cajou Night came around there was hardly anyone left to vote, but when the votes came in, the survivors had decided overwhelmingly in favour of Krag. Ivory was crowned and the very next day Ollin's churches were closed down all across the city, while altars to Krag were erected in their place.

Few ordinary non-magical people wanted to come to a city where he ruled. The life of a Scrap was not one to be coveted. Of course, technically, the people of Baton Noir and the Burnt Bones Country had the choice every year to change their minds and give the country back to Ollin. But the Royalty charms system came in as soon as the war finished and no one wanted to go up against the magical elite, powerful and ruthless as they were. And so the city had stayed Krag's domain. Many magical people also moved away, often to a different province altogether.

The Grand Smoky Railway Station closed its doors after a few years of dwindling tourism and then slowly fell to rot and ruin, causing the locals to rename it the Ghost Station. Even the pier itself was crumbling. Built alongside the railway station, it had once boasted elaborate mooring posts, carved alligator heads snarling ferociously from the top, with a painted boardwalk and elaborate cast-iron lamp posts. Now the posts were covered in moss and algae, the paint had long since peeled from the boardwalk and the lamp posts were dark and strung with hundreds of strings of red cajou beads, the colour of the vampires.

Flickering candles lined the length of the wooden walkway, leading all the way to the station itself. The main doors were propped open and Jude walked through into the lofty ticket hall. Candles flickered within the building too, reflecting off the hundreds of crystals still strung from the dusty chandelier above them.

It was a huge thing and Jude peered at it uneasily in the gloom, not wanting to walk beneath it in case the rusting cord holding it up snapped. She could make out the outlines of balconies from the floors above, as well as velvet drapes hanging in tatters from the walls. The candle-lined path had been cleared away, exposing the exquisite tiles beneath depicting trains and steamships, hot-air balloons and maps, dirigibles and compasses – from a time when travel had been exciting and glamorous. Aside from the path, though, the rest of the floor was covered in dirt and dust that had built up over some fifty years, as well as broken glass from the windows above and pieces of plaster where parts of the ceiling had caved in.

It was all frightfully unsafe but vampires did love a Gothic, dramatic setting and Jude wasn't surprised that they still wandered into the building. She hurried across the dark ticket hall, through to the platforms on the other side. They too had fallen into disuse and neglect, and the ever-present moss had crept over some of the railway lines, as if the swamp was trying to reclaim the Ghost Station. Jude could spot the odd disused railcar slowly rotting away in the dark, and the air stank of iron and decay. A warm wind whistled down the platform, tugging at Jude's dress like fingers clutching at the silk. She looked left and right, trying to get her bearings and work out where to go.

And that was when she saw the feather lying on the tracks. Large and blue, it almost seemed to glow in the moonlight. The next moment, the wind picked it up and it fluttered down the tracks. Jude looked back and quickly spotted another feather.

"Where are they coming from?" she muttered, a bad feeling stirring in the pit of her stomach.

She set off down the platform, following the trail of feathers until she turned a bend and immediately saw the girl lying on the train tracks.

CHAPTER TEN

Ivory had explained that Etienne had taken some of the abandoned railcars and restored them to their former glory and Jude could see them up ahead, several feet away. There were seven in total and even in the moonlight Jude could see they'd been waxed and polished. Beaded lamps shone in the windows, which were hung with red velvet drapes. Jude could hear piano music and laughter from within. No one cared that a teenage girl lay on the tracks outside.

Hiking up her long skirt, Jude hopped down beside her. She had brown hair that was tumbling out of her bun, a blue dress and a matching feather boa. The dress was torn at the shoulder and the boa lay crumpled on the ground, shedding feathers in the breeze. Twin puncture wounds on the girl's neck still bled, leaving thin trails down her neck. She was conscious and Jude helped her to sit up, propping her against the side of the platform. She couldn't have been more than fifteen. A Subject charm jingled against other cajou charms at her wrist. And a bruise was already blooming over her right eye. The night was as warm and close and sticky as ever, but the girl was shivering.

Jude felt the anger rising up inside her, begging to be let out. She clicked her fingers to try to get the girl's attention. "Hey," she said. "You in there?"

The girl just gazed back at her with an expression that was almost resentful. It occurred to Jude that no matter what she did, there would probably be no saving the girl – she might already be one of the doomed lost souls that were gobbled up by Baton Noir every day.

You're right, Ivory whispered. *This one already belongs to Old Esther.*

As if the thought of her name had summoned her, the legba of lost souls herself was suddenly there – right there on the tracks – hunched possessively over the slumped girl and hissing at Jude, who fell back with a cry.

Old Esther looked just as Jude had always imagined her, with an ancient body so crippled and bent that she could only barely drag herself along with the aid of a stick. Up close, Jude could see how her teeth were blackened with decay and drool hung in strings from her lips. Her skin was cracked with age, her fingers were bent with rheumatism and her eyes were wild and mad and feral. In spite of herself, Jude trembled.

Quick! Ivory said. *You have to present her with an offering.*

Each legba was supposed to be presented with their own unique gift if they appeared in physical form or took possession of another person. Baron Lukah was given a bottle of swamp whisky, for example, while Amelia – the legba of beauty – expected perfume and tiny fairy cakes. Jude had no idea what Old Esther's offering was until Ivory said, *Teeth! You have to pull out one of your teeth and give it to her.*

Are you crazy? I'm not giving her a tooth! Jude thought back, as the legba stretched out one deformed hand towards her mouth, grasping and clutching.

Then get the hell away from her! the cajou queen replied.

Jude didn't need telling twice. She scrambled to her feet and dragged the girl on to the platform. When she glanced back down to the tracks, the legba had gone.

"Come on," Jude said to the girl. "Let's find somewhere for you to sit down."

The girl didn't reply but she allowed herself to be led back to the Ghost Station, where Jude located a bench and sat her down on it.

"Wait here," Jude said, wrapping the feather boa round the girl's shivering shoulders. "I have some business to attend to, but once I'm done I'll take you back to the Hurricane Quarter and find you a doctor. OK?"

The girl shrugged, which Jude took as agreement. She left her on the bench, staring at the dancing shadows made by the candles, and made her way back down the tracks to the Fang, where she presented the stolen invitation to the doorman.

He waved her through and she stepped into the first railcar. A waiter immediately handed her a red drink in a champagne flute and Jude didn't need to look too closely to know that it was blood, thick and clotted.

The car had clearly once been a saloon for serving cocktails and nibbling hors d'oeuvres. There was a bar in the corner and the velvet seats were arranged in booths. The windows were all closed and the air was horribly warm and stuffy. The red velvet everywhere simply added to the sense of claustrophobia in the close, narrow space. A musician belted out jazz tunes on a small piano to the fifteen or so vampires in the car.

You must get to the end of the train, Ivory urged. *Etienne's railcar is at the end.*

Jude put down the glass of blood on a nearby table and squeezed her way past the throng of vampires as best she could. They were all elegant and beautiful, and many of them eyed her with a mild sense of surprise as they caught her scent and realized she wasn't one of them.

When she got to the fourth car Jude saw Etienne himself, dressed in a dark blue suit with a white cravat, lounging in a chair by the window and watching the female saxophone player in the corner with a hungry expression on his face.

Here Jude also saw the 'rare item' the invitation had spoken of. Ivory had been right. Displayed in a glass case at the end of the railcar was the coin she had seen through Ivory at the Blue Lady. It gleamed there looking dirty and unassuming, and it was hard to believe that it was actually one of the most powerful items known to cajou. There was a placard beneath the coin with four words painted on it in elegant red lettering:

Cajou Queen's Murder Weapon

I was right, Ivory breathed.

Jude frowned. *But … surely he can't just be auctioning it off like that? I mean, I know the cajou Royalty are powerful but even Etienne can't get away with this in broad daylight, can he? Surely the coin must be evidence?*

Perhaps he has managed to bribe the police, the cajou queen replied.

Jude knew it was likely. Most of the police were Subjects, after all. Probably all of them. She couldn't recall ever seeing a Scrap in uniform.

It hardly matters now, Ivory went on. *You must get to his drawing room. Once we have his hair I can perform a spell to—*

Ivory broke off as Etienne suddenly called out, making Jude jump, "You there!"

She turned, afraid that he was speaking to her. Perhaps he knew, somehow, what she planned to do. But he was looking at the waiter.

"My glass is empty," Etienne said in a cold voice.

The waiter – a small, middle-aged man with a slight limp – hurried forward to refill it. Etienne lifted it to his lips, took a sip and then said, without looking at the waiter, "I won't have slovenly service at the Fang. Get out."

The waiter hesitated. Only for a moment – but it was enough. Etienne sprang from his chair so fast that Jude barely saw him move. Suddenly he was beside the waiter, his tall body looming over him in the narrow space.

"I ... I'm sorry, sir—" the waiter began, but that was as far as he got before the vampire grabbed him by his lapels.

In one smooth movement Etienne took the wine bottle from the waiter with his left hand and used his right to grip the back of the smaller man's neck. Then he slammed his head down into the side of the table.

Once, twice, three times.

Four, five, six.

Jude closed her eyes to block out the sight as she felt that familiar sense of rage boiling up inside her. How she longed to intervene and do *something* rather than simply standing and watching it happen along with everyone else.

But what could Jude do? What could anyone do? Ever since the war, Royals had ruled Baton Noir. Sometimes it felt like they ruled the whole word. And no one had the guts to stand up and say enough was enough.

Finally Etienne let the waiter go and the man slumped on to his knees, his lips and nose a bloody mess. A couple of his teeth lay on the floor beside him. The green witchstone in his Subject charm had lost its light. The waiter scrambled unsteadily to his feet. He was still trying to apologize as he backed away, the words bubbling over his torn lips.

"I know where you live," Etienne said as he retook his seat in the booth. "If I ever see you here again I will have your daughters slaughtered."

The waiter flinched and then hurried from the railcar. Throughout the whole exchange, the saxophonist had continued to play without missing a note. Jude wondered how often something like this happened at the Fang.

She kept her head down as she made her way to the next car. When she got to the seventh, she saw there was a sign over the door: *No humanity charms beyond this point.*

Aside from the ugly affair with the waiter, the atmosphere in the first six cars had been fairly civilized, with their champagne flutes and evening gloves and smoky jazz. But the seventh car was an altogether different story. Some of the vampires in it were completely naked, for a start. Some seemed to be drugged up, high on something. Most of them were feeding from human Subjects with pale skin and frightened eyes. There were no champagne flutes. Just ripped skin and bloody lips.

Etienne's dressing room is at the end, Ivory said inside Jude's head. *Keep going.*

Have you been here before? Jude asked her, wondering how she knew so much.

Etienne wouldn't permit it, Ivory replied. *But he couldn't prevent me from standing on the platform and watching. He doesn't own the entire Ghost Station. Head for the drapes.*

Jude saw there were velvet drapes marking the end of the car. A sign saying *Private* was pinned to the cloth but she slipped quickly behind the drapes, praying that the vampire clients in the room would be too stoned to notice and that their human victims would be too preoccupied with having their blood drained.

It was still a risky move, though, and she felt her heart speed up in dreaded anticipation of being caught. Her gloved fingers gripped the door handle, but when she pressed down it didn't budge.

"It's locked."

Of course it is, the cajou queen replied.

Remembering the magic word Ivory had used before, Jude bent down to the keyhole and whispered, "*Skelekey*."

Once again, the delicious sensation of black magic fizzed through her fingertips, and she couldn't help a small shiver of pleasure.

It's not so bad, is it? Ivory whispered. *A little taste of black magic.*

Opening a locked door is hardly black magic, Jude replied. But deep down she felt worried. She shouldn't get any pleasure from cajou at all. She shouldn't grow used to it.

She pressed down on the door handle and this time it opened into Etienne's private dressing room. She stepped in, being careful to draw the door closed behind her. Ivory repeated the spell and the lock clicked back into place.

Jude's hands were sweating inside her gloves as she fumbled around for a light switch. At last the glow of light filled the car and Jude saw that it was part office and part dressing room. A carved wooden desk stood at one end and Etienne had filled the rest of the space with racks of clothes, full-length mirrors and a plush velvet couch. There was a small sink over in the corner, with soap and a comb lined up neatly beside it.

Thrilled to have discovered the comb so quickly, Jude hurried over to take it, only to find that it didn't hold a single hair.

Not one! Ivory hissed, and Jude could feel her anger and disappointment.

"One of his sworn enemies is a cajou queen," Jude said. "Perhaps he got in the habit of not leaving hair around the place to be hexed with! You should have thought of that."

I didn't think he'd continue to take such precautions once I was dead, Ivory protested.

Before Jude could reply, there came the sound that she had dreaded since first entering the room – the quiet click of a key turning in the lock.

CHAPTER ELEVEN

There was only one place to hide in the whole room, so Jude threw herself under the desk, her bare shoulders pressing painfully into the wood and her boots wedged tight against the other side. She'd be discovered instantly if anyone came round the front. She could only hold her breath and pray that didn't happen.

"—isn't going to be much use to her, is it? She's dead, after all." Jude recognized Etienne's voice. He sounded exasperated. "So what harm is there in it? Well? Aren't you going to say anything?"

"It appears you have enough to say for the both of us."

Jude almost gasped out loud at the sound of that second voice. It was one she knew immediately – one she had heard twice a week for over a month now, talking softly to her through the wire mesh of the screen in the Owlery, a voice she would recognize anywhere.

The Phantom. But how had he even known about the party when he hadn't got the invitation?

Jude couldn't help staring at the wooden front of the desk, hoping for some small crack to peer through and get a glimpse of him. All those weeks of being in the same room and she'd still never actually seen him with her own eyes. It was hard not to be curious, especially given what everyone said.

"No, really," Etienne went on. Jude heard the creak of furniture as he sat down, presumably on the couch. "Since you clearly have an opinion on the matter, share it with me, please. What harm is there in auctioning the coin?"

"It's ghoulish," the Phantom replied.

"As I pointed out to the police, it can hardly be returned to its rightful owner now, can it?" Etienne said. "Given that it belonged to the murderer."

"I rather thought the rightful owner might be you," the Phantom said.

Etienne gave a short laugh. "Well, you're in a charming mood this evening, I must say."

"It should have been returned to Ivory's family once the police released it," the Phantom said.

"Perhaps, but I was the one who found it and that gives me some right to it, I suppose? The police seemed to think so at any rate."

"Of course they did," the Phantom replied. "They're sell-outs."

"Subjects, you mean," Etienne corrected.

"You must do as you see fit," the Phantom said. "But I don't care for it."

"I would have preferred you not to fraternize with the woman who ruined my life, but there we are. We each have our own cross to bear."

"I was not fraternizing with Ivory," the Phantom replied shortly.

"No? So you didn't ask her to come and visit you at Moonfleet on a regular basis?"

"She did come to Moonfleet but you know full well what that was in regard to. You also know I would never have asked her were I not desperate."

"Still the same old savage, I take it?"

Jude frowned, wondering what he was talking about.

"Quite," the Phantom replied. "But I did not come here to speak of that."

"No, you came to lecture me about something that's none of your damned business," the vampire replied pleasantly. "Are you sure I can't persuade you to have something to eat?"

"I am not hungry."

The vampire sighed. "Well, fetch yourself a drink at least. Bottom desk drawer."

Jude felt her stomach plunge into her boots. If the Phantom came round to the front of the desk then she would see him and he would most certainly see her.

You stupid girl! Ivory groaned. *You should have worn the beauty charm. Then he wouldn't have recognized you.*

What difference would it make? Jude hissed back. *He'd still expose me!*

"I am not thirsty," the Phantom said.

"But I am," Etienne replied, his voice suddenly hard. "Fetch me the bottle, can't you?"

"I am not your servant, Etienne," the Phantom replied in a growl. "And good thing too. I saw the state of that waiter who was leaving as I came in. Your handiwork, I presume?"

Despite his words, though, Jude could hear the creak of footsteps as he walked over to the desk, and her hands bunched up into fists at her side as her mind tangled itself into knots desperately trying to find a way out.

"You're a fine one to talk," Etienne drawled. "Given the atrocities that have gone on in your house. That business in your attic – a ghastly affair by anyone's standards. People accuse me of being a monster, but in truth I don't believe I could ever be half so ruthless as you've shown yourself to be. And to someone you proclaimed to love, no less."

The footsteps were almost at the desk now and Jude's heart raced in her chest. Her palms became slippery, her breath hitched in her throat and it was hard not to groan aloud. She gritted her teeth, preparing to be dragged from the desk by her hair, dreading the thought of broken noses and picking up teeth off the floor…

And then he was there. Frozen halfway down to reaching for the bottom desk drawer. Slim and elegant, wearing a beautifully tailored charcoal-grey suit. Despite her dread of this moment, and how it would play out, Jude couldn't help her eyes flying straight to the Phantom's face. A face she had been dying to see for ages and that everyone said was hideously deformed, a grotesque horror that kept him mostly confined to Moonfleet.

In that first instant, she thought that a demon's face stared back at her – the skin a deep, dark red, the colour of blood clots. But then she realized that he was wearing a Cajou Night mask. It covered his face, starting at his forehead and coming down over his cheeks and nose to end just above his mouth. In fact, his lips and chin were the only part of him on display – even his hands were inside gloves. The small bit of skin she could see was pale, like porcelain, his lips were wide and his black hair fell to his shoulders. His eyes, behind the mask, were a smoky-grey, and Jude thought she saw them widen in surprise at the sight of her. Through the eyeholes of the mask, she could just about make out that the skin around one of his eyes was mottled and that the lower eyelid sagged downwards, exposing the inner red eye socket.

For an endless moment, they just stared at one another, and Jude couldn't help trembling. If he gave her away, she was done for. The Phantom hesitated for barely a moment before he yanked open the bottom drawer and pulled out a bottle of moonshine, along with a cut-glass tumbler.

"What happens at Moonfleet," he said, straightening up, "is none of your affair."

"I could say the same to you about the Fang," Etienne replied.

"When is this auction going to be anyway?" the Phantom asked, moving round the desk and out of Jude's sight.

"Next week. Gives me time to drum up as much interest as possible beforehand. You know, if you get enough people in then you can make almost as much in bar takings as you will on the auctioned item itself."

"Is business really that bad," the Phantom asked, making no attempt to disguise the contempt in his voice, "that you must keep afloat by auctioning off macabre murder weapons?"

"Macabre murder weapons are immensely popular in Baton Noir," Etienne replied. "Just you wait. People will pay good money to come and gawk at the weapon that finished off the cajou queen."

"I can see there's no talking sense to you," the Phantom said. "Let's go back out. I was enjoying the jazz."

"Sometimes I think that's the only reason you come here any more," Etienne grumbled.

Fortunately, the vampire seemed only too glad to return to his club and another moment later the door closed and they were gone, leaving Jude alone.

That bastard! Ivory hissed. *How I hate him!*

Jude didn't reply as she scrambled up from behind the desk and then hesitated beside the door. Fortunately, it had a little peephole set into it, which allowed her to see through to the other side. After giving it five minutes, Jude used the magic word to unlock the door and hurry through before locking it behind her again.

As discreetly as she could, she slipped out from behind the curtain and began making her way back through the railcars.

But we haven't got what we came here for, Ivory protested.

You saw his comb, Jude shot back. *The only way I'm getting some of Etienne's hair is if I pluck it from his head myself. And I'm not doing that. Not after what I saw him do to that waiter. We'll have to come up with another way.*

Ivory didn't seem to have an argument to that because she fell silent. As Jude strode down the train, she glimpsed Etienne lounging in the same booth as before, but there was no sign of the Phantom. She went straight to the exit, stepping out into the warm night air with relief.

And then a gloved hand clamped down on her arm.

"There you are, my dear."

Jude looked up into the Phantom's glowering red demon's mask and had to force herself not to shrink back. The mask itself was an ugly, fearsome thing. How much worse must his real face be that he would choose to cover it with such a hideous visage?

"Allow me to escort you back to the station," he said.

His voice was level, almost pleasant, and Jude realized that he was talking for the benefit of the nearby doorman. Those slate-grey eyes, though, were steely hard and cold as he stared at her. Despite the warm night air, Jude shivered. It was beyond strange to be so close to the Phantom like this, with no screen to separate them. He was not much taller than Jude herself and slender, almost thin, yet it was an elegant thinness rather than a scrawny one. There was a sort of repressed energy about him – like a coil that longed desperately to spring. And when Jude took the arm he offered her, she could feel the tension in his body and the hardness of the muscles beneath his jacket sleeve.

They started off down the tracks together and the Phantom spoke as soon as they were out of earshot of the doorman.

"What can be the meaning of this?"

Jude desperately wracked her brains for an explanation, but coming up with nothing decided to go for the defensive approach.

"Only the other day you said that what I do when I leave Moonfleet is my own affair."

The Phantom breathed out hard through his nose. "Fortunately, the doorman knows me, or else I may not have got in at all tonight. Etienne was adamant that an invitation had been sent to Moonfleet. You broke in," he said. "And you stole it. Is that not so?"

Jude couldn't help but squirm. "It … it wasn't premeditated," she said at last. "But it was wrong. And I'm sorry."

"Apology not accepted," the Phantom snapped. "Why are you wearing that Royalty charm? You're a Citizen."

Jude was glad that he'd used the word "Citizen" rather than "Scrap", but she had no idea how to reply. The Phantom stopped on the tracks and gripped her wrist to force her to stop too.

"You must listen to me; I am serious," he said. "Whatever is going on, do not cross Etienne Malloy. He is … unbalanced. And do not ever think of setting foot in Moonfleet Manor again. It isn't safe. How dare you go against my instructions like that? I cannot think what possessed you to do such a thing."

Jude opened her mouth to reply, but before she could do so Ivory seized control of her tongue and spoke in her rasping old voice.

"Don't bully the girl, André. And as for what possessed her – that would be me. The cajou queen."

Jude thought she saw the Phantom's eyes widen behind his mask. He let go of her abruptly. "No," he said. "It cannot be. Ivory Monette?"

"There's only one queen of Baton Noir, darling," Ivory replied.

Would you stop that? Jude thought furiously at Ivory. *I can speak for myself.*

She shoved the cajou queen aside with a mental effort. "I'm sorry," she said. "Sometimes she manages to take control of my tongue."

"So it is true?" the Phantom replied. "You're possessed by the cajou queen?"

"She wants to find out who murdered her," Jude replied.

I've thought of something I need from him, Ivory said. *Something he can do. Tell him.*

He won't want to help, Jude thought back.

Tell him or I'll speak for you.

"She says she wants your help," Jude said reluctantly.

"Does she indeed?"

Tell him if he doesn't help then I'm going to reveal his secret.

Jude hesitated. How on earth would he react if she said such a thing?

"Well?" the Phantom said quietly. "There is something else she wishes to say to me, is there not?"

Jude sighed. "She … she says that if you don't help then she's going to reveal your secret."

The Phantom had gone absolutely still. "I see."

A dark shape fluttered above their heads and Jude

looked up sharply, squinting into the night. Something large and leathery rustled past in the shadows, just out of sight.

"This is not the place to talk," the Phantom said. "Come to Moonfleet tomorrow. Go straight to the Owlery."

No. To the front door, Ivory said. *He will allow us inside.*

"Ivory wants us to go into Moonfleet itself," Jude said.

"That isn't permitted," he snapped.

I will not talk business in a filthy Owlery, Ivory said. *Tell him the whole city will know his secret if he doesn't allow us into the house.*

Jude groaned. "I'm sorry, but she's saying that she'll tell everyone your secret if you don't let us into the house."

The Phantom made a growling sound in the back of his throat. "Goddamn you, Ivory Monette!" He shook his head, breathing hard. For long moments he was silent. "Very well. You will come into the house. But I will not be held responsible for anything that happens. Now, let's go. I must get back – Paris will be waiting for me."

Jude followed the Phantom along the tracks, her swamp boots knocking off pieces of rust and cajou moss. She couldn't shake the conviction that they were being watched. Several times she glanced back over her shoulder, but there was only disused track stretching along behind her.

It's Etienne's vampire bats, Ivory said.

The Phantom must have been aware of them too, because he glanced up and the next second flung out his gloved hand towards them. There was a burst of silver light, and then a flurry of feathers as a ferocious-looking hawk owl flashed past, tearing after the bats above like it meant to rip them apart.

Jude's mind immediately flew to that night six months ago, when she'd broken up with Leeroy. She'd had tea with Sharkey and his grandmother and then arrived home to find Leeroy waiting for her on her balcony, drunk and angry.

"Where the hell were you?" he'd said, the smell of beer sour on his breath. "I've been waiting here all evening."

"How was I supposed to know? We didn't have any plans to meet—" Jude began.

"So you thought you'd sneak off the moment my back was turned?" he snarled.

"I didn't sneak off anywhere! I just had dinner with my friend."

Jude felt suddenly exhausted by the conversation, knowing exactly how it would play out, as it had so many times before.

"He's after you!" Leeroy said. "Just can't wait to get into your pants. If he hasn't already. And I'm sick of it." His mouth set. "I don't want you to see him any more."

Jude gaped at him. "He's my best friend. I can't—"

"If there really is nothing going on between you then you won't mind not seeing him again," Leeroy said, a crazed look of triumph on his face. "How many times have you slept with him? You slut!"

Jude felt the sting of the word and tears filled her eyes against her will. "We've … never even kissed," she said, but it came out as a whisper. What was the point? She knew he would never believe her, whatever she said. "I can't do this any more. I think … I think we need to … break up."

For a long moment, he just stared at her, his eyes bloodshot in the dark.

"You ungrateful bitch!" he said in a hoarse voice.

Suddenly he no longer looked handsome to Jude at all. It was like she could see him clearly for the first time and she knew what she had to do. The certainty of it was a relief after all the months of agonizing about how she could fix things between them. It was a glorious thing to feel her resolve harden inside her as she realized she no longer wanted to fix it. She no longer wanted Leeroy and hadn't wanted him in some while. Whatever love there might once have been was dead.

"Get out," she said. "I don't want to—"

He lunged at her before she could finish. Suddenly his hands were wrapped tight round her arms and he was shaking her so hard that she bit down on her tongue and blood filled her mouth. "*Bitch!*" he hissed. "You worthless, ugly, useless *bitch!*"

Jude tried to twist out of his grip but he was stronger than her, and she could see a terrifying wildness in his eyes. She didn't know what he would have done if the silver owl hadn't arrived. It swooped at them so fast that Jude didn't get the chance to see it properly. She only knew that it gave a terrible shriek and then attacked Leeroy like a deranged thing, tearing at him with its claws and beak so that he fell to the ground, arms raised protectively over his head as blood ran down his wrists.

It only lasted a few seconds, and then the bird left as suddenly as it had arrived. Leeroy staggered to his feet, and with one last furious look at Jude fled down the stairs to the street. As she wiped blood from her chin, Jude searched the sky for the bird, but it had completely disappeared.

Now, on the train tracks, she said, "What the heck was that?"

"A hawk owl," the Phantom said briefly. "It'll chase away the bats. Temporarily."

"But ... it looked like it was made of moonlight..."

André is descended from Krag, Ivory said inside her mind. *The night legba. His descendants can do strange things with moonlight sometimes.*

The Phantom offered nothing more about the owl and they made their way back to the train station in silence. When they arrived, the girl Jude had left there was gone.

"You came by boat?" the Phantom said.

"Yes, but there was a girl. She was hurt. I promised I'd take her back to the Hurricane Quarter with me."

"Pointless," the Phantom said, dismissing the idea with a wave of his gloved hand. "If she's one of Etienne's girls then she'll already have gone back to him. There's no saving such a person."

Jude clenched her hands by her sides. "You'll save any owl that comes your way but won't lift a finger to help a human girl?"

The Phantom paused and his voice softened just a

little. "A person has to want to save themselves first," he said.

"Well, I promised," Jude said. "I'm going to look for her—"

"You are not." The Phantom cut her off, his voice hard once again. "You're going straight home. You will not meddle in Etienne's affairs any more than you already have."

Jude thrust her anger down deep. "Fine," she said, doing her best to sound meek. Contrite. Both things she had never been in her life. "Whatever you say."

She followed the Phantom over to the pier and recognized his swamp boat tied up at the other end.

"Come at eight tomorrow morning," he said curtly.

Jude thought of her pa and how she'd have to get him up and dressed and breakfasted first.

"I can't come at eight," she began. "I have to—"

"Don't be late," the Phantom said.

And without another word he walked down the pier to his boat.

You arrogant bastard! Jude thought, glaring at his back, feeling a sudden rush of resentment.

Well said, dear, Ivory remarked.

Jude hopped down into her own boat and made a show of starting up the engine but the Phantom

161

was so convinced his orders would be obeyed that he didn't even linger to make sure she left. Instead he gunned his engine and shot straight out into the canals. Eager to get back home to Paris, Jude supposed. She shook her head and scrambled back on to the pier.

What are you doing? Ivory demanded.

"Going back to look for that girl," Jude replied.

You shouldn't. André is right. There's no helping her. Girls like that don't want to be helped.

"You don't know her!" Jude shot back. "You don't know anything about her. I made a promise and I'm going to give her every opportunity to come back with me, to get away from this place if she wants to."

She couldn't help thinking of the crying child at Moonfleet and how she had just left her there without even trying to find out if she was all right. She wasn't about to do the same thing again.

It is tempting fate to go back, Ivory warned. *All for the sake of a girl you don't even know, and who will not want to be saved.*

"I don't care," Jude said, striding along the wooden boards. "I'm going to have a quick look around the station. If she's not there then so be it, but I can spare her five minutes before I abandon her in this awful

162

place with that monster. Whoever she is, no one deserves that."

She walked back into the Ghost Station and spent the next ten minutes poking into its dark corners, but there was no sign of the girl. Perhaps she really had gone back to the Fang. Jude decided to have another look around the pier and started to walk back across the ticket hall. She was almost at the exit when a cool voice spoke behind her.

"Giving up so soon?"

Jude turned and saw Etienne standing there, gazing straight at her with his hands in his pockets.

CHAPTER TWELVE

"You're looking for Mary, aren't you?" Etienne said. "She's returned to the Fang, of course. She never would have left with you."

"Oh." Jude swallowed hard. Her heart was already starting to speed up inside her chest even before a large shape detached itself from one of the balconies above and flapped down to perch on one of the gargoyle's heads. Finally Jude could see it clearly and it was indeed a large vampire bat.

"She's too important to me you see," the vampire went on, taking his hands from his pockets. "She serves many functions. Cleaning my office, for example. Do you not think she does a good job?"

"I … I imagine she does," Jude said.

"Come now, madam," Etienne said with a slow smile that exposed his vampire canines. "Don't be coy. You *know* she does. You were giving my office quite a thorough examination, in fact."

Jude's heart seemed to stop. She could feel the blood draining from her face, hear Ivory gasp inside her head.

"Oh, yes, I knew you were there," Etienne said, taking a step closer. "I heard your heart beating the moment I walked through the door. Why do you think I sent André over? I thought he'd drag you out by your hair and save me the trouble, but then he developed a sudden case of selective blindness. Imagine my surprise. But *why* would he do such a thing? For some girl he doesn't know?"

Etienne walked closer and Jude forced herself not to take a step back. She could feel Ivory's emotions – a mixture of fear and love and yearning – all blazing away inside her.

"Unless," Etienne went on softly, "he *does* know you?"

The vampire was right in front of Jude now and peering at her closely. Suddenly his pupils dilated alarmingly. "Well, I'll be damned," he said in a voice as soft as smoke. "The bats told me they'd heard Ivory's voice but I didn't think it could be true. That explains why André didn't give you away." Jude was painfully aware of the vampire's strength, and his menace, and his size, as he leaned his head towards hers and said,

"I did not expect to see you again until we were reunited in one of the hells, my darling."

Some unseen shape shifted above them and the warm air stirred as dark wings kissed the night. Jude wondered how many bats were up there.

"Do you remember that day fifty years ago?" Etienne asked. "Here. In this station."

Immediately the deserted building shifted and changed. The dirt and grime fell from the walls, the chandelier sparkled in the sunlight that poured through the spotless windows. The decay and the debris and the decline were all gone and, in their place, a magnificent space glittered around them. Beautifully dressed people hurried to and fro on their way to trains; the ticket counters gleamed, the brass lamps shone and the floor tiles were waxed and polished. Jude could smell the smoke and oil of the steam engines, could hear their piercing whistles over the background hum of chatter.

Etienne stood before her but this was a different Etienne. A humanity charm hung alongside the Royalty one at his wrist and a top hat shielded his face from the sun. His blue eyes were warm as he looked down at Jude. Only he wasn't really looking at her – he was looking at Ivory. Jude caught their reflection in a gold-framed mirror on the wall behind and saw Ivory as she'd once been – young and beautiful, with a headscarf tied around her mass of black hair. Her purple dress clung to her in all the right places and her eyes were dark and bewitching, full of a pure, uncomplicated love as she gazed up at the vampire.

He leaned down so that his lips were beside her ear. "You are the one true love of my soul, Ivory Monette," he whispered, his cool breath tickling her skin. "I would do terrible and unspeakable things in your name. I would burn down the whole goddamn world if you asked me to."

The next moment, the sunshine, the steam and the echoes of glory all fell away, leaving nothing but ashes and ruin in its place. The dark, deserted train station flickered in the candlelight, like the sad ghost of the thing it had once been. Etienne stared down at her with his ice-blue eyes and there was only a cold anger where love had once thrived.

"It is you, isn't it?" Etienne peered at her closely, as if he might be able to glimpse Ivory behind Jude's eyes. "I can hear your heart beating beneath this girl's. How are you doing this? How are you not dead?"

"I am dead," Ivory replied, taking over Jude's tongue to speak in her own voice. "I fashioned a leapfrog poppet to pull my soul into a living person."

"Good gods," Etienne said softly. "Why?"

"So I could find how who murdered me. And make them pay."

The vampire gave her a strange look. "You think it was me," he said.

"Wasn't it?"

Etienne turned away and said, "What ghastly things we have done to one another, my dearest. That day at this train station fifty years ago feels like it was somebody else's life. I wanted to hurt you, I will admit that. After how you hurt Jackie I would gladly have wounded you, destroyed the things you loved, injured you in any way I could think of. But gods help me, I never could have murdered you. Not even after what you did." He gave a humourless smile. "You wanted to undo me completely and you succeeded, did you not? The Etienne you loved is dead and gone. You buried him with your own hands."

Jude felt Ivory's remorse and regret shuddering right down to her bones.

"I felt the moment you were killed," Etienne went on. "Warped and toxic and twisted as our bond had become, it was still there, and I felt it happen, somehow." He frowned slightly, his gaze distant.

"As if some part of me had been ripped away. When your granddaughter started shrieking about the door being locked, I knew what we'd find. Someone hated you so much they were prepared to sell a little piece of their soul to put you in the grave. And it couldn't have come at a better time for me. You see, the Fang has drained me dry. To the brink of ruin. The auction for this coin will pay off my debts. Allow me to start again. I suppose I should thank you." He looked at her. "I was not involved in your murder. But I don't imagine you'll take my word for it, will you?" He yanked a strand of hair from his head and held it out to Jude. "Take it. Work your magic spells. Much good they ever did you."

Jude hesitated a moment, unsure of whether or not she should trust this gesture. Could it be that easy, after all? Was he really just going to give her what she wanted?

She reached out and took the hair, slipping it into her inner pocket, alongside the gris-gris bag. And then, slowly, she turned round to go, but before she could take a step, Etienne said quietly, "Aren't you going to ask about Jackie?"

Jude felt a ferocious flare of jealousy deep in her stomach from Ivory. Even after all these years, the cajou queen still couldn't bear to hear the other woman's name on Etienne's lips.

"That devilish snake you conjured out of your black soul still lives inside her, you know," the vampire went on. "Sometimes, when I go to visit her, I see it there. Wriggling beneath her skin, gliding up, then down. Like it's looking for a way out. One time it went up her neck to her face and I suppose it must have knocked against her right eye because all the blood vessels in it suddenly burst. She gave this great howl. I hear it still. I asked the doctors about removing the vile creature but they fear it has become a kind of symbiont and she wouldn't survive without it."

Jude licked her dry lips. "I … I'm sorry—"

"There was an accident at the asylum last week," Etienne went on, as if she hadn't spoken. "Jackie managed to get hold of a razor blade. Thought she'd cut the snake out herself, you see."

Jude clenched her teeth. "Is she—?" she began.

"Oh, she's alive," Etienne replied. "They got the razor off her. But do you know what happened during the struggle?"

Jude met Etienne's eyes and knew immediately that something awful was about to happen.

CHAPTER THIRTEEN

He lunged for her at the same time as she turned and raced towards the exit.

A dark monster came down from the lofty ceiling. Wings unfurled, claws scraped against stone and hundreds of bats descended on Jude in a cloud of fangs, beady black eyes and guttural squawks. She felt their wings in her hair and their teeth nipping against her skin, and although she screamed and lashed out blindly, she couldn't find her way past them.

The whole entire world was just bats. Bats and bats and bats.

But then they parted like a curtain as Etienne strode through them and gripped both her bare arms in his gloved hands, hard enough to leave bruises.

"Enough," he said quietly.

The bats scattered instantly, melting away into the shadows once again. At the same time, a reassuringly familiar weight appeared on Jude's shoulders and she realized that Beau had materialized, as if somehow sensing the danger she was in. He opened his jaw wide and hissed at Etienne – a savage, menacing sound.

The vampire snarled back. "That damn snake never did like me!" he said. "I'd chop it to pieces if I thought it would hurt you but given that you care only for yourself, what would be the point?"

The candlelight reflected strangely in Etienne's eyes, making them seem like mirrors. He put one hand on the back of Jude's neck and then gripped her wrist to bring her gloved hand to his mouth. From a distance it would have seemed like a lover's gesture, as if he meant to kiss her palm. But suddenly he snapped her finger straight back. There was a crunch and a tearing, and then there was blood, warm and oozing, and a blinding pain that exploded inside Jude's skull.

Beau lashed out at Etienne, biting him on the wrist, but Ivory was shrieking: *Cajou venom doesn't work on vampires! The gris-gris! Use the goddamn gris-gris!*

Etienne was grinning at her, baring his vampire fangs as he raised Jude's hand. Perhaps he meant to snap another finger. Perhaps he was going to break all of them. The first finger was certainly broken. Jude could see the bone sticking straight out of the tear in her glove, impossibly smooth and pale and white beside the scarlet flecks. The sight of it made her gag so she tore her eyes away, reached into the concealed pocket of her dress with her uninjured hand and flung the gris-gris at Etienne. A surge of Power raced down to her fingertips as she threw it and the charm burst apart in the vampire's face, scattering its contents.

Etienne jerked back, raising his hands with such a shriek of pain that Jude knew it must have been more than a few roots and bit of red pepper that had struck him. There'd been black magic tied up in the bag as well. When he lowered his hands, panting, his eyes were milk-white.

The blindness won't last! Ivory said. *Get out! Get out now!*

Jude ducked out of reach of his flailing arm and raced for the exit. The gris-gris spell seemed to be affecting Etienne's vampire bats too, because they flapped around erratically overhead, as if unsure of where they were, and this time Jude was able to get through them.

You should have sacrificed that chicken, Ivory whispered inside her mind. *He probably wouldn't have been able to sense me if you had.*

Jude ignored her as she sprinted to her boat, thankful for her trusty swamp boots. She leaped in, revved up the engine and steered the boat away from the Ghost Station. She'd just turned down the nearest canal, beneath the shelter of the overhanging swamp moss and cajou ivy, when a great cloud of angry vampire bats burst from the station in a flurry of dark wings that made the night sky tremble.

♛

Jude raced the boat as fast as she dared down the canal to the Gargoyle Bridge. When she realized there was no sign of the bats following them, she slumped back in her seat, cradling her bleeding hand. It throbbed like anything but worse than the pain, the shock or the blood was the thought of her music and how she needed that finger to play. What if the break was too bad to mend? Music was the most essential part of her soul. She couldn't have that ripped away from her too, she just couldn't.

She found herself sinking down under the weight of an old familiar gloom – that big black octopus of despair, pushing its oily tentacles into her heart, mind and soul, looking for weaknesses to be exploited, cracks it might shatter apart and fears to be dwelt on and agonized over. And Jude thought that she couldn't do this any more, couldn't take the constant struggle and hardship of it. When she looked down at her hand, the piece of bone sticking out through her bloodied glove made her feel all wobbly and she longed to sit back and relinquish responsibility.

But there was no one to hand responsibility *to*, that was the trouble. That had always been the trouble. There would be no handing the burden over to someone else. Not now, not ever. It was up to Jude, just like it always was.

For a long while she concentrated on slowing her breathing. There was no sound but for the cool clink of the zombie bottles knocking together overhead and the soft sighing of the cajou ivy in the warm breeze. She could feel the bulging eyes of the clay zombie heads all staring down at her from the nearby bridge and it felt like all the hundreds of poppets clustered around the swamp trees turned their blind button eyes on her too, waiting for her to make up her mind, watching to see what she'd do next. A dark ripple shuddered past the side of the swamp boat and Jude knew there was probably an alligator gliding unseen beneath the black water.

She took a deep, shuddering breath. First things

first, she had to get somewhere safe. She'd lingered too long in the canal as it was – even now she could see the tendrils of cajou ivy taking an interest and reaching out their vines towards her like fingers.

She gunned the engine and set the boat moving once again. Her apartment was so far away, and she couldn't bear the idea of the long journey, so she made for Papershell Pecan Street instead. Sharkey shared a cottage there with his grandmother, right on the water. And in that moment Jude really, *really* needed a friend.

Finally she reached the pier. Beau seemed to have disappeared as Jude scrambled from the boat and staggered to Sharkey's back door alone. Ivory was saying something inside her head but Jude couldn't concentrate on the cajou queen right then. Her ears were ringing and she was shivering despite the warm night air.

She hammered on the door with her good hand, over and over again. The lights were all out and she supposed it must be late, but she really wasn't sure how much time she'd spent in the Ruby Quarter.

Finally the door opened and Sharkey's grandmother stood there. A tiny woman, dressed in her nightshirt, with fluffy white hair puffing out around her ears and a gigantic rifle gripped in two shaking hands, aimed straight at Jude. Her eyes widened when she saw who it was and she quickly lowered the rifle.

"Judy-lou!" she exclaimed. "Good gods! What happened?"

"Mops!" Sharkey shouted from the hallway behind. "I said don't open the door till I'm there!"

"You were takin' too long with that dressing gown!" she yelled over her shoulder.

"A guy can't answer the door in the buff, Mops," Sharkey said, hurrying up behind her in a brocade-trim robe. Sharkey had a great love of fancy things and tended to splash out on them whenever he had any spare cash.

His mouth fell open in shock at the sight of Jude and without asking any questions he squeezed through the door and put a steadying arm round her.

"What happened?" Mops asked again.

"Oh." Jude held up her bloody glove. "A vampire broke my finger."

Suddenly the idea seemed terribly funny and Jude heard herself give a weird-sounding laugh that, once started, she didn't seem to be able to stop.

Sharkey pulled her to his chest, kissed her head and said, "There now. Laugh as much as you want to if it helps, darlin'. Let's get you inside."

She soon found herself sitting in the cosy kitchen with a steaming mug of chicory coffee before her. The fire in the stove had burned down to embers but Sharkey soon had it stoked up again, while Mops set down a bowl of water and cleaned and bandaged Jude's finger, carefully padding round the broken bone.

"Good-for-nothins," she muttered, shaking her head. "Them vampires are just a big ol' bunch of good-for-nothins. This is gonna need a proper doctor."

"Not tonight," Jude said. She thought of Sofia and said, "I have a friend who can help me in the morning."

"How did you get that close to a vampire anyway?" Sharkey asked. "You're the smartest girl I know – you oughta have enough sense not to be tangling with vamps. And why are you dressed all fancy? Your telegram said you were too sick to come to practice. What's going on, Jude?"

Jude was too tired, hurt and defeated to think of an excuse on the spot, so she told them – about the poppet, Ivory Monette and what had happened at the Fang.

"Why didn't you say something before?" Sharkey demanded. She couldn't quite tell if he was angry or offended, or both.

"I didn't want to involve you in it," Jude said.

"Besides, what good would it do? What difference would it make? You're not a witch doctor, or a vampire, or—"

"No, I ain't, but the one thing I am is your friend, you muttonhead," Sharkey said. "And sometimes having a friend around can be a help, even if they don't have any magical powers."

"This is dangerous, Sharkey!" Jude gestured at the bloody, torn glove lying on the scrubbed wooden table. "You're my best friend in the world. I'd never forgive myself if something happened to you because of me. Or you, Mops."

Sharkey's grandmother shook her head. "Judy-lou, I love you, but you say the most dumb-ass things sometimes. We're family, ain't we?"

Jude felt a small glow of warmth flare up inside her. They were, after all, the closest thing she had to a family after her pa now.

"Of course Sharkey will help you," Mops went on. "Hell, if I had a cajou queen trapped inside of me, I'd expect the both of you to jump to it quick-smart if you didn't wanna whoopin'. You'll stay here tonight. And we'll talk about what's to be done in the mornin'."

"But my pa—"

"Your pa can cope without you for one night," Mops said firmly.

Jude wanted to protest that he'd be worried but the truth was he probably wouldn't even notice she'd gone. She collected her bag from the boat to change back into her dungarees before settling down in the spare room. She'd stayed there before, and it was much warmer, nicer and more comfortable than her own room back home. There was a lot more love in this house and it was something you could sense the moment you stepped through the door.

Sharkey held her close when saying goodnight. "I love you, you know," he said.

"I know." Jude squeezed his arm. It sometimes felt as if Sharkey was the one constant in her life. The one thing she could truly rely on. "I love you too," she whispered. She suddenly felt a wave of remorse, for waking them in the middle of the night, for involving them at all, for not being stronger, for not having herself together. "I'm—"

"Don't you even think of sayin' you're sorry, girl," Sharkey interrupted her. "I ain't sorry one bit." He kissed her on the temple and said, "Just get some sleep, yeah?"

"OK."

Sharkey was still shaking his head as he walked out of the door. "Muttonhead," he said cheerfully as he closed it behind him.

Jude climbed into bed and tried to sleep, but her mind kept replaying the evening over and over again and her finger throbbed. To make things worse, she kept thinking she could hear bats flapping around in the dark outside, brushing their leathery wings against the window, trying to get in. An hour or so after she'd lain down, she realized Beau was on the bed with her, curling his large body round her in a way that was strangely comforting.

"How did he get here?" Jude asked. "And how did he appear before, in the Ghost Station?"

He can sense where I am, and so where you are, Ivory said. *He's never far away. And he can use the spirit world to travel around. It seems like he's taken a bit of a shine to you. In fact, he's been more affectionate to you than he was with me in recent years.* She sighed. *I suppose he never quite forgave me for killing Betty.*

"But ... then why didn't he appear at the Blue Lady?" Jude asked. "When you were murdered?"

The cajou queen was silent for a moment. Then she said, "I'm not sure. Perhaps ... perhaps he sensed that he wouldn't be able to do anything against a magical attack? It hardly matters now anyway."

The snake tucked his flat head into the groove of Jude's shoulder and she felt the same glow of warmth as before, her fear lessened and so did the piercing pain in her finger. She ran her fingers slowly down the snake's smooth skin. With him there she suddenly felt safer and the thought of bats no longer troubled her.

"Thank you, Beau," she said.

The warmth from the snake glowed a little brighter and soon afterwards Jude fell asleep.

CHAPTER FOURTEEN

Jude woke the next morning and had a few blissful moments before she remembered everything that had happened the day before.

Are you there? she immediately said inside her head to Ivory, trying to work out if she could feel her.

Still here, Ivory replied. She sounded half-asleep, as if she too had only just woken up. She even yawned as she added, *You'll not be rid of me that easily.*

Jude sat up and rubbed her eyes, wondering how long she'd slept. There was sunlight streaming in through the windows, warm and pleasant on her skin.

What happens to you when I fall sleep? she asked, wondering.

I'm not really sure, the cajou queen said. *But I think your sleep drags me into sleep too. And when you wake up, your thoughts duly wake me.*

She didn't sound all too happy about it, but added,

It makes sense, I suppose. As the host, you take priority.

Jude was relieved to hear it. She hated to think of the cajou queen being aware and awake inside her mind while Jude herself was oblivious.

Before she could say anything further to Ivory, there was a knock at her door.

"You can come in," she called.

Sharkey entered, carrying a wooden tray with a cup of coffee and a plate of warm beignets on it.

"Morning," he said cheerfully. "How's the hand?"

Jude looked down at her bandaged finger. It ached a little but nowhere near as much as she would have expected. Carefully, she unwound the bandages. Beneath them, her finger was still bloodstained but there was no longer any bone sticking out. The skin looked black and blue, swollen and bruised, but it wasn't ripped. And her finger hurt but it wasn't broken.

"He's healed it," she said, staring at her hand.

"Who?" Sharkey asked, startled.

"Beau. He was here last night. Where's he got to?"

She threw back the bed sheets and, sure enough, there he was. It only occurred to Jude in retrospect that it might have been wise to give Sharkey some warning about the twelve-foot-long albino cajou python. Her friend swore and the breakfast tray

184

fell from his hands with a crash. Beignets rolled off under the bed and coffee spread out across the floorboards. Seconds later, Mops burst into the room with her shotgun.

"It's OK!" Jude said, leaning down to pick up the snake and hold him to her protectively. "It's all right. This is Beau. The snake I told you about last night. He's not dangerous. Look, he healed my finger."

She held up her hand for them to see. To her relief, Mops lowered the shotgun. Jude lifted the snake on to her shoulders, comforted by the solid weight of him there.

"Thank you, Beau," she said. It seemed like the most natural thing in the world to draw his neck over to her face and plant a kiss on top of his flat head.

Sharkey gave a shudder. "Gives me the creeps, that thing," he said. "Are you sure it's safe?"

"I'm not really sure of anything," Jude replied with a sigh. "But I don't think Beau means any harm to anyone."

They cleared up the coffee and retrieved the beignets from the floor. Jude attacked her breakfast with gusto. She found she was ravenously hungry, but as she gobbled down her food she thought of her pa, at home on his own, and immediately felt guilty.

"Thanks for everything, Sharkey, but I better go see what's happening with my pa," she said.

"Then what?" Sharkey asked. "Back to Moonfleet, is it?"

She sighed. "I suppose so. There's something Ivory wants the Phantom to do."

"I'll come with you."

"Sharkey," Jude began. "I'm not sure that—"

"Ain't gonna do a bit of good arguing with me about it," he cut her off with his lazy drawl. "I know where the old cursed mansion is. If you don't come and get me, I'll just wander over there on my lonesome and start banging on doors and hollering for folks."

Jude tried not to smile. "All right." Secretly, she couldn't help being a little pleased. It would be a relief to have an ally there. "But look, I don't know how the Phantom will take it. He might not want to let you in. I'll meet you there, but just give me an hour or so to check on Pa first, OK?"

Sharkey nodded. "Sure thing. See you at Moonfleet in a couple of hours."

Jude said goodbye to Sharkey and his grandmother, then went down to her boat, gunned the engine and headed for home. When she reached the pier, Beau immediately slithered off towards the drainpipe, making his way to the balcony. Jude trudged up the steps to her front door and smelled smoke. She threw open the door to the sight of her pa wrestling with a frying pan that was on fire.

She hurried across the room and pushed him out of the way before grabbing the pan, dumping it in the sink and turning on the faucet. The pan hissed and spat out a few droplets of burning oil that scalded Jude's arm.

"Are you all right?" she demanded, looking at her pa who was slumped back against the kitchen counter.

"Yeah," he grunted. "Goddamn thing caught alight."

Jude glanced at the blackened pan. She felt guilty, yes, but she was also sick of having to be here all the time. Sick of being anchored to a grim situation that only ever seemed to get worse and worse.

"Sit down," she said. "I'll fix you some breakfast."

Her pa was staring at her hand. She didn't think her finger was broken any more but it was still swollen and bruised enough to draw attention.

"Fighting again." He glared at her. "I was worried sick when you didn't come home. You're going to ruin your life, you know. The only one of us to get out unscathed and you're just going to throw it all away, like it's nothing."

Jude looked up at him sharply. "Is that why you hate me?" she asked. "Because you think I got out unscathed?" She could feel the sudden danger of tears and furiously willed them to stay locked away inside where they belonged as she hissed, "Did it ever occur to you that being the survivor who has to pick up the pieces is its own nightmare? That I have a special kind of hell all of my own?"

She was breathing too hard, going down a road she didn't have time for. With an effort, she drew herself back. "Look, let's not ... let's not get into this right now. Things are the way they are. Talking won't change that. Sit down and I'll make breakfast."

Some part of her longed for him to protest. To take her arm and *insist* that they talked. To at least try to make things right between them. But perhaps it had all been broken for too long, and there was no saving it now. Not unless Jude carried out her end of the bargain and Ivory then did as she'd promised and healed him. There might be some hope for them then.

Her pa grunted, pulled out a chair and sat down at the table. He didn't say another word until Jude put a plate of food in front of him.

"Toast is burnt," he said.

"Too bad," Jude replied.

They ate in silence. Once they'd finished, Jude followed her pa to the bathroom to go through their usual routine. He had his back to her as she entered the room, but she caught sight of his face in the mirror on the opposite wall and his expression took her breath away. There was such an agony of raw despair there that Jude could feel her chance of saving him slipping away, despite everything she was trying so hard to do and all the hundreds of tiny ways she endeavoured to help him. It wasn't working, and suddenly she could feel Baron Lukah's shadow so strongly in the room that she almost expected to see the legba there in the corner with his pipe, his smoked glasses turned impassively in her direction.

It made a great sob want to rise up in her throat but she thrust it back down again and reached for her father's one remaining arm, her fingers curling around the worn fabric of his sleeve.

"You can talk to me," she blurted out. "Really. Look, I know things are bad. Really bad. I know you're suffering and I know life seems hopeless to you sometimes. I know you've gone to dark places I can't even imagine. And I want to help, but I don't know how. I just..." She floundered, trying to find the right words, the ones that might somehow make a difference. "I just want you to know that I'm here and I love you and I'll listen. If you want to talk then I'll listen." Her hand tightened slightly round his arm. "Please, Pa," she said. "I'm right here."

Her pa looked at her and it seemed to her as if maybe she had broken through. He seemed to really see her rather than simply gazing through her, and for those seconds it was like he was finally back in the room.

But then his focus shifted and he said, "Nothing left to say, Jude. Let's just get this over with."

He shook off her hand and stomped towards the sink. Jude took a deep breath to steady herself, but still felt shaken up as they went through their usual routine. She helped him to wash and dress and all the while she could sense that he resented her. She knew he must feel humiliated that she had to help him clean himself, that she had to see him naked, even help him on the toilet sometimes if it was a really bad day. And he turned that humiliation around on her, as if she was to blame, as if she had caused this situation somehow. It was a thankless task that she seemed doomed to repeat over and over again. If she hadn't had music as an escape, she thought she might have gone mad herself by now.

She prayed with all her soul that the cajou queen would make good on her promise.

You do your bit, Ivory whispered, clearly hearing her thoughts. *And I'll do mine.*

Even though the cajou queen was speaking the words Jude wanted to hear, she didn't particularly appreciate the intrusion or the reminder that Ivory was there, listening to all her most personal, private thoughts. It was an intolerable situation to not even be able to retreat to the quiet privacy of your own mind. Jude determined that she must help Ivory as quickly as possible so she could go back to just being herself once again.

Finally her pa was washed, dressed, fed and installed in his chair. He hadn't spoken another word to her all morning.

"I'll see you later," Jude said.

His right hand trembled where it lay on the armrest but he didn't say anything and eventually Jude left. She could only help him by helping the cajou queen.

Her swamp boots clattered noisily on the steps as she made her way down to the street, where she paused for a moment to collect herself, to straighten her shoulders and get back into fighting mode.

Jude Lomax does not give up, she thought fiercely to herself.

And despite all the fear and unpleasantness of the last few days, this was a new morning. The sun was warm on her face and she was glad to be back in her familiar dungarees, with the smell of gumbo from the store below their apartment filling the humid air. She breathed it in deep, tilted her face towards the sun for a moment and strained her ears for the sound of a jazz band playing somewhere. It was faint and muffled, but there as always.

She straightened up, squared her shoulders and set off in the direction of Moonfleet Manor.

CHAPTER FIFTEEN

Sharkey was waiting for her outside the gates when she arrived, dripping with his usual assortment of cajou charms. He beamed at her as she approached.

"Was startin' to think I might've been stood up," he said.

"Sorry. Pa was in a difficult mood this morning."

"No matter. Gave me time to read the papers."

Jude realized he had one in his hand.

"Seen the headlines?" he asked.

"No," Jude replied. "I haven't had much time for reading recently."

"Well, this one might interest you. Here, take a look."

He handed it to her and Jude saw that the front pages were full of the fact that Ivory Monette's granddaughter, Charity, didn't seem to be able to see or communicate with the legba. There had been long meetings between her and the town's Mayor, a cruel bully of a Subject named Rufus Seething, which all appeared to have ended badly due to Charity's inability to pass on messages from the cajou spirits.

It's because my spirit is still here, Ivory said inside Jude's mind. *The legba appear only to me.*

Jude repeated what the cajou queen had said and Sharkey nodded. "Thought that might be the case," he said.

Jude rifled through the pages to get to the rest of the article and saw that some aggressive journalists had managed to follow Charity into her boyfriend's hospital room. Attached to various machines and drips, he looked even worse than when Jude had seen him in Ivory's vision back at the Blue Lady – lying grey, wasted and skeletal on the bed.

"Charity Monette's boyfriend, Wade Andrews, lies seriously ill and is not expected to make it to Cajou Night," the paper excitedly proclaimed.

The photo next to it showed Charity trying to push the photographer out of the room. Jude would have been furious if someone had shoved their way into her dying loved one's hospital room like that but Charity didn't so much look angry as heartbroken, small and hopelessly lost. Jude felt an unexpected pang of pity for her.

Does she have any other family in Baton Noir? she asked the cajou queen.

No, Ivory replied. *Her mother abandoned cajou and ran off. She's alone.*

Jude frowned. Ivory did not seem all that worried or concerned for her granddaughter. For a moment, her tone had almost sounded glad…

Of course I'm not glad, Ivory snapped, overhearing Jude's thoughts. *But I can't pretend I feel any grief for Wade. He's a waste of space and she's better off without him.*

Jude took one last look at the photo and it seemed to her that there was a bit of a wild look in Charity's tear-filled eyes as she tried to wrestle the photographer out. It was the sort of raw desperation Jude recognized. There was only so far a person could be pushed before they had to push back. Or break down altogether.

Still frowning, Jude passed the paper back to Sharkey, who tucked it into his pocket and said, "I guess it's already crossed your mind that if her spirit is still inside you come Cajou Night, then you might be crowned queen rather than Charity?"

Jude stared back at him. It hadn't occurred to her at all.

"That's the last thing I want," she said. "The whole point of this is to get *rid* of Ivory."

It wouldn't work anyway, Ivory said. *An ordinary human can't contain any spirit, let alone a cajou queen's, for very long without there being … well … consequences.*

What kind of consequences? Jude thought back, alarmed.

Never mind about that. If you help me quickly enough then you'll never have to find out. Just don't go getting any ideas. You enjoy the power you get from being a cajou queen – there's no hiding it from me. I can feel it. So don't you start thinking you're going to hold on to it forever because Power like this isn't for the likes of you.

Some small treacherous part of Jude couldn't help wondering about what she might be able to achieve with Ivory's Power – for herself, for her father, for Baton Noir. But then she would become one of *them*, one of the cajou elite she had spent most of her life despising. And she'd be stuck with Ivory's ghost rattling round inside her head, never having a moment's privacy or a single secret thought.

Not an attractive prospect, is it? Ivory said.

No, Jude replied. *Don't worry. I have no desire to*

become the next cajou queen.

"Come on," she said out loud, pushing open one of the wrought-iron gates. "Let's get this over with."

Sharkey ambled along beside her, hands in his pockets, as if they were off for a picnic rather than about to knock on the front door of Moonfleet Manor. In fact, Jude didn't get the chance to knock because the front door was thrown open at her approach. The Phantom had clearly been watching out for her and now stood framed in the doorway before them. Once again he wore a perfectly tailored suit, this time in a dark navy colour. When she thought how much it must have cost, she had to push down a flare of resentment at the sight of it.

"Good morning," Jude said.

"You're late," the Phantom replied.

"I'm not," Jude said at once. "For the simple reason that I never agreed to be here at eight o'clock in the first place. I had my pa to see to first."

"I don't know who this person is and I don't care," the Phantom said, gesturing at Sharkey. "He can't stay."

"You know I'm getting pretty fed up with everyone's demands and ultimatums," Jude said. "So I think I'm going to start issuing a few of my own. To start with, my friend Sharkey can stay for however long he's prepared to be part of this freak show. Also, as soon as this business with the cajou queen is over, I quit. Playing the trumpet for you, that is."

"Quit?" the Phantom repeated. "You can't."

"I can and I just did."

The Phantom paused before saying, "All right, your friend may stay. We will discuss your employment here later." He stepped back from the doorway. "Well, come in then," he said, before muttering under his breath, "if you think you can bear it."

Jude and Sharkey glanced at each other before stepping over the threshold into Moonfleet Manor. Jude couldn't help her eyes going straight to the looming staircase, half expecting the crying girl from before to be there, but there was no sight nor sound of her. The door closed behind them with such a heavy thud that Jude jumped.

"A word of warning about the house before we go any further," the Phantom said. "It is ... not like other houses. As I'm sure you are aware, it was built by madmen, and some of their voices echo here still."

"You're saying the house is haunted?" Jude asked.

The Phantom turned his red mask towards her but it was too dim in the hallway for her to see his eyes clearly.

"It's not just that it's haunted," he said. "It's cursed as well. Forsaken." He shook his head. "I fear there is no explaining it to someone who hasn't experienced it, but you'll find out for yourselves soon enough. Do not wander off. Do not go poking into corners that do not concern you. And do exactly as I tell you at all times. Am I clear?"

"As mud," Sharkey said cheerfully.

"Perfectly clear," Jude said. "Now, could we get on? The sooner we find out who murdered Ivory, the sooner I'll get what I want from her and she'll finally leave me in peace."

"You cannot trust the cajou queen," the Phantom replied. "Whatever it is she's telling you to do, whatever it is she's promising you—" He broke off suddenly, staring. "What happened to your finger?"

Jude glanced down, remembering that it was bruised and blackened and about twice its normal size. "Beau healed it for me afterwards, but Etienne broke it," she said. She looked up at that implacable red mask. "Yes, I went back, after you left. For the girl. I didn't find her but Etienne found me. He knew Ivory was there. He knew I'd been under his desk too."

The Phantom was silent for a long moment. Then he shook his head and said, "That was an unspeakably stupid thing to do. You were lucky to escape with your life. It also explains why I received a telegram from Etienne this morning. He seems to believe that Ivory and I are in league together, plotting against him. He's told me not to come back to the Fang because I won't be welcome there."

Ivory swore an oath inside Jude's head.

But I wanted André to purchase the devil's coin from Etienne! she exclaimed. *That was the entire point of coming to talk to him today.*

When Jude repeated what she had said, the Phantom shook his head. "I won't be admitted to the Fang for the auction. I couldn't buy the coin now, even if I wanted to."

What did you want it for anyway? Jude asked.

To give back to the swamp devil, of course. And in return get from him the name of the person who made the bargain with him to murder me.

All right, well the coin is off limits, Jude said. *What do you want to do now?*

Ivory paused, then said, *We'll go see the swamp devil anyway.*

But if we don't have the coin to return to him then what makes you think he'll tell you who he made the bargain with? Even if we did have the coin, he might not be willing to tell us anything.

Let me worry about that, Ivory replied. *You just need to get us to the Black Bayou.*

Jude sighed. "Ivory wants to go to the Black Bayou," she said to the others. "To find the devil's wishing well."

"Out of the question," the Phantom replied immediately. "The bayou is full of dangerous things. They are—"

"We will go into the bayou, André," Ivory said, taking over to speak through Jude. "And we will take your paddle steamer to get there. If you don't assist me in this then I swear I will tell this girl your secret."

Jude hated the sensation of hearing the cajou queen's husky voice coming out of her mouth but beneath her anger and irritation at being taken over once again Jude felt a vague puzzlement at the cajou queen's choice of words. Before she had mentioned exposing the Phantom's secrets to the city in general but this time she'd mentioned Jude specifically.

The Phantom made an impatient gesture and turned away.

"Very well," he said. "We will go to the Black Bayou. And may the gods have mercy on us all."

Jude managed to wrestle back control of her tongue

but the effort had caused a sheen of sweat to break out on her hairline.

"Gods, I hate it when she does that," she began. "It's really…" She trailed off.

"What's wrong?" Sharkey asked at once.

"I don't know," Jude said. "I feel … a bit … weird."

"Perhaps you should sit down?" Sharkey said.

Jude tried to reply but her mouth was suddenly full of nails. They pierced her tongue and cheeks as she struggled to spit them out, but they just kept coming and coming. She was vaguely aware of Sharkey gripping her shoulder and saying something but she couldn't concentrate on anything other than not suffocating on the endless torrent of nails. Finally it ended and Jude was left wiping blood from her lips and gasping.

There you are, Ivory said softly. *I told you there'd be consequences.*

"What the hell was that?" Sharkey demanded, staring down at the pile of bloody nails.

"Ivory said the human body doesn't like having a spirit trapped inside it," Jude said. "And that there would be side effects."

Her mouth tasted like iron and blood.

"We should go," the Phantom said, gazing down at

her. "The Black Bayou is a forsaken place. I wouldn't dare linger there after nightfall."

Excellent, Ivory said, and Jude could feel her glee warming her blood. *It is a fortunate thing that André has taken a shine to you, my dear. Otherwise I most likely never would have been able to enlist his help, even with the aid of blackmail.*

What's that supposed to mean? Jude demanded.

Do you really not know? André Majstro – the Phantom of Moonfleet himself, the monster who cares for no one and nothing – has developed some kind of affection for you, a grubby Scrap, a nobody, Ivory said, each word brimming with spite. *I was never quite sure of the extent of it, the nature of it, or indeed the reason for it, but I had a fairly good idea there was* something *there. And it seems my instincts were right.*

You're talking garbage, Jude replied. *I don't think he even likes me. He just enjoys jazz music.*

Yes, but why you? Ivory said. *Did you not think it strange? There are plenty of talented musicians in Baton Noir. They're ten a penny. Why would he seek you out in particular?*

Jude didn't have an answer to that. She *had* wondered about it. But it had come at such a good time for her. It had provided regular money when she needed it most, and she hadn't liked to think about it or examine it too closely.

You're mistaken, Jude finally said.

I've known André Majstro a long time, Ivory replied. *More years than you've been alive. I know what I know.*

The cajou queen's words played over and over in Jude's mind. She did not believe for a moment that the Phantom had developed any kind of fondness for her but she couldn't help remembering her pa's insistence that there would be some price, something else that the Phantom wanted from her, and now she wondered whether perhaps he might have been right after all.

CHAPTER SIXTEEN

Half an hour later, they were on board the paddle steamer that Jude had so often glimpsed from the grounds. Although it had clearly once been a grand thing, it was not in much better condition inside than it was on the outside. The boat was a relic from before the war, back when music was the only god worshipped down the Razzmatazz River. Ollin adored music and was best friends with the legba of music, Papa Louis. But Krag's best friend was Ira, the legba of chaos and storms. And so after the war the old Jazz Quarter became the Hurricane Quarter, with storms tearing through with disheartening regularity.

Jude had always thought it testimony to the spirit of the city that even Ira's storms couldn't stop the party for very long. The Blues Quarter had come off worse, though. As it transformed into the vampire's Ruby Quarter, most of its honky-tonks and jazz joints were closed down to make way for the midnight supper clubs and gambling dens it was now known for.

As she stepped on to the old paddle steamer, Jude could see a music lover's soul was evident in its decor, from the portraits of famous jazz musicians hung along the walls, to the musical notes carved into the balustrades, and brass trumpets stamped on the wooden panels. And there were tributes to Papa Louis everywhere you looked, bronze statues, oil paintings and wooden carvings. But it was all chipped and worn, dirty and uncared for.

"You may go where you like," the Phantom said, "but be aware that the first-class swimming pool down below was infested with rats last time I looked."

Jude shuddered. "Perhaps we'll just stay up on deck," she said.

It took them an hour or so to pass through first the neon-lit areas then the industrial units of the meatpacking district. The Phantom went into the wheelhouse to steer the boat and Jude and Sharkey sat on the rusted desk outside, watching as the scenery passed by.

Once they'd gone beyond the built-up areas, the view consisted of nothing but swamp trees and cajou ivy – except for one single, solitary man standing on the opposite bank, gazing straight at them. He wore a top hat and a waistcoat and lazily smoked a cigarette as the light reflected off his glasses.

Jude nudged Sharkey. "Do you see that man?" she asked, gesturing across the water at him.

Sharkey looked right at him but slowly shook his head. "I don't see no one," he said.

"I was afraid you'd say that," Jude replied. "I think it's Baron Lukah."

She couldn't see his eyes behind the smoked glasses but she felt sure he was looking straight at her. And then a moment later, he lifted a hand and pointed at his eyes before slowly raising his arm to point at her.

I see you…

I know that you're there…

Jude felt Ivory flinch inside her.

Baron Lukah is waiting for you, isn't he? Jude said, keeping her eyes on the legba until the boat rounded a corner in the waterway and he was lost from sight. *That's why he was watching me in the Fountain District the other day.*

He's looking for me, Ivory agreed. *He knows I gave him the slip.*

207

Jude couldn't help but shudder. The last thing she wanted was the legba of death himself coming after her.

How does that work anyway? Jude asked. *Is he just going to keep following you or what?*

After all, plenty of people weren't ready to go but that didn't mean they could escape their fate when their time came.

Let me worry about Baron Lukah, Ivory said.

Jude tried to push the legba out of her mind and before long they'd reached the Black Bayou. It was quite different from the Firefly Swamps where Jude had lived as a child. Those had glowed with the light from hundreds of golden fireflies but the Black Bayou was soulless and lightless, even in the middle of the day. A great dark swamp, choked up with ancient trees and creeping moss and hanging cajou vines.

Sharkey gave a low whistle through his teeth. "Damn," he said. "This really is a forsaken place."

Jude had skirted the edges of the Black Bayou before, but like most people had always been wary of venturing further inside. For one thing, it wasn't just an ordinary bayou. The legend went that during the war even the sky itself had shaken and trembled at the terrible violence happening in the Burnt Bones

Country down on the planet below. Even the fire devils had fled. And eventually it was bad enough to displace Sheba, the legba of nightmares, who'd fallen from the sky to land in the bayou, where she had melted away into the water. And now the place had gone all twisted and strange.

"Watch out for the cajou ivy," Jude murmured as one sneaking tendril slid over the railings towards them. She aimed a kick at it with her boot and it retreated quickly enough, but she didn't trust it not to come flying back the moment their eyes were averted.

The trees smothered a lot of the sunlight and they had to squint into the shadows in order to make out the waterways, which spiralled in all directions.

"How are we ever supposed to find the right one?" she asked.

"I heard that if you wanna throw a coin in the wishing well then you need to visualize it in your mind," Sharkey said. "That's how you find it."

"I heard the same thing, but none of us are going to throw any money in the well," Jude replied. "So that's not going to work, is it?"

The Black Bayou was a huge expanse that stretched for miles on the outskirts of Baton Noir. There was probably no one in the country who had explored it properly. A few foolhardy adventurous types had attempted to chart it, but the problem was the waterways seemed to move around from one day to the next, as did the trees and landmarks. And given that the bayou was basically a self-contained lake that didn't lead anywhere, there was really not much point venturing into it unless you wanted to find the wishing well.

It was steaming-hot and Jude could already feel sweat running down her back and making her palms slippery. The sound of tree frogs rang in her ears, and the air smelled sweet and damp, like decay. As the paddle steamer went deeper into the bayou, Jude noticed that, like the trees lining Squid Ink Canal, these ancient branches had also been hung with black magic items – only they weren't zombie bottles this time but skeleton dolls and shrunken heads.

Skeleton dolls were like cajou poppets, only with even more sinister intent. You didn't create a skeleton doll because you wanted to hex or injure someone. You made one only if you wanted to see somebody dead. About the size of Jude's palm, they dangled from the branches, their bleached bones clicking and clacking together as their grinning skulls turned this way and that in the breeze.

Even worse were the shrunken heads, with their eyes and lips sewn shut, rubbery skin and protruding lower jaws. Cajou legend said that you should shrink your enemy's head immediately after their death in order to protect yourself from their vengeful spirit. Their faces were so distorted and odd-looking that it was hard to believe they had ever once been real people, and Jude couldn't help shuddering as they went by. Some of them had hair sewn back on, long braids threaded with charms and beads, or little tufts of dark fuzz that stood straight up in the swampy heat.

"Barbaric," Sharkey murmured as they went past.

Jude tried to keep the wishing well at the forefront of her mind, but it was hard when she kept thinking she could see dark oily things moving between the trees.

"Does anyone else see those?" she asked.

"What?"

"There's something there." Jude pointed to a nearby marshy bit.

"Could be alligators," Sharkey said, frowning. "Plenty of gators in the bayou. Along with turtles, frogs, birds—"

"No," the Phantom said from behind them. "They're nightmares."

"Nightmares?" Jude repeated. She'd heard of Sheba's nightmares but had always hoped they were more myth than fact. She groaned. "They're real?"

"They are," the Phantom said. "Listen."

It took Jude a little while to make it out beneath the clicking of the skeleton dolls and the sighing of the trees and the churning of the water behind them. But then she realized that the frogs she'd heard earlier had gone quiet and in their place there was a sort of humming. It was high-pitched and warbling and it made Jude's head ache.

"There's one." Sharkey pointed and Jude caught a brief glimpse of a many-tentacled thing disappearing into the water with a splash.

Jude peered down at the water. The entire swamp could be crawling with them for all they knew. It was too murky to see beneath the surface but a couple of times she saw a sudden ripple, the flash of a fin or a whiskery mouth reaching up from the depths.

"Don't allow any of them to touch you," the Phantom ordered. "They grow fat off whatever nightmares you already have and give you new ones in return. And watch out for the flying ones."

The moment he said it, Jude realized there were warped creatures fluttering between the branches of the swamp trees. They moved too quickly for her to see them properly; odd, unnatural, jerky movements. But whatever they were she could tell they were all deformed things with two heads, bald skin or too many teeth.

"You should concentrate on the well," Sharkey said in a whisper. "Hard as you can."

Jude summoned up all her resolve and tried to imagine the devil's wishing well in her mind.

But it was no good. The Black Bayou had realized they were there and it was looking at them, peering closer, reacting, wondering about them. Branches of cajou ivy unfurled from the trees and reached out towards the boat, forcing Jude and Sharkey to shrink back from the railings. The water around them began to churn and foam, as if some monster flailed unseen beneath. The cajou ivy ignored them and made straight for the paddlewheel, tangling itself in the spokes like a great hand squeezing its grip tight, causing the old boat to groan in protest and forcing the Phantom to kill the engines. He stepped out of the wheelhouse to join Jude and Sharkey.

"There's nothing I can do," he said. "The swamp has us."

CHAPTER SEVENTEEN

The bayou is alive, Ivory whispered inside Jude's mind. *It may just be curious about you.*

And then it happened all at once − a sudden, unnatural cessation of sound. Gone were the tree frogs, the nightmare humming, the slithering of the vines, the clicking of the skeleton doll bones and the churning of the water. It was as if someone had flipped a switch.

"There's one right there!" Sharkey pointed.

A gruesome thing was perched in one of the lifeboats. Part bird and part reptile, it had a scaly, bony body, with black-feathered wings ending in sharp claws, and a cruel, twisted beak on both of its jackal heads. Jude thought of the jackal on Baron Lukah's cane and shuddered. But worst of all each head must have had a dozen eyes − each one of them as milky and blind as an ancient spider's.

As if sensing their gaze, both its beaks opened at once, like it was about to hiss at them, but instead that weird humming noise started up again. Jude felt a strange pressure on the back of her eyeballs and her head ached worse than ever.

The next moment the nightmare had raised one of its claws and one by one began to dig out its blind eyes. They popped out with a horrible wet sucking sound, falling down to roll around in the bottom of the lifeboat.

"Why … why is it doing that?" Sharkey asked, transfixed.

Before anyone could reply, another nightmare flapped overhead, landing with a thud on the deck, followed by two more that tentacled their way up the side of the boat, sprawling with wet slaps on the boards. The nightmares were a sickening mix of teeth and suckers and jaws, humming their weird discordant song louder and louder.

Jude glanced at the wheelhouse, thinking they could shelter in there, but the cajou ivy was tangled in the doorway, holding it open.

"We're trapped," the Phantom said. "We should—"

But he was interrupted by one of the nightmares suddenly whipping a tentacle at Sharkey, wrapping it round his ankle and jerking his feet out from under him before dragging him, yelling, halfway across the deck.

Jude made to follow but the Phantom's hand clamped down on her shoulder.

"Wait," he said. "It's not—"

Jude threw him off and ran across the deck. The creature had slithered up to the side of Sharkey's face and suddenly wrapped its tentacles round his throat. There was a wet sound as its suckers fastened on. Sharkey gave a yell and then the thing started slobbering and sucking at his ear. The next moment, it had coaxed out a long string of what looked like saliva but as it left the ear it turned into a large greasy bubble with images moving around inside it.

Jude could see an image of Sharkey inside the bubble, trying to play his saxophone. There was no sound coming from it but every time he tried to play, he couldn't remember how. Sharkey had told her about it before, it was one of his most common nightmares.

Jude reached down, dragged the creature off and threw it over the side of the boat. Another nightmare came slithering over and she aimed a kick at it with her swamp boot. It landed right in the soft, fleshy part of the creature with a horrible squelching sound but instead of falling to the deck, the nightmare burst apart into more than twenty versions of itself.

"What the—?"

"If you strike them, they multiply," the Phantom said, appearing at her side.

The next moment, one of the nightmares clamped its teeth round Sharkey's leg and ripped out a chunk of flesh. Her friend's scream of pain went through Jude like a blade. She grabbed the nightmare and threw it off but the damage was already done. And there were more of the things slithering across the deck towards them. They were trapped.

"How are we supposed to fight them off?" Jude asked.

"You can't," a female voice said.

Jude looked up and saw a woman in a dark blue evening gown sitting on the railings, lazily swinging her feet back and forth. She was beautiful but she was also depraved and insane. Jude could see it in the depths of her eyes, the twist of her mouth and the strange sing-song lilt to her voice.

"Who are you?" Jude asked.

"Who are you talking to?" the Phantom said beside her.

"That woman on the rails."

"There's no one there," the Phantom replied.

Jude realized she was looking at a legba.

"You're Sheba," she said. "Aren't you?"

"That's right," the legba of nightmares replied.

And then Beau appeared on her shoulders and an image immediately filled Jude's mind – a vision of the snake unhinging his jaws to swallow a nightmare down whole.

Just at that exact moment, one of the awful creatures took a flying leap, heading straight for the Phantom's chest. Jude's hand flashed out and she grabbed it by the tentacle in mid-air. "Stop!" she cried, her voice ringing across the bayou.

The nightmare had been leaping so fast, how the heck had she managed to catch it? Perhaps she was tapping into some of Beau's snake prowess somehow? She could certainly feel the snake's excitement through the pounding of her own fear as she stared at the devilish thing dangling from her grip, its tentacle slick and slimy beneath her fingers. She knew what Beau wanted her to do, so she tossed the nightmare up to him in one fluid motion.

There was a distinct *crack* as Beau unhinged his jaw, opening it astonishingly wide, and allowed the entire creature to land in his mouth. It thrashed, tentacles wriggling everywhere, but Beau swallowed it down greedily. Jude could feel the lump of it on her shoulders, still struggling from within the snake's bulging belly.

Sheba clicked her fingers and the nightmares that had been crawling towards them suddenly stopped in their tracks, tentacles twitching. Slowly the legba got down from the railings, her bare feet landing on the deck, her dress stirring round her ankles.

"A cajou queen!" she exclaimed. "Here in our humble bayou. I dare say we should be honoured, my children." One of the nightmares slithered up her leg to her arms. She cradled it, crooning over it like a small child. "Your snake is large and powerful," the legba said. "But he can't eat all of my nightmares. Not in their hundreds."

Jude became aware that even more of them had appeared. The flying ones rustled feathers and leathery wings from the railings and the branches of the trees overhead.

"We don't mean any harm," she said, walking closer to the legba, her hands spread in what she hoped was a non-threatening gesture. "We're just looking for the devil's wishing well."

"Ah, the devil," Sheba replied. Her eyes glittered violet in the strange half-light of the swamp. "The swamp devil lights the way for those who wish to make a bargain with him or return one of his coins. But since none of you want to make a bargain yourselves and you do not have a coin, you won't find the wishing well."

"What makes you think none of us want to make a bargain?" Jude asked, walking closer to the legba. "Or that we don't have a coin?"

"Because if you did then you wouldn't have found your way to me," Sheba said. "The truly desperate ones go to him. Everyone else is mine. That's our agreement."

"In that case, you'd better let us go," Jude said. She was right at the railings with the legba now, close enough that she could see the flecks of black in her purple eyes. "We're not here for you. And I don't think you want to break the terms of your bargain?"

"I do not," Sheba replied. She fixed her strange violet gaze on Jude and stepped right up to her. "But your snake ate one of my children, so you owe me something first, girl."

Jude was immediately wary. "What can I give you?" she asked.

"It isn't what you can *give* me," the legba replied, her voice as smooth as a length of cool silk. "It's what you can *take* with you."

Jude frowned. "But—"

And that was as far as she got before Sheba gripped her arms and with an inhuman strength lifted her over the railings and threw her down into the murky water below.

CHAPTER EIGHTEEN

The moment of falling seemed to stretch on for an eternity. Jude's mind was full of Daryl and how this feeling, this sense of unspeakable dread, must be the exact same thing he'd experienced in his last moments as he'd plunged down into the swamp.

She hit the water, which knocked all the wind out of her like a punch to the guts, and then greedy fingers wrapped round her and dragged her down beneath the surface. She was vaguely aware that Beau's weight had left her shoulders and assumed the snake must have vanished back into the safety of the spirit world.

She couldn't tell which way was up and which was down. The entire world was just water, so brackish and full of thick choking weeds that Jude couldn't see more than a foot in front of her. Her flailing hands brushed the rusty hull of the paddle steamer, as something scaly swept past her leg and a pointed fin jabbed her elbow.

There were things in the water with her. Nightmare horrors of the kind she had glimpsed on the deck with Sheba. Even the water itself was thick and slimy and too warm, as if she were inside the belly of a gigantic beast, surrounded by stomach fluids that would dissolve her skin and hair and soul as they digested her.

She kicked hard and her head broke the surface. She took in a great shuddering gasp of air and then a life preserver from the boat landed in the water beside her head with a splash. She grabbed on to it, relief tingling through her just as a tentacle curled round her ankle and yanked her sharply downwards. Her hand slipped immediately from the smooth surface of the preserver and streams of bubbles flew up past her face as she was dragged back down.

There was a sudden flash of white and Jude realized that Beau was in the water with her. The great snake shot towards her ankle, striking out at the octopus-nightmare, which flinched away, releasing Jude in the process. Beau pressed close against her trying to create a barrier, but there were too many nightmares. The water was teeming with them. Tentacles and fins and maws and whiskers and smooth reptilian skin, all desperate to get to Jude, all pressing up against her in the dark.

Jude felt the change as Ivory took control of her body and began to struggle and thrash in the water, evidently as desperate to reach the surface as Jude was herself. But her struggles only succeeded in lowering them deeper beneath the surface and Jude's hands brushed the weeds and plants that grew on the riverbed. Ivory tightened Jude's grip round something smooth and cold, yanking it up from the silty bed.

What are you doing? Jude thought at her furiously. *You're going to get us both killed!*

She wrestled back control and had almost reached the surface when one of the nightmares found a way past Beau. It was one of the smaller creatures, about the size of Jude's hand. It looked like some kind of deformed, warped, twisted fish, with bulging toad's eyes, fat, swollen lips and a pale, anaemic body. Jude felt it brush the back of her neck and she lashed out at it with her hands while her lungs burned and screamed for oxygen, but the thing slipped through her fingers and began to push its bulbous head into her ear.

Reeling with shock she couldn't prevent a reflexive gasp for air. The sludgy water of the bayou rushed into her mouth and down her throat and it was like drinking mud and sand, but it was nothing compared to the excruciating agony of having the nightmare force its way deeper and deeper inside her head.

It felt like half her face was being ripped off and the entire right-hand side burned in agony. Jude felt fins tear and teeth nip and was sure the nightmare must be destroying her ear and the inside of her head, but the water filling her lungs made it hard to think straight. She was suddenly sure she could hear Sheba's laughter down there with her, warped and distorted by the water.

I'm going to die in this bayou, she thought hopelessly, with sudden, terrifying clarity. *Half drowned and half ripped apart by monsters. Just like Daryl.*

For a flash of a moment she even thought she saw her little brother there in the water with her, still wearing the bow tie he'd donned for her birthday, half his face torn away by gators, smiling a skeleton grin and reaching out one mangled hand...

But then there was a stream of bubbles as someone landed in the water beside her. Jude saw the red mask and realized it was the Phantom. One of his arms reached around her, he pressed her to his side and seconds later Jude's head broke the surface and the Phantom was pushing her up over the side of one of the paddle steamer's lifeboats to land with a thump on the wooden floor, which was still scattered with the glistening eyeballs of the nightmare.

Sharkey was already there, staring at her, pale-faced, with both hands clamped to his bleeding leg. Jude put a hand to her ear where the nightmare had burrowed in, fully expecting to feel blood and flesh, perhaps even the smooth bone of her skull where the skin had been ripped away. But her skin was unbroken beneath her fingers, her hair sticky with swamp rather than gore. She tried to speak but only coughed up more gunge, choking on the rancid taste of the bayou.

The boat tipped as the Phantom dragged himself into it. The movement dislodged the mask from his face and he lunged after it desperately. The mask clattered to the floor of the boat, sliding over towards Jude. Despite herself, she couldn't prevent her eyes going straight to his head but he'd already turned away from her, one hand covering his face. The other he held back blindly towards her. His shirt had ripped and Jude saw that his entire forearm was covered in scars left by vicious burns.

"My mask," he said in a hoarse voice. Jude saw that his hand trembled slightly. "Please."

She hurriedly scooped it up, the wood smooth and warm beneath her fingers, and pressed it into his waiting hand. He immediately put it back on and, when he turned round, Jude saw that there was a nightmare on his neck.

She cried out a warning but it was too late. The creature latched on and dragged out a bubble, the same way it had with Sharkey. The Phantom grabbed the monster and threw it into the water, but not before Jude saw the image inside his nightmare. Her mind recoiled in disbelief. That couldn't possibly be one of his nightmares. It didn't make sense. But she couldn't spare a thought for it just then. Her head throbbed and she clutched it in her hands.

"What's wrong?" the Phantom said sharply.

"I thought that… I thought the nightmare had somehow managed to—"

She broke off with a gasp as an explosion of pain went off like a firework inside her mind. It was so bad that she reeled backwards and it was only the Phantom's hands on her shoulders that prevented her from falling straight into the water. But the bayou seemed to be spinning and spinning all around her and she could *feel* the nightmare wriggling around inside her head, probing its whiskery mouth into every corner, poking its sharp fins into sensitive bundles of nerves that sent white orbs flashing and popping in front of her eyes.

"Tell me what's wrong!" the Phantom said.

But Jude couldn't speak. She instinctively tried to clutch at the Phantom, but he was no longer there. Jude staggered to keep her footing as she suddenly found herself in the mirrored parlour of Sofia's store, where the witches performed their private spells.

Belle was there, sitting at the covered table with her fortune-telling cards spread before her.

The sudden silence and stillness made Jude's head spin after the noisy chaos of the swamp.

"Don't worry," Belle said. "I've taken Krag's card out." She held it up for Jude to see before slipping it between the pages of a large spell book that rested on the table at her elbow.

"What?" Jude frowned, trying to work out what was going on.

"I only want to tell people about the good things that are going to happen in my readings," Belle went on. She looked up at Jude and said, "Well, come on then. Take a seat."

Jude wanted to reply that she didn't want to take a seat and that she didn't want to have her cards read either. But her legs were already walking over to the table and she found herself sitting down. Belle's cat, Dazzle, leaped on to the table at the same time and sat down regally on top of the spell book, surveying the scene with eyes that were as impossibly blue and beautiful as Belle's.

"Now, let's find out about your love life," Belle said.

Jude immediately thought of Leeroy's cruel fingers and even crueller words. She shuddered. "I don't want a love life," she said.

"Nonsense, Jude," Belle replied. "All girls want lovers."

She spread three cards on the table. When she turned the first one over, it was the one card neither of them had expected because it had already been removed from the pack – Krag, the prince of the cool legba.

"That's a neat trick," Jude said. "How did you get it out of the book?"

Dazzle was still sitting on top of the tome and hadn't moved the whole time.

Belle stared down at the card, her face pale. "That was no trick," she said.

She reached out and quickly flipped over the remaining two cards to reveal two more Krags, identical to the first.

It must be some kind of joke pack, Jude thought.

Belle frowned at her. "Your love story will be a great

and powerful thing," she said. "But your soulmate has a terrible darkness inside him. One that could rip him apart and take the whole world with it."

Jude wanted to remind Belle that she'd said she only told people about the good things in their future. But a movement in the mirror caught her eye and when she looked up she thought she caught a glimpse of a horse's sleek, muscled body flashing past in the reflection. But that wasn't possible. Horses had been forbidden in Baton Noir for years.

She shook her head. It must have been a trick of the shadows. All of this was just a trick.

"There's no such thing as soulmates," she said, looking back down at the Krag cards before her.

It wasn't the infamous legba himself that drew her eye so much as the horde of chaos horses gathered behind him – glossy black creatures with death in their eyes and red flames snorting from their noses. The terrifying beasts that would one day bring about an end to the world.

A snorting noise made Jude look up and then she was on her feet so fast that her chair fell backwards.

The great dark horse was there, right there behind the mirror, real fire flaring from its nose, real malevolence in its eyes as it came closer and closer.

Jude wanted to run but found herself rooted to the spot.

She couldn't move. Not even when the monster of a horse reared up on to its hind legs, not even when the glass smashed beneath its hooves and the shards flew out to pierce her face, blind her eyes and slash her skin.

Blood filled her vision and all she could hear was the *clip-clop* of hooves as the chaos horse forced its way through the broken mirror, into the room and right out into the world.

And there was absolutely nothing Jude could do to stop it...

CHAPTER NINETEEN

Jude felt the cold before anything else. It was a soul-chilling, bone-deep cold, not something she had ever felt before in the permanently warm Baton Noir. For a confused moment, she wondered whether perhaps she might be dead and lying in a grave. Surely that could be the only explanation for how she could be feeling cold *inside* her skin and even inside her head.

Her eyelids felt like they'd been glued shut, but she managed to peel them open and found herself lying on a lumpy couch in front of a fireplace in an unfamiliar room. As she sat up she felt Ivory stir inside her mind, the cajou queen's disorientation mixing with Jude's own.

Moonfleet, Ivory muttered. *We're in Moonfleet.*

Jude looked around and saw that Ivory was right. She'd never seen this room before but she could tell immediately that it belonged to Moonfleet Manor because the window looked out on to the grounds where she could see the cajou tree and, beyond that, the Owlery. With relief, she realized that the chaos horse scene she'd just witnessed was nothing more than a new nightmare, given to her by Sheba's horrid creature.

Now she was in a large drawing room with floor tiles the same absinthe shade as she'd seen out in the hallway and a fireplace made from black cajou wood. Jude saw that the faces of the damned were carved into it and she shuddered as she looked at their anguished expressions and eye-rolling suffering. She heard the Phantom's words inside her head once again: *built by madmen...*

The walls were lined with portraits, and all the painted faces gazing down at her were, quite clearly, members of the Majstro family. They were all dark oil paintings, angry smudges of greys and greens and blacks, but there seemed a strange stillness to many of them as if they might move at any moment, and Jude was sure she could feel the prickle of their eyes watching her. They were all noticeably good-looking, as was common with descendants, and many had the same smoky-grey eyes as the Phantom.

As if this thought had summoned him, André himself suddenly opened the door and walked in carrying some clothes.

"Oh, good," he said, when he saw she was awake. "How are—"

"Where's Sharkey?" Jude asked, scrambling to her feet.

Her dungarees were still damp from the bayou, which explained how cold she was, and also why she smelled like fish and swamp slime. She felt dirty, tired and small.

"He's at St Germaine's hospital on Praline Street," the Phantom replied. "He will be fine," he added quickly. "But his leg is being treated. He will need to stay there for a day or two." He gestured at her vaguely and said, "I am sorry about the wet clothes. Paris is not here. And I didn't like to presume…" He trailed off, a note of uncertainty in his voice that Jude hadn't heard before.

"It's fine," Jude said quickly. "Even if she had been here, the last thing I want is to be undressed by your girlfriend."

"Paris would be most put out to hear herself referred to as such."

"Your whore, then." Jude surprised even herself with the note of venom in her voice. But she'd just recalled the nightmare she had seen Sheba's creature drag from the Phantom and anger bubbled up in her now. She knew that he hadn't been truthful with her.

"There are things we must discuss," the Phantom said with a sigh. He put the pile of clothing down on a nearby chair. "But first you should change."

"Isn't there somewhere I can shower first?" Jude asked. She didn't think she'd ever felt dirtier in her life and a mansion like Moonfleet must have dozens of bathrooms.

The Phantom paused, then said, "I regret not."

Jude crossed her arms over her chest. "Why?" she said.

"The upper floors of the house are … not accessible at the moment," he said.

And then Jude heard it, the faint sound of sobs coming from somewhere beyond the room.

"That girl's on the stairs again, isn't she?"

"She is no girl," the Phantom replied.

Jude walked across the room and pushed past the Phantom to stick her head out into a gloomy corridor. It stretched away before her, sconces flickering on the walls, casting a dancing light over the dark green tiles. The sound of sobbing was clearer now and this time Jude realized that there were words too – the same phrase, repeated over and over again.

"Why did I do it?

Why? Why?

Why did I do it?

Why did I do it?"

"It certainly sounds like a girl to me," Jude said, looking at the Phantom.

"It is my sister," he said. "Violetta."

He beckoned her back into the portrait room, drawing the door closed behind him.

"Violetta!" Jude repeated. "But Violetta Majstro is the one who tortured those servants in the attic."

She couldn't help glancing towards the window at the dark cajou tree in the grounds outside, its crooked branches spread out against the afternoon sun, like spindly spider limbs.

"Yes," the Phantom agreed. "Violetta died and my father, in his madness, decided to chop down the cajou tree from which she'd hung. A new tree appeared in its place overnight. It refuses to be removed, you see. But the wood from the original tree was made into the double staircase you saw in the hall. And Violetta's spirit is often there on the stairs. On a bad day, she will not let anyone pass. Today is a bad day. That is why I cannot offer you a shower. A change of clothes will have to suffice. I'll be just outside the door when you're done."

And with that he turned and walked out, closing the door behind him.

Is it really Violetta on the staircase? she asked Ivory.

I believe so, the cajou queen replied. *A wild and wretched spirit, by all accounts.*

Jude shuddered and was about to pick up the clothes when a painting caught her eye and frowning she went to take a closer look. It was of a young man and two girls, standing on the lawn outside Moonfleet. Jude could see from the dates that it had been painted sixty years ago.

The painted girl staring from the canvas was no more than fifteen years old, pale with light blond hair tumbling over her shoulders. She had a delicate beauty, with her angular face and rosebud lips. Beside her stood a younger dark-haired girl of perhaps six or seven. And behind them, one hand placed on each of their shoulders, was a man. He was tall and slender, dark-haired and handsome. And even though he wasn't wearing a mask Jude immediately recognized the grey eyes gazing out at her from the canvas. Her breath caught in her throat.

"Is that…?"

André, Ivory replied. *Before he became the Phantom.*

Jude stared at the painted figure. Like all the other

Majstros, he was incredibly good-looking and she wondered what could have happened to his face to make him want to cover it up.

Do you know? she asked Ivory.

Perhaps he annoyed the wrong person in a fight, the cajou queen suggested.

Jude looked back at the painting. There was something fierce and protective about the way he had a hand on each of the girls' shoulders – a sense that he was holding on to them tightly, as if fearing they'd be taken from him. And there was something about the look in his eyes too, a sort of resignation and knowing. An acceptance of something dreadful.

Jude's eyes went to the brass nameplate and she saw that the two girls were also Majstros. She'd never heard of the younger one, Enid. Perhaps she'd moved away or died years ago. But the second sister she knew very well – all of Baton Noir did. It was Violetta Majstro, the evil perpetrator of the horrors in the attic.

Seasoned police officers had apparently had nervous breakdowns as a result of what they'd seen all those years ago. Terribly mutilated bodies, ravaged by cajou acid burns, flies' eggs laid in open wounds, maggots eating people while they were still alive. There was one woman who was said to have had all her arms and legs removed and gold coins sewn behind her eyelids. And a man was found chained to the wall with a stick protruding from a hole that had been drilled into his skull. The stick, they said, had been used to 'stir his brains'.

A warped and evil bunch, the Majstros, Ivory said, as if reading Jude's thoughts. *And no wonder. They're descended from Krag, after all. Their wickedness manifests itself in different ways, but they're all touched by evil, or warped by the madness of the moon eventually. Take Julian Majstro over there.*

Jude turned away from the group portrait to look at another nearby painting of a dark-haired man in a grey silk suit.

Blackmailer. Swindler. Slave-trader, Ivory said.

Jude recalled Ivory's claim that the table in the Ghost Room was laid for Julian. She saw again that shadowy twitch of a robe, the glimpse of bony ankle…

And Dorian Majstro, Ivory went on, *that handsome man in the hat. Pirate. Thief. Gambler. Next to him is Vincent Majstro. Smuggler. Arsonist. Merchant of flesh—*

"That's enough!" Jude whispered. "I don't want to hear any more."

But I haven't told you about the best one yet, Ivory protested. *Over in the corner—*

"Would you shut up?" Jude hissed. "I don't care about the Majstros."

She snatched up the clothes. All the painted eyes in the room seemed to stare at her and she thought she saw Violetta actually blink.

Jude hastily turned away and dressed as quickly as possible, trying to ignore the prickling sensation of all those eyes fixed on her. As she slipped out of her dungarees, a small object fell from the inside pocket, landing with a clatter on the floor. Jude bent to pick it up.

"Oh my gods," she said, holding it to the light. "It's a bone flower."

Made entirely out of one smooth piece of bone, the white flower was cool to her touch. Extremely unusual, Jude had never seen one in real life but knew they were said to grow in Sheba's shadow.

She suddenly remembered how Ivory had taken control of her body for those moments in the water, and how she'd felt her grab on to something on the riverbed and pull it up.

"Why did you do that?" she said to Ivory. "It wasn't exactly the most convenient time for picking flowers."

I don't know, it was instinct, Ivory replied. *I was just trying to grab hold of anything that might be useful.*

Jude wasn't at all sure she believed her. The words sounded just a little bit too rehearsed.

Really, Ivory said, obviously sensing her doubt. *I just grabbed hold of whatever was in reach. You may as well keep it. It's pretty.*

"It's valuable," Jude replied. "Bone flowers fetch handsome prices for cajou spells. Perhaps Sofia will buy it from me."

She slipped it into her pocket for safekeeping. The clothes were clearly Paris's, a pair of fitted black jeans and a beautiful white silk shirt. Jude felt ridiculous in them. She was not as well fed as Paris and had never had her curves to begin with. The jeans seemed to hang off her hips, making her feel bony and scrawny, and the white shirt became smudged and dirty the moment she put it on. These were a beautiful person's clothes and Jude felt her own plainness intensely, like she was a child playing at dress-up.

It doesn't matter what you look like, Ivory said. *You shouldn't be worrying about whether André will think you attractive.*

I'm not! Jude said, her face going hot.

You cannot trust the Phantom, Ivory insisted. *He is dangerous.*

He saved my life, Jude replied. *And he said pretty much the same thing about you remember.*

Her head ached and she felt suddenly tired. How she longed to be back on her little balcony, sipping a cold mint julep and playing jazz into the evening. But that wasn't an option so she called for the Phantom to come in.

The door immediately opened and he stepped into the room. It was impossible to read his expression behind his mask but Jude was sure she must make the most ludicrous picture in Paris's clothes, like a pig dressed in silks, and she lifted her chin slightly to compensate. At the same time, she couldn't help recalling Ivory's words from a moment before. The cajou queen was right. What the heck did her appearance count for at a time like this? It certainly shouldn't matter one jot what the Phantom of Moonfleet thought of her.

"I saw your nightmare," Jude said, determined to get herself on track. "Back at the bayou."

She recalled it now, the image she'd glimpsed inside the bubble. It was one she knew well, one that haunted her own dreams. In fact, it was one of *her* nightmares.

There'd been the wooden pier, the candles flickering in jam jars hung from swamp trees, the birthday balloons, and Jude herself, standing alone in her party dress, looking around desperately, screaming for help that was never going to arrive in time as her little brother was eaten by alligators in the water below.

"Yes," the Phantom said slowly. "I thought you might have."

"Well?" Jude said. "What's the explanation? You weren't there. So how do you have one of my nightmares?"

"I was there," the Phantom replied. "Although you didn't see me."

"All right," Jude said stiffly. "Why were you there?"

The Phantom crossed his arms and looked down towards his boots. "Can it be that you don't already know?" he asked.

"Know what?"

You should have let me finish, Ivory whispered.

Almost against her will, Jude felt her eyes slide over to the portrait in the corner of the room. A deep flush of heat rushed up her face. She recognized the man immediately, how could she not when his face was branded on to her soul? She heard his voice inside her head once again:

Well, well. Is it somebody's birthday?

And then Ivory was laughing softly, each giggle like a nail driven into Jude's skull.

Theodore Majstro, the cajou queen laughed. *Drunkard. Drug addict… And child-murderer.*

"My father killed your brother," the Phantom said. "To punish your father for an unpaid debt. By the time I got there it was too late to stop him. But it is a scene that has haunted me ever since. The sound that those gators made … well, I expect you still hear it too."

"But … but Pa always said it was some warlock from outside the city," Jude began. "Why would he lie?"

But even as she asked the question, she already knew. Her pa had lied because he knew that one day Jude might seek revenge for Daryl and he hadn't wanted her anywhere near the Majstro family.

"Where is your father?" she asked.

"He died in the madhouse," the Phantom replied. "Five years ago."

She looked at him, and it suddenly infuriated her that she couldn't see his face and wasn't able to read his expression.

"So what's going on here?" she said. "Why did you ask me to come to Moonfleet in the first place?"

The Phantom rubbed at his neck and Jude could practically feel his discomfort.

"I felt … a sense of responsibility towards you," he said. "Because of what my family took from yours."

244

Jude thought of the food boxes left on her doorstep, the strange sensation she'd always had of someone watching over her.

"You're the angel," she blurted out before she could stop herself.

The Phantom raised his head. "I beg your pardon?"

Jude immediately felt foolish. "It's just … how I used to think of the mystery person who left the food."

"There are no angels in Baton Noir," the Phantom replied in a strange voice. "Only devils."

"But you are the one who left the boxes?" Jude pressed.

"Yes," the Phantom replied.

"And you would linger beneath my balcony too sometimes."

The Phantom paused. "I did not mean to," he whispered. He ran a hand through his hair and said, "It's just that your music was … so beautiful. And as you can see, there is not much beauty here. At Moonfleet."

Jude glanced at the dark oily portraits on the wall and couldn't help another shudder. It felt as if all the Majstro villains were sneering down at her. She wrapped her arms round herself, feeling suddenly exposed and vulnerable, as if all her defences had been stripped away, leaving her weaknesses laid bare.

"I wish you hadn't done that," she said, struggling to keep control of her emotions. "You had no right to spy on me."

She thought of all the times she'd had to go into her pa's bedroom to clean up piss or drag him out of bed. The times he'd come out on to her balcony to rage at her for some trivial offence and how she had so often been at her wits' end not knowing what to do or how to handle it. She recalled how often she had sat out on her balcony weeping in despair. She saw her life through the Phantom's eyes and it looked more pathetic than it had ever seemed to her before.

"I suppose you think I'm just … a complete failure of a person," she said.

Perhaps it was the stress of the last few days, but to her dismay she suddenly felt tears filling her eyes and it seemed to take every last ounce of her willpower to blink them away and her entire throat ached with the effort. She supposed the Phantom must have noticed because there was a silence in the room that seemed to stretch on interminably, but Jude simply couldn't look at him.

Finally he spoke. "I admire you more than any person I've ever met."

Jude looked up, wondering whether he was mocking her. He couldn't possibly mean it. Not after what he'd seen.

"That … isn't funny," she said, her face burning. "You know as well as I do that my life is an absolute, shocking mess—"

"But you don't give up."

"I *did* give up!" Jude cried. "For a while. After Leeroy. He … he's this boy who—"

"He is vermin," the Phantom said in a cold voice.

Jude looked at him sharply and then she remembered how Leeroy had sat with her on the balcony sometimes and realized the Phantom may have heard some of the things he'd said to her. That he'd know who Leeroy was and how Jude had allowed him to treat her and speak to her. Like she was nothing. Like she was worthless.

"You … you were there the night I broke up with him, weren't you?" she said. "You sent the owl."

"I was afraid he would hurt you."

"I always thought I was … such a strong person," Jude said. "But it was like he had some kind of power over me for a time and it took every bit of energy I had to get away from him. That's … that's the bit I hate most about myself. I should have…" She shrugged angrily, not knowing how to vocalize the mix of helplessness and shame that swirled round inside her, even after the break-up. "I shouldn't have let him make me forget who I was."

"Well," the Phantom replied. "We are all of us guilty of that from time to time. Sometimes it seems to me that these days I am more mask than man." He glanced at Jude and said, "We wish that our sorrows were simple and straightforward, but that is not the way of things. Is it, Jude?"

She thought of her pa and his bitterness and grief and ruined body. She thought of all the times he'd broken her heart and how fiercely she still loved him anyway.

"No," she said. "I guess not."

"I asked you to play at Moonfleet because I enjoy your music and thought it could be some extra money for you. But if I behaved badly in bringing you here, which I suppose I have, then I can only apologize."

Jude took a deep breath. "No," she said. "I understand. It's fine. You're not responsible for your father. I suppose I should thank you. For the food boxes. For the job here at Moonfleet. For saving my life today. I am … in your debt."

"You are not," the Phantom replied stiffly. "Not by

any means. I should never have allowed that trip to the bayou to take place today. I let myself be cowed into silence by Ivory because I feared she would reveal my secrets to you. I won't make the same mistake again. Ivory must do as she sees fit. I can't control what she chooses to tell you, but the truth is that I would always have helped you, even without her blackmail."

He took a step closer. "I only ask that no matter what she reveals, you will at least try to accept that I have always had a good reason, at the time, for the things that I have done." Behind his mask, Jude saw his grey eyes flick to the portraits on the wall. "All my life," he said, "I have done my utmost not to be like them."

Jude nodded. "I believe you."

You're a fool, Ivory sneered inside her mind.

Be quiet, Jude snapped. *Life's complicated. It's not always possible to do the right thing, even when you desperately want to.*

Stupid girl, Ivory replied. *I would tell you what I know about the Phantom right here and now, if only to protect you. But then you'd most likely refuse to have anything more to do with him, and we need him for what's to come next.*

And what's that? Jude replied.

Well, you heard Sheba, the cajou queen said. *We must*

have that devil's coin. Without it we'll never get through to the wishing well and I'll never find out who murdered me. Therefore we're going to have to steal the coin. From Etienne. And the Phantom is going to help us.

CHAPTER TWENTY

To Jude's surprise, the Phantom did not immediately dismiss the idea of stealing the coin from Etienne when she told him what Ivory had said.

"Yes," he replied. "I had anticipated that was what we would have to do. And I've thought of how we might do it."

"How?" Jude asked.

"By summoning the aid of the Thief. Ivory must know a spell to call him."

One of the cool legba, the Thief was, as his name suggested, a master criminal who delighted in taking things that did not belong to him. He was said to be thin, a bit of a joker and would immediately pocket any object that was given to him.

"Before we do anything," Jude said. "I'm going to visit Sharkey in hospital."

There isn't time for that! Ivory hissed. *Cajou Night is tomorrow!*

Cajou Night? Jude thought back. *What's that got to do with anything?*

N–nothing particularly. It's just that time is marching on and, like I told you, a human body doesn't like having a spirit trapped inside it. You could become ill. And then you'd be no use to me at all.

It seemed to Jude that Ivory had stumbled over her words a little but she didn't have time to puzzle over it.

Whatever, she replied. *Your concern for my health is touching, but I'm fine. It'll take me five minutes to look in on Sharkey. Then we'll go and buy the things we need for this spell to summon the Thief.*

The Phantom said he would accompany her to the hospital.

"They wanted to arrange payment then and there but I was in a hurry to get back to Moonfleet so I just handed over my wallet."

"Thank you," Jude said, as it suddenly occurred to her that she hadn't expressed her gratitude yet. "For seeing that he was taken care of and—"

But the Phantom shook his head and cut her off abruptly. "Please," he said. "It was the least I could do."

It's an act, Ivory said inside Jude's mind. *You mark*

my words. One day, you'll see.

Jude ignored her as she went outside with the Phantom. St Germaine's was only a short walk away and was a much better hospital than Sharkey would have been able to afford himself. Jude felt a terrible anxiety sloshing around in the pit of her stomach with every step. What if Sharkey was angry with her? She should never have allowed him to come to the bayou in the first place.

They arrived at the hospital and headed to the reception desk, where the Phantom collected his wallet and Jude was given directions to Sharkey's room.

"I hope you find him well," the Phantom said.

Jude sighed. "He shouldn't be here at all. People are getting hurt because of me."

"People are getting hurt because of Ivory," the Phantom corrected her. "I should return to Moonfleet. Meet me there when you have the ingredients you need."

Jude nodded. "All right. I'll see you later."

He turned and was about to go when a horribly familiar voice called out, "Oh my gods, Jude, have you lost your mind? What the hell are you wearing?"

She slowly turned round, knowing who she would see, smirking before her. Sure enough, Leeroy stood in the corridor, as handsome as ever with his golden-blond hair, his blue eyes and his perfectly straight nose. His lips curled into a sneer as his gaze rested on her. To make matters even worse, his friend Ollie was there too, and Jude knew that would make Leeroy determined to show off. There was nothing she could say or do that would prevent him from putting her down in front of his friend. She had known that they worked in a hospital in the Fountain District but why oh why did it have to be this one?

"That outfit looks like it belongs on a Pearl," Leeroy said. "Talk about a pig dressed in silks!"

And there it was, the reason why he was able to make her feel so worthless. It was because he echoed her own insecurities straight back at her. Why, she'd had that exact same thought just an hour earlier when she'd first put on the clothes. It was as if Leeroy could see into her soul somehow and held up a mirror that Jude had no wish to look into.

Little rat, Ivory said. *You know, I could tell you how to make a vinegar jar that would sour his life. All you need is a personal item of his, a few herbs and some red pepper to put in a glass jar with his name on it. Then you fill it with vinegar, call his spirit into the bottle and shake it when the moon is full—*

I'm not making a vinegar jar! Jude snapped, cutting her off.

She took a deep breath but before she could say a word there was a dark blur of movement and suddenly the Phantom was no longer by her side – he was gripping Leeroy round the throat with one gloved hand and then lifting him, one-armed, to slam against the wall. Leeroy tried to speak but only a gurgle came out as his face turned purple and his dangling ankles drummed helplessly against the plaster.

"You will not speak to her," the Phantom hissed in a tone so icy-cold that Jude felt goose bumps creep across her skin.

"Let him go, you maniac!" Ollie cried.

The Phantom ignored him, didn't even turn round as Ollie rushed at him. His spare hand just flew up at the last moment so that Ollie practically ran into his fist, taking the hit directly to the throat and staggering back with a gurgling sound.

"You will not speak to her," the Phantom repeated, still looking at Leeroy. "You will not look at her. You will not think of her. Ever again. Am I clear?"

Leeroy tried to nod, but it was impossible for him to move and both his hands clutched desperately at the Phantom's.

"For god's sake, let him go!" Jude hissed.

The Phantom released his grip immediately and Leeroy slithered to the floor, gulping for air, his throat swollen and red. People were shouting and Jude was afraid that security guards might appear at any moment. But the Phantom had already turned away and was stalking out of the hospital.

With one last glance at Leeroy, Jude hurried after him, catching up just outside the entrance at the same time as a security guard

"Hey!" the guard called. "We had reports that someone just— Oh!" He broke off as the Phantom turned round and he saw his mask. "S-sorry to bother you, Mr Majstro."

And that was it, the guard went back into the hospital without another word of reproach. There were no consequences of any kind. After all, André Majstro was cajou Royalty and Leeroy Lamar was only a Scrap.

"Come here." Jude gripped his wrist and tugged him down a nearby side street. It was one of the Fountain District's many residential streets, lined with immaculate white-columned mansions nestled away behind wrought-iron fences. Jude stopped beneath the cool shadow of a papershell pecan tree. It was the first time she'd ever deliberately touched the Phantom and he snatched his arm away from her now as if she'd burnt him.

"What the hell was that?" Jude demanded.

"He was being rude," the Phantom replied.

"So? That doesn't give you the right to grab someone by the throat! And I don't need you to fight my battles for me either!"

He made an impatient noise and turned away from her.

Finally he said, "If I did wrong, then I apologize."

Jude thought back to all her previous encounters with the Phantom. He had always seemed so completely in control of himself and his emotions before. This had been different. She'd heard the venom in his voice as he'd spoken to Leeroy – it had seemed personal.

I did try to tell you that you had somehow broken through to that shrivelled-up heart of his, Ivory said, sounding smug.

But surely she had to be wrong?

"Do you…" Jude began, frowning. "You don't … have feelings for me. Do you?"

She fully expected the Phantom to deny it immediately. Perhaps even point out her plainness, the difference in their status or her undesirability in general. But instead there was a long pause.

"I have tried so very hard not to," he said at last. "But … the more I resist, the worse it proceeds to get."

"But … but I don't understand. You've got Paris. She's a million times prettier than I am—"

"We have never been in a romantic relationship," the Phantom said. "Besides, Paris has not yet developed her soul. There can be no comparison with your kindness and loyalty and beautiful spirit." He didn't look at her as he went on, "Ivory may have guessed at some of this, so I would prefer you hear it from me, assuming she hasn't already said something." At last, he turned his head, his grey eyes watching her from behind the mask. "I want you to know that you are perfectly safe. I would never…" His voice caught in his throat. "Never dream of acting on my feelings. I will not contact you. I will not pester you. After this is all finished, you need never see me ever again. I give you my word."

"But I—"

"Now, I really must get back to Moonfleet," the Phantom said. "And Violetta."

He walked off before Jude could say anything. Not that she had any idea what she *would* have said. Her mind buzzed with it all. Ivory started to make some snide remark but Jude cut her off out loud, drawing the attraction of a couple of passers-by.

"Would you shut *up* already?"

Get on with it then! Ivory sniffed. *You're supposed to be getting supplies for the spell, not mooning about on the street, with the Phantom of all people!*

I wasn't mooning about, Jude snapped.

The sooner you see your friend, the sooner we can get a move on, Ivory said.

Jude pulled herself together, walked back to the hospital and went in to find Sharkey. There was no sign of Leeroy this time and she shoved her ex from her mind as firmly as she could, along with the disconcerting conversation with André.

When she reached Sharkey's room, she was relieved to see that he was sitting up in bed. His leg was bandaged where the nightmare had bitten him but he smiled when he saw her and waved her over for a hug.

"I thought you might be angry with me," she said, drawing back and taking the nearby seat.

"Angry with myself, more like," Sharkey replied. "Can't believe I went and got myself monched by one of them horrors." He gestured to his leg. "Not much use to anyone like this, am I? And worst of all, I guess I won't be able to play in the band for Cajou Night tomorrow."

Jude felt another flash of guilt. She knew that Sharkey and his grandmother would have been relying on that fee every bit as much as she was. But then she recalled the bone flower still in her pocket. It was a valuable thing and she knew she'd have no problem selling it in Baton Noir.

"Listen, don't worry about the money," she said to Sharkey. "I can make it up to you."

Her friend immediately started to protest, so Jude drew the strange flower from her pocket to show him.

"I grabbed this in the Black Bayou," she said. "Or rather Ivory did. Once I've sold it we can split the— Argh!"

The rest of her sentence disappeared in a little yelp of pain as she felt a sudden pressure building behind her eyes and tasted iron on her tongue.

The bone flower is not for selling! Ivory's voice hissed angrily inside her mind.

"What's wrong?" Sharkey asked, reaching forward to grip Jude's shoulder.

"Nothing," she said, although her head still ached. "It's just Ivory."

Why are you so concerned about that flower? she asked the cajou queen. *I thought you said you picked it up by accident?*

I did, but that doesn't mean we can't use it, Ivory replied. *An item like that holds a lot of magical power. We might need it. So don't you dare think of selling it until this is over!*

Jude frowned. It seemed to her that Ivory was acting strangely over this flower.

You've seen your friend, Ivory said, *and now we really must go. There are things to be done.*

Jude turned her attention back to Sharkey. "Don't worry about the money," she said again. She stuffed the bone flower back in her pocket. "One way or another, I promise I'll make it up to you."

CHAPTER
TWENTY-ONE

As soon as she'd left the hospital, Jude set about collecting the things on Ivory's list. They needed graveyard dirt again, but at least this time there was no sign of the Gravedigger when she entered the cemetery. From there she went on to Sofia's store in Mojo Alley. The streets were absolutely packed with revellers preparing for Cajou Night and Jude had to shoulder her way through the throng.

Belle was there, looking as lovely as ever in a pink silk top and spotless white jeans. Her blond hair was swept up into a high ponytail and several gold hoops adorned one ear.

The witch's face fell at the sight of her. "Oh," Belle said. "You're here."

"Shouldn't I be?" Jude asked.

"It's just that Sofia has gone off to find you," Belle replied. "She left about twenty minutes ago. Said she had something to tell you. She was in quite a hurry too – it seemed like it was important."

"Well, it'll have to wait, whatever it is," Jude replied. "My hands are full right now. Can you help me find this stuff?" She handed over the list Ivory had dictated to her. "I need it for a spell."

Belle frowned as she scanned down it. "What kind of spell?" she said.

"It's … it's personal," Jude said, unsure whether Sofia would have told Belle about Ivory, and reasoning that the fewer people who knew about it, the better.

But then Belle glanced at her and said, "It's something to do with the cajou queen, I suppose?"

"Sofia told you?"

"Sofia tells me everything. There wouldn't be much point doing otherwise. It's quite difficult to keep secrets from a witch who has the sight."

"Right," Jude replied. "Well, you know why I need these ingredients then."

Belle looked back down at the list in her hand. "We have the jar, the herbs, the red wax and the black cat fur," she said. "But we don't stock graveyard dirt, stolen or irreplaceable items, or cajou ivy."

"That's OK," Jude said. "I'll just take what you have."

She selected the things she needed and went up to

the counter. As Belle ran each item through the cash register, she kept casting strange looks at Jude.

"What is it?" Jude said.

Belle looked startled. Her eyes flicked to Jude again as she handed the paper bag across the counter.

"It's just that…" The witch hesitated for a moment, then seemed to make up her mind. "Sofia said you might come to the store. And if you did then she wanted me to check whether there's anything she can do to help with this … cajou queen situation."

"And?" Jude said, sensing that there was more.

Belle looked her in the eye. "And I want you to stay away," she said. Her pretty face was troubled as she went on, "Look, I don't mind Sofia being friends with a Scrap—"

"A Scrap?"

"Sorry, sorry." Belle lifted a hand, causing her beauty charms to jingle together. "I meant Citizen, of course."

"Of course."

"I don't mind Sofia being friends with you," Belle went on. "But look, this thing that you've got yourself mixed up in could be very dangerous and the truth is that I've always sensed something very big and … dark … in your future. And when I do readings for Sofia, sometimes I sense a little bit of that darkness

264

in her future too. And I know that it comes from you. So I'm asking you to please leave Sofia out of this. She's my ... well, I love her. I'm just trying to keep her safe, that's all." She gave Jude a pleading look and said, "You can understand that, can't you?"

"Sure," Jude replied. "It's OK. I have a plan. And it doesn't need to involve Sofia."

"Thank you," Belle said. "I'm really not trying to be mean, honestly. It's just you have to look out for the people you love, don't you?"

Jude picked up the paper bag. "Yeah. It's all right, I get it. I'll see you around."

She left the store, leaving Belle still looking uncomfortable behind her.

We don't need Sofia anyway, Ivory said.

Jude knew that but she still felt a small, sharp flash of hurt at the way Belle had just spoken to her. She recalled how the witch always sat in the Royals section of streetcars and liked to frequent Royals-only bars and jazz clubs. And even though she'd always been perfectly pleasant and polite to Jude, she'd never exactly been friendly. Even the offer to read her cards was, it seemed, only because the witch had sensed something in Jude's future that she wanted to know more about.

Don't worry about Belle, Ivory cut in on her thoughts. *Worry about the rest of our spell ingredients. The cajou ivy we can get from Moonfleet.*

And what about the stolen or irreplaceable items? Jude asked.

There's a store just down the street, Ivory replied.

Really?

Or course not! Ivory said. *The stolen item is something you'll need to steal yourself. Preferably from a loved one because that will give it more power. The Thief is not the easiest legba to summon. If he were then people would be doing it all the time. To increase your chance of success, the objects you place in the jar have to have as much magical energy as possible. And the item he steals will only belong to you temporarily.*

What does that mean? Jude asked.

You'll only have it for a short while. Then it will return to its original owner. The more powerful your spell, the longer you'll get to keep it.

Well, that just makes the whole thing completely pointless! Jude said.

For us, it won't matter, Ivory replied. *We only need the coin long enough to find the devil.*

Jude sighed. *And the irreplaceable object?*

That must come from you, Ivory said. *The more precious*

266

it is, the more powerful it will be.

I'm a poor Scrap who has nothing! Jude replied impatiently. *What do you suggest I sacrifice?*

You could offer him time, Ivory said.

Time?

Some years off your life, the cajou queen said. *So if you wanted to give him two years, for example, then you would just write 'two years' on a piece of paper and put that into the jar…*

Absolutely not, Jude replied. *I won't give him two days.*

You could give him some of your musical talent? Ivory suggested.

Not that either.

Well, you'd better think of something, Ivory said in a cold voice. *Otherwise you'll be breaking into Etienne's mansion and stealing the coin yourself.*

Jude sighed and headed for home, mentally going through a checklist of her belongings. She didn't have much in the first place, let alone something irreplaceable. But there was *one* thing she could think of…

The sun was setting as she headed back and the lights were coming on to cast their neon glow over the sweating cobbles. Jude let herself into their home and found her pa exactly where she'd left him. She hurried straight to the bathroom, eager to get washed and changed before he could start asking questions. She shoved her dirty clothes deep into the laundry basket before grabbing a clean pair of dungarees from the closet. It was a relief to be clean again and Jude felt almost human as she towelled off her hair. After that, she quickly made dinner and she and her pa ate in silence – the atmosphere between them even more stilted than usual after their argument that morning.

Eventually, Jude said, "Why didn't you tell me the truth about who really killed Daryl?"

Her pa slowly put down his fork. Jude wondered whether he might deny it but he simply said, "Who told you?"

"Does it matter?" Jude replied.

Her pa chewed on his lip. "Trying to protect you," he grunted at last, not looking at her. "Thought you might take it upon yourself to go after him one day. Suppose there's no harm in you knowing about it now. Theodore Majstro is dead. Died in the madhouse." He straightened up in his chair slightly. "And there's another reason I didn't tell you," he said, seeming to force out the words. "Shame. Plain and simple. Majstro was the only person who'd lend to me. Business had been slow and I was scared we'd lose the house, see? But I knew that family were a depraved bunch. I knew and I went there anyway." He looked Jude straight in the eye. "That's why I lost my temper that time you talked about going to Moonfleet," he said. "That family is wicked. If you'd gone there, something awful would have happened to you." His voice fell to a whisper. "I could just feel it in my bones."

Jude didn't say anything for a few seconds.

"Well," she said. "Thank you for admitting the truth now." She got up to clear the plates.

"Your friend was here earlier, by the way," Pa said.

Jude turned round from the sink. "What friend?"

"That witch friend. Said she had a message for you. I told her to leave a note in your room."

Jude tidied away and then went into her bedroom where she immediately noticed the Ivory Monette poppet. Its clothes had been removed and, even more strangely, it had been nailed face down to her dressing table. When Jude walked closer, she saw something she hadn't seen before when the doll had been dressed. There were words stitched into her back with black thread – two words, in fact:

Jude Lomax

And alongside it, a note from Sofia. Ivory protested

inside Jude's mind, took over her hands, grabbed the note and ripped it in half.

No! Jude cried, wrestling back control with all her mental effort. She slammed the two pieces of the note alongside each other on the table. She could still just about read it, despite the fact that it had been torn:

Jude,

I discovered this while examining the poppet. There's a tiny bit of magic left inside so I've nailed her down so that she doesn't reclothe herself before you get back.

I thought you must have had some kind of connection to the poppet for this to work. Do you remember, I asked you about it?

Well, this proves that Ivory Monette chose you. She chose you before she died. It wasn't random. For some reason, it was always going to be you.

I don't know what it means, but I thought you should know. I'm at my apartment all afternoon if you need me.

I hope you're OK.

Love, Sofia xx

CHAPTER
TWENTY-TWO

Jude swore out loud.

"What the hell is this?" she said to Ivory. "You told me it was random but you picked me right from the start! Why?"

It's really not such a big deal, Ivory said sullenly. *I simply needed someone who had access to Moonfleet.*

"Moonfleet?"

And the Phantom. I knew I'd need his help if I ever found myself in this position. André has money, resources, boats. Even if he hadn't run into you at Etienne's club, it was always my plan to ask for his help eventually.

"Paris has access to him too," Jude said. "Why didn't you write her name on the poppet?"

Because the Phantom doesn't care about Paris! Ivory said. *He cares about you, as you now know full well. Besides which, Paris wouldn't have come to my funeral and passed beneath the charm gates.*

Jude recalled how Sharkey had told her that Ivory Monette's will had asked for the Done and Dusted Brass Band by name and how odd she'd found that at the time, given that their band was hardly the best or most prestigious in Baton Noir. Certainly not the kind of band you'd expect to play at the funeral of the cajou queen herself.

"You set me up," Jude said, as realization dawned. "I suppose Pa was right. Something awful *did* happen because I went to Moonfleet."

Something great may happen too, Ivory pointed out. *I didn't tell you that I'd chosen you specifically because I didn't want you raising a ruckus. But look, we're so almost there. All you have to do is summon the Thief and then we can find the devil's wishing well.*

"Oh, is that all?" Jude replied sarcastically.

Let's just get on with it, Ivory snapped.

For a moment, Jude thought about ignoring Belle and Ivory and going to find Sofia. But what would be the point? She had the Phantom to help her with summoning the Thief. And Sharkey had already been hurt because of her. Belle had been right – there was no need to endanger Sofia too.

Still scowling, Jude walked over to her bed, lifted the pillow and picked up the photo of Daryl. She'd taken this one herself in an attempt to capture the fireflies she loved so much. Daryl had run into the shot at the last moment and showed up slightly blurred on the pier. She remembered she'd been really cross with him for ruining the scene, had shouted something about how he always spoiled everything.

"This is the only photo I have of my brother," she said to Ivory. "Is that precious enough for you?"

Years from your life would have been better, but I suppose we might try with that, the cajou queen replied.

Jude stuffed the photo into her pocket then checked that her pa was still in his chair before she tiptoed into his room. This was the bit that hurt the most. It was one thing to give up something of her own, but to take from her pa one of the very few precious things he owned was a different story.

It'll help him in the end, Ivory whispered. *Just remember that.*

As Jude rummaged in her pa's chest of drawers, she told herself that Ivory was right. It would be worth it to take away some of his pain. That's what this whole thing was about. She found what she was looking for, right at the back of the drawer. It was a locket on a delicate silver chain.

"My mother's," Jude said to Ivory. "There's photos inside of Pa and Daryl and me."

Will he miss it?

"He'll be devastated. And…" she swallowed, "and if I give this away too, then it means we'll have no photos of Daryl left. We'll never be able to look at him again."

Perfect, the cajou queen replied.

♛

Jude hid her trumpet under the bed before gathering up the things she needed for the spell, including the items from her altar, and stuffing them all into her empty trumpet case. She told her pa she was going out to practise with the band for the upcoming Cajou Night celebrations. Then she took the streetcar to the Fountain District and went straight to Moonfleet Manor. She could feel her nerves all wound up tight as violin strings at the thought of seeing the Phantom again after the things he'd said to her that day. She didn't know what to make of it, how to feel or what to think. For now, the easiest thing seemed to be to shove it all to one side and deal with it later, once things had calmed down.

Moonfleet Manor hunched, brooding in the

moonlight, as Jude drew near and she could see the cajou tree spreading its dark branches against the sky. She didn't dare approach it by herself in case it tried to throttle her, so she went up to the front door and slammed the metal knocker down on the wood.

It seemed to take an age for it to be answered and she started to wonder whether the Phantom was actually in at all. But then the door swung open and there he stood. The first thing Jude noticed were the spots of blood on his white shirt collar. Then she saw that his gloves were ripped and bloodstained at the edges.

"What happened?" she asked, staring. "Are you all right?"

The Phantom followed her gaze and shoved his hands into his pockets. "Fine," he said. "It's just that Violetta is … in a wild mood today. As I said earlier."

"A *ghost* did that?" Jude said. Her eyes flicked to the shadowy staircase over the Phantom's shoulder.

"Never mind about Violetta," the Phantom said. "Did you get everything you need for the spell?"

"Everything except the cajou ivy."

"All right. Wait a moment."

The door closed again, leaving Jude on the porch alone. The Phantom returned a few minutes later with a new pair of gloves and some shears.

"Cajou trees are difficult at the best of times," he said. "And ever since it became the Hanging Tree, it seems to have some kind of link with Violetta. So you'd better stay well back and allow me to do this."

Jude followed him across the lawn and they were about twelve feet from the tree when the Phantom held up his hand and said, "That's close enough."

Jude stopped and watched as he went the last few steps. This was the nearest she'd ever been to the cajou tree, and even in the moonlight she could see that it was a strange thing indeed. Not only was it warped and twisted, branches growing out at strange, impossible angles that made Jude's head ache, but there were pins, needles and nails embedded into its black trunk too. Jagged stitches of thread tied the leaves to the branches, which glimmered with buttons and were hung with strange dark feathers. Multi-coloured cajou beads dangled in bunches like berries, and the roots crawled out over the grass towards them as if they were gnarled fingers. Sticky trails of red and black wax ran down the trunk like sap. And the tree smelled of tar, blood and black magic. It was shocking to think that such a monstrous tree could have appeared overnight like that.

And then there was the cajou ivy, twisting slowly round the trunk, slithering down the branches in snake-like coils.

The moment the Phantom approached, one of the vines shot out and wrapped itself round his wrist. He took a sharp step back and in the same movement raised the shears to snip the vine. It came loose, still attached to his sleeve, and he quickly moved away from the other vines, which were already stretching towards him.

"Will this do?" he asked, turning to Jude and holding up the vine, which was perhaps two foot in length.

Perfect, Ivory breathed.

"Yes," Jude said. "Now we're ready to perform the spell."

Under Ivory's direction, she set up her altar on the lawn, then proceeded to place the items in the summoning bottle. She felt a deep cut of loss as she put the photo of Daryl in there, and then hesitated over her mother's locket. She would never be able to look at Daryl's mischievous freckled face again and she knew that her memory of him would grow dimmer and dimmer until she would no longer be able to see him at all and then it would almost feel like he'd never existed.

But Daryl was dead and there was nothing left to be done that could help him. Her pa, though, was very much still alive, and Jude was determined to follow this road all the way through to the end, so she forced the locket into the bottle. Ivory then directed her to write the Thief's name backwards thirteen times on a piece of paper, which she rolled up and pushed into the bottle too.

Now wrap the ivy round the bottle, Ivory instructed.

Jude did as she said, expecting to have to fasten it with something when she got to the end, but the vine pulled from her hand and shot eagerly into the bottle, as if it could sense the magic sizzling away in there. Its stitched leaves pressed against the inside of the glass, hiding the other objects from sight and sealing up the neck.

What happens now? Jude asked Ivory, expecting her to recite a spell and that would be that.

Instead the cajou queen said, *You have to bury the bottle at a crossroads.*

Crossroads?

It's the only way to summon the Thief. If it were anyone else doing the spell he'd need to take possession of someone present in order to communicate but you'll be able to see him without that.

Jude looked up at the Phantom, who was standing a few steps away, watching her. "She says we need to go to a crossroads. Where are we supposed to find one of those?"

"We have one here, as it happens," the Phantom replied. "At Moonfleet."

"Where?"

The Phantom gestured over his shoulder. "In the family graveyard. One or two of the Majstros have dabbled in cajou over the years. The graveyard was specially designed to have a crossroads at its centre."

A crossroads in a graveyard of all places! Ivory exclaimed. *How perfect!*

Jude packed up the altar and picked up the bottle then they made their way over to the graveyard, which was situated on the other side of the house. Iron lamp posts stood at regular intervals with electric lights illuminating the path. Like most of the cemeteries in Baton Noir, this one had its graves above ground in stone tombs and crypts. Jude noticed marble statues of various legba – such as the Gravedigger and indeed Baron Lukah himself – keeping an eye on everything. And as they walked past the ornate crypts, Jude recognized some of the names from the portrait room and couldn't help wishing that Ivory had not shared so much of their disreputable histories with her.

They made their way past the graves to the crossroads at the centre. A small shed structure stood to one side and the Phantom reached into this for a shovel.

"Do you need to dig the hole yourself?" he asked.

Yes, Ivory said.

"I do," Jude replied.

The Phantom handed over the shovel. "Just be careful," he warned. "All manner of ghastly things have probably been buried at these crossroads over the years."

It was not a cheering thought and Jude dug a small hole as quickly as she could, worried that she might drive the shovel into a skull and dig up a skeleton at any moment. Once she had a hole large enough to conceal the bottle, she pressed it inside before covering it over. When it was completely buried, Jude straightened up and brushed dirt from her palms.

Now what?

Now we wait to see whether the items you placed in the bottle will be enough to tempt the Thief, Ivory replied.

And how long will that take?

Before Ivory could reply, a voice spoke from the roof of the crypt above them.

"Well, well, well. This looks like it's going to be interesting."

Jude looked up and saw a lanky man sitting on the roof of Dorian Majstro's crypt with his long legs hung over the edge, lazily drumming his ankles against the wall as he gazed at them with a sly grin already spreading across his thin face.

The legba of theft wore a shabby suit that looked as if it had seen better days. His waistcoat had been patched and mended in multiple places. His brogues were scuffed at the toes and desperately in need of a good polish and his shirt cuffs were stained with ink. Jude recalled that when he wasn't engaged in robbery the Thief was said to be an enthusiastic writer of poison-pen letters.

He had long dark hair that hung in lank strands past his shoulders, and a thin, pale, wolfish face, with sharp cheekbones. A pair of pince-nez sat on his long nose and he pushed these up as he looked down at the items in his hands. Jude realized it was her photograph and her pa's locket.

"A picture of a dead brother," the Thief said. "And a pilfered locket that once belonged to your mother and has been stolen from your father." He looked over his glasses at Jude. "You have my attention, little girl," he said. "What would you like me to steal?"

"Is he here?" the Phantom asked, noticing that Jude's gaze seemed fixed on the crypt.

She nodded. "I'd like you to steal a devil's coin," Jude said. "Belonging to a vampire named Etienne Malloy."

The legba looked back down at the photo and locket, holding them up and testing their weight for a moment.

"Yes," he mused. "That can be arranged." He looked at her and said, "But you will not have it for long. Not unless you're prepared to sweeten the pot with some years of your life thrown in."

"How long will I have the coin without doing that?" Jude asked.

The Thief pursed his lips for a moment. Then he said, "An hour is all I can promise, I'm afraid."

Jude was worried Ivory might start protesting that an hour wouldn't be enough time to go back into the swamp and attempt to locate the wishing well but, to her surprise, the cajou queen said:

That will suffice.

"An hour is enough," Jude said to the Thief.

He raised his eyebrows. "Are you sure?" he asked. "If you were to throw in just six months, I could extend your ownership to three weeks."

"No," Jude said. "Thank you. An hour will do."

The Thief shrugged his bony shoulders and slipped the photo and locket into his pocket. "Have it your own way," he said. "So do we have a bargain?"

"Yes," Jude replied.

"I need you to say the words."

"I would like you to steal the coin for me."

"It would be my special pleasure." The Thief got to his feet. "The coin will be yours by tomorrow afternoon."

Afternoon! Ivory exclaimed. *Why does it have to be the afternoon? Ask him if he can get it now.*

What does it matter? Jude asked, surprised.

But she looked up at the Thief and said, "Can't you get it sooner?"

"Surprisingly enough I have other things to do besides running errands for you, Miss Lomax," the Thief replied, straightening his tie. "You will have the coin tomorrow afternoon. Possibly early evening."

Then he snapped his fingers and was gone.

CHAPTER
TWENTY-THREE

Jude returned home and spent the night in her own bed. As she dressed the next day, Ivory grumbled continuously about the delay in getting the coin but since there was nothing much that could be done about it Jude ignored her. She was about to leave her bedroom when Ivory suddenly said, *You're wearing different dungarees today.*

"So?" Jude replied.

Get the bone flower from the pocket of your old ones, Ivory said. *We should take it with us.*

"What is it with you and this flower?" Jude muttered as she grabbed it from her old dungarees and stuffed it into a pocket. She still couldn't shake the feeling that there had been something a bit odd about the way the cajou queen had appeared to deliberately take them down deeper into the bayou when they'd been in the water. As if she'd been after the flower all along...

Hearing her thoughts, Ivory said, *Oh, don't be so suspicious! I grabbed it out of instinct.*

"So you said," Jude replied.

And we should take it with us in case it's useful later, that's all, the cajou queen replied. *Besides, if you leave it lying around then Beau might eat it. He's partial to magical flowers.*

Jude glanced at her bed and saw that the great snake had indeed appeared there, snoozing contentedly in a big coil. She was too keen to get to the hospital to visit Sharkey to argue about it any further.

When she arrived on the ward, she was relieved when her friend told her that the injury was healing well enough and they thought he'd be able to go home the next day. They whiled away the day playing cards and talking. It felt good to have a reprieve from the constant onslaught of cajou madness, although given that tonight was Cajou Night, it was hard to avoid it completely. Even the hospital had been decorated with strands of cajou beads and jazz records scratched away on every ward.

When lunchtime came and went, Ivory started getting twitchy, dwelling on how and when the coin would be delivered by the Thief.

He'll probably just know where I am, Jude said. *He is a legba.*

I think you should go back to Moonfleet, Ivory insisted. *That's where the summoning spell took place so that's most likely where he will return.*

Jude resisted at first, not much relishing the idea of hanging around in Moonfleet Manor's private graveyard but the cajou queen was so insistent that Jude said a reluctant goodbye to Sharkey and made her way to Moonfleet. She arrived on the doorstep just as Paris came storming out of the front door, the Phantom close behind her.

"—not spending another moment in this house of horrors!" she was saying.

The Phantom reached out a gloved hand to grip her wrist. "Please don't go," he said in an oddly strained voice. "I will double your fee."

"Not for all the money in the Majstro vaults!" Paris snarled, snatching back her hand. "You're a … a monster to ask me to do it in the first place. And she's a raving lunatic who belongs in an asylum. If you want to lock people up that's your own affair. It's a wicked—"

"Be quiet!" the Phantom snapped, suddenly noticing Jude. He flicked his gloved hand at Paris and said,

"I accept your resignation. Leave and don't come back."

Paris turned on her heel, saw Jude and scowled. "You'll get out too, if you have any sense," she said, before storming off down the driveway.

"What was all that about?" Jude asked, staring after her.

"It's of no consequence," the Phantom replied. "There was a job I'd hoped Paris might do for me. It was always a long shot and … it turns out it is not going to be possible after all."

There was such a note of utter dejection in his voice that Jude said, "Is it something I can help with?"

Then she remembered that Paris was a Pearl from the Pearl House and there was only one type of job that the Phantom was likely to have had in mind for her. The moment the words left her mouth, she blushed furiously.

Seeing her reaction, the Phantom gave a humourless laugh. "It is not what you think," he said. "But it is not something you can help with either."

"What did she mean about someone being locked up?" Jude asked, recalling the words and feeling suddenly uneasy.

The Phantom turned away. "She was talking of Violetta," he said.

"But she said something about the asylum—"

"You need not concern yourself with it," the Phantom replied. "Has the Thief brought the coin yet?"

"No, not yet. Ivory wanted me to come here in case he came back to the same place."

"Then we will wait in the graveyard," the Phantom said.

Jude followed him across the lawn but she couldn't shake her feeling of unease. Paris had made it sound as if there was a prisoner in Moonfleet. Plenty of people talked about there still being a lunatic left in the attic but Jude had thought those were just stories. Still, she couldn't help glancing at the dark windows staring out like eyes from the top floor of the house. She recalled what Ivory had said:

If you knew the truth you wouldn't even want to be in the same room as him...

She directed her thoughts to the cajou queen.

Do you know anything about this? she asked.

About what? Ivory replied, in far too innocent a tone.

What Paris was saying. Is there a prisoner at Moonfleet? Is that the secret you've been blackmailing him with?

Just concentrate on getting the coin, Ivory replied. *We have more important things to worry about than your crush on the Phantom right now.*

I do NOT have a crush! Jude replied, hating how childish Ivory had made her sound.

Stop going on about him then.

Jude dropped the matter as they walked into the graveyard. There was no sign of the Thief and there continued to be no sign of him for the next hour. As the second hour crawled slowly by, Ivory began to get more and more restless inside Jude's head.

Why are you so on edge? Jude snapped. *What's the rush?*

What's the rush? Ivory sneered back at her. *The rush is that I've had it with this! Everything is taking too long and I must find out who murdered me so that they can be appropriately punished! Plus there's no telling how long your frail human body will hold out before my spirit overcomes it completely.*

Jude shuddered. It was hardly a cheerful thought.

Another hour went by and the sky had started to darken before the Thief finally appeared, back where he had been before on top of Dorian Majstro's crypt, the devil's coin glinting dully between his long fingers. He gave a mocking bow when he saw Jude, bending his lanky body so low that his nose almost touched his toes. Then he straightened up and tossed her the coin.

"Your plunder, my lady," he said. "Have fun."

Jude caught the coin in both hands and, when she looked up, the Thief had gone.

Finally! Ivory hissed, gazing down at the coin in Jude's hands.

Now what? Jude asked her.

Tell the Phantom we need a boat, Ivory said. *The paddle steamer is still trapped in the swamp and that little lifeboat will never do. He must get another one from somewhere quickly.*

When Jude told the Phantom what Ivory had said, he nodded. "I know where to get one," he said. "We'll go there now."

No, Ivory said. *You must stay here. There's another spell I need you to do. It'll help us find the wishing well.*

"Ivory wants me to stay here and do another spell."

"What kind of spell?" the Phantom asked.

"She says it'll help us find the wishing well."

The Phantom stared back at her, his eyes narrowing behind the mask. "Why did she not do this spell the first time we went to the bayou?"

Jude listened for Ivory's answer, then said, "Apparently it can only be done at a graveyard crossroads. She didn't know you had one."

The Phantom paused for a moment. "I'd prefer you didn't stay at Moonfleet by yourself."

290

Jude was about to reply when she felt a sudden strange gurgle in her stomach. The next second she felt a weird feeling of pressure building inside.

"What the—?" she began, but that was as far as she got before almost doubling over with a gasp.

There were *things* inside her stomach, living things. She could feel them scrabbling over each other, pushing, prodding and poking, like they were trying to find a way out.

"What's happening?" the Phantom demanded as Jude fell forward on to her knees.

But she couldn't speak. She could only heave desperately, and before long she felt large lumps working their way up her throat. Then they were in her mouth – scrabbling over her tongue, falling from her lips to land with a wet splat on the ground.

Jude stared in horror at the slimy toad in front of her. Before it could right itself, Jude heaved again and a second toad came out, quickly followed by a third, and a fourth, and a fifth. Soon there were thirteen toads before her in a glistening pile of webbed feet and bulbous eyes and green leathery skin.

Jude sat back, exhausted, wiping slime from her chin as the toads hastily scrabbled away among the graves. Her mouth tasted of the bayou and she longed for a glass of cold water to wash it away.

"What the hell was that?" the Phantom asked, crouching before her, his grey eyes searching her face from behind the mask.

I told you that an ordinary human can't take cajou possession indefinitely, Ivory whispered. *Too much black magic in the blood, you see. Make no mistake, if my spirit stays inside you much longer, you will die. We're running out of time, girl.*

"It's Ivory," Jude said. "She says I'll die if her spirit doesn't leave soon. I think you need to go and get that boat."

"Very well." The Phantom shook his head. "But stay in the grounds until I return. Don't go anywhere near the house."

"I won't," Jude promised.

She watched him go out through the front gates then said to Ivory, "All right, how is this spell going to work? Do we need to go and buy some ingredients or—"

There is no spell, Ivory replied.

"But you said—"

I only said that to get André out the way.

"Why?"

Because I'm going to tell you what his secret is.

CHAPTER
TWENTY-FOUR

Jude was silent for a moment, the warm evening air ruffling her hair.

"Why the sudden change of heart?" she asked.

I'm not a monster, Ivory said. *Whatever you may think of me, there are some injustices that even I shudder to behold. And this one has lain heavy on my conscience. I knew of the suffering that went on within Moonfleet but did nothing to lessen it. With the Phantom out of the way, this is perhaps the only chance I will ever have to right this wrong, so I will share the Phantom's secret with you and you'll be horrified as any decent person would be. You'll want nothing more to do with him but you must promise to put aside your disgust and work with him long enough to catch my murderer.*

"It's not as if I have much choice about that," Jude replied, recalling the toads.

A few hours ago, you asked me if there was a prisoner

at Moonfleet, Ivory said. *Well, the answer is yes. There is. André keeps a child locked up in the attic.*

Jude recoiled. "I don't believe you," she said.

You heard what Paris said as she left. André recruited her to be a jailor. And it's why he first asked for my help too. He wanted me to perform a spell to make the child lose a memory — something she saw that she shouldn't have. I came to care for her. I told the Phantom I needed more time with her to come up with a suitable spell. I thought of going to the police but I didn't want to make an enemy of a Majstro. So I was a coward and did nothing, and now I'm asking you to help me make amends for one of the most wicked acts I ever committed.

Jude wanted to doubt her, and yet there was a real note of what appeared to be anguished desperation in the cajou queen's voice.

"What memory did he want you to erase?" she asked.

The child saw his face, Ivory said. *Without his mask. And his real face is something that no one is allowed to see. He's a proud man and couldn't bear it, couldn't bear for her to spread the word about what she'd seen.*

Jude's mind whirred frantically as she tried to gather together everything she knew about the Phantom. He *was* strongly attached to his mask. He didn't even like to be seen with it very much. She could imagine that he would react badly to someone seeing his true face. But would his reaction really be so extreme as to lock up a child?

"I just … can't believe that André would do such a thing," she said.

If you don't believe it, then what harm is there in checking? Ivory replied.

Jude glanced up at the grey stones of Moonfleet. "I promised that I wouldn't go back into Moonfleet. And I don't have a key…" she began, before remembering the skelekey spell and falling silent.

The Power will get us in, Ivory replied. *Please. I know you have no reason to trust me, but please believe me when I say that there really IS a child locked up in there. We can free her before the Phantom returns. A chance like this will never come around again. If you refuse to help her now then you will have to go the rest of your life knowing that there's a tortured soul locked away in Moonfleet because you were too afraid to act when you had the chance.*

Jude thought of the crying girl on the stairs that she had simply walked away from. The fact that she was a murderous ghost didn't really help since Jude hadn't known that at the time. And then there was the teenage girl back at Etienne's club. Abandoned to her fate with the vampires, Old Esther and the other doomed lost souls. The waiter in the Fang she had longed to help but had prioritized her own mission instead, while telling herself that there was nothing she could possibly have done anyway. Well, maybe that excuse wasn't going to work here. Because she *could* go into Moonfleet and check whether Ivory was telling the truth or not, and she would never get the chance again.

She gritted her teeth. "All right," she said. "Show me how to get inside and I'll take a look at this attic of yours. But I'm not promising anything. And I'm not releasing anyone until I've spoken to the Phantom. If there *is* someone locked up in there, then I can only think that he probably had a good reason for it."

Even as she spoke, though, she couldn't help wondering what reason could possibly be big enough to justify locking up a child, especially if their cell was somewhere as cursed and haunted as the grisly attic of Moonfleet Manor undoubtably was.

Beau appeared on Jude's shoulders as she walked back through the grounds and she reached up a hand to rub his head, glad of his presence and reassuring weight. When she reached the front door she wasn't surprised to find it locked in multiple places. She had to say the word *skelekey* several times before the door swung open, revealing the dark interior of Moonfleet's main hallway. The double staircase loomed before them, the cajou wood gleaming, dark and wet. Jude took a step towards it but Ivory immediately stopped her.

Not that way. Violetta might not let you pass.

As soon as she'd spoken, Jude heard the subdued whispering start up again.

"Why did I do it? Why did I do it?"

She didn't relish the idea of going past the ghost, especially when she recalled the mad eyes from the portrait and the terrible things the girl had done in the attic. Every inch of Jude's skin prickled at the thought of setting foot in such a place.

There's another staircase, Ivory said. *At the back of the house. Go down that corridor there.*

Jude did as the cajou queen had said, glad to leave the whispering ghost behind her. It was dark and Ivory had to use Jude's tongue to speak out loud: "Luminé."

The candles lining the walls immediately lit themselves, providing enough light for Jude to make her way down the corridor. It felt deeply wrong to be in the house without the Phantom, not just because she was trespassing but also because in the deserted quiet she felt as if the house was watching her. There was a sense of a deep breath being held in. Waiting.

Part way down the corridor, the green floor sloped away from her unexpectedly and Jude stumbled, putting her hand against the wall to steady herself. The tiles weren't cold and hard as she'd expected but soft and warm, and – just for a moment – it felt as if they pressed out against her hand, like the house itself was breathing…

Jude snatched her hand back in alarm.

Is Moonfleet Manor alive? she hissed at Ivory. *I mean the house itself?*

Who knows? Ivory replied, which Jude did not find a very comforting response.

Ivory directed her down the corridor to the kitchen, where she found the other staircase. It had clearly been used for servants, back when servants still worked at Moonfleet. Unlike the cajou staircase, these stairs were plain and simple and led straight up to the second floor. Jude got a glimpse of another corridor stretching away from her before Ivory said, *Don't stop here. Carry on to the attic. The stairs go all the way up.*

Jude did as she'd been told, her wariness increasing with every step. The worn wooden stairs creaked loudly beneath her swamp boots and the air became ever staler. There were no windows and the electric lights were feeble. It was hot and muggy inside the house too, and Jude could feel sweat start to form at her hairline. It was like breathing the air inside a crypt, like being sealed up with ghosts and old bones, like feeling the clutching hand of Baron Lukah hungrily reaching out for you…

Perhaps it was the thought of the death legba putting ideas in Jude's head, but she suddenly thought she heard the *tick-tock* of the pocket watch he carried, counting down mankind's allotted time, and the touch of dry fingers running over her cheek…

She cried out and jerked back against the wall, almost dislodging Beau, raising her hand to ward off an invisible foe.

Stop that! Ivory snapped. *Don't think about Baron Lukah. He's already hunting me as it is. I don't need you sending out thoughts to him like a beacon!*

"Sorry," Jude gasped. "I didn't mean to. I just … suddenly felt like he was on the stairs with me."

She glanced back the way she'd come and for an instant thought she saw a twin flash, like light bouncing off a pair of smoked glasses.

It's only a few more steps to the attic, Ivory said. *Just get on with it. We're running out of time.*

"All right!" Jude wiped a sheen of sweat from her forehead and carried on. It felt dangerous to turn her back on the shadowy staircase behind her and her boots clattered noisily in her haste to reach the top. Finally she reached a long narrow landing, with just one plain wooden door standing before her. Something about it made Jude shudder, as if an echo remained of all the horrors that had taken place behind it. It was, unsurprisingly, locked, so Jude whispered the magic word. But the door remained sealed fast.

It has magical protections on it, Ivory said. *They can only be removed by the person who placed them there. Fortunately for us, that was me.*

She took over Jude's tongue and whispered the magic word in her own voice. There was the dull click of a lock sliding back. Jude reached out and tried the handle. The door swung open easily, revealing the attic within.

CHAPTER
TWENTY-FIVE

Jude expected the attic to be dusty and dark, filled with cobwebs and shadows. Instead it was a clean space, softly lit by the golden glow of several lamps. Thick rugs lay on the floor and bookcases lined the walls. There were elegantly upholstered chairs in one corner, arranged to create a sitting-room area. In the opposite corner was a bed, along with a wash basin and a toilet. An open chest revealed a large selection of toys, including what appeared to be a perfect replica of the Ghost Station. Crouched before this, holding a beautiful toy steam engine in one hand, was a little girl.

Jude recognized her from the painting she had seen downstairs. She'd been the other girl with the Phantom and Violetta. She wore a blue silk dress and her dark hair was tied back in a neat ponytail, fastened with a bow. Her skin had the too-pale look of someone who hasn't seen the sun for a long time but she was an exceptionally pretty child nonetheless, with long dark lashes and deep indigo eyes. For a moment, she and Jude simply stared at one another. Then the girl slowly got to her feet and as she did so, there was the clinking of iron.

Jude saw there was a metal cuff locked round the girl's ankle, attached to a cruel-looking chain that stretched into the centre of the room, where it was fastened to a large metal loop on the floor. The bare skin round the girl's ankle was red-raw and there were bloodstains on her feet. Jude's insides seemed to shrivel up inside her at the sight. Beau sensed something was wrong too, because he raised his head from Jude's shoulder and let out a vicious-sounding hiss.

I told you, Ivory said, triumphant. *I told you there was a child locked up in here.*

"Are you Enid?" Jude asked, remembering the name from the painting.

"Yes," the girl replied. She had a quiet, serious voice to match her small, solemn face. "Who are you?"

"My name is Jude," she said, putting one hand up to quieten Beau. "Jude Lomax."

"Are you going to be the new Paris?"

"No." Jude shook her head. "I'm a friend of Ivory's."

The girl's face lit up for a moment, but then she frowned and said, "Is that true?"

"It's true, my dear," Ivory said, using Jude's tongue to speak in her own voice. "I've come to set you free."

Hang on a second, Jude said, pushing Ivory away. *I haven't said I'll do that yet.*

What possible reason can you have not to? Ivory snapped.

Jude hesitated. It was a fair question. And yet her gut instinct told her not to trust Ivory. After all, if Enid was a Majstro then that meant she was a descendant too. And descendants didn't age in the same way that people did. Jude had seen her looking exactly as she did now in a painting that had been created sixty years before, which meant that she wasn't a child at all. Jude could feel how tense Beau was through her shoulders, which instantly made her wary.

"Oh please," the girl whispered, tears suddenly filling her eyes. "Please let me out of here."

"Did André put you here?" Jude asked.

"Yes. He's my brother."

"Why did he lock you up?"

"I saw his face," Enid said, echoing what Ivory had told her earlier. "Without the mask. It's the one thing he can't forgive."

"How old are you?" Jude asked.

She paused and Jude couldn't help thinking that she was weighing up whether or not to tell her the truth. "It's hard to tell," she said. "You lose track of time when you're locked away in an attic with nobody to talk to. But Paris worked it out and told me that I turned seventy-four earlier this year."

You lied, Jude said to Ivory, feeling strangely triumphant. *You said a child was locked up in here.*

Descendants aren't like us, Ivory replied. *Enid's aging froze when she was seven. She has all those years' worth of memory and experience but, in many ways, she IS a child still. Besides, what does it matter? She's a prisoner here against her will. The only decent thing to do is set her free.*

"I know my brother can seem … kind," Enid said. "And he is sometimes. But he can also be monstrous, just like the rest of us." She gestured at the attic around her. "This is how André's wickedness manifests itself."

Jude shook her head. She didn't know what to do. She wanted to trust the Phantom, yet it was hard to imagine any explanation that could justify this. The attic had been made comfortable but it was a prison just the same.

"He's had me locked in here for years," Enid said.

"And I've asked so many people to help me during that time. Servants that have come and gone. Paris. Ivory. Nobody was brave enough to go against the Phantom of Moonfleet Manor. No one is prepared to risk anything to set me free."

Jude thought again of the girl on the train tracks at Etienne's club and the hundreds like her who suffered every day in Baton Noir. Many people, she suspected, wanted to see change, but they weren't prepared to do anything about it. She hated that she was probably in that category herself. And yet she couldn't help thinking that there must be *some* reason the Phantom had done this, something more than being angry because his sister saw his real face.

"I even managed to call out to visitors in the grounds a few times," Enid went on. "That's why he chained me to the floor, so I couldn't reach the windows, and he covered them up with thick drapes." Her eyes suddenly swam with tears. "Have you ever stopped to appreciate how glorious a thing it is to feel the sun warming your face? I haven't felt that for so long. Oh, please won't you just open the window so I can feel it?"

"It's night time," Jude replied hoarsely.

Tears spilled over the girl's eyelids and ran down her cheeks. "The moonlight then," she whispered.

"Some fresh night air. If you're not going to set me free, at least let me enjoy that before the Phantom finds out what you're doing and throws you out."

The air in the room was dreadfully stale, the awful musty, sticky smell of suffering and captivity. Jude walked over to the nearest window. What harm could it do when the girl was chained to the floor like that? Even so, she was careful to take the long way round so as to stay out of her reach. Descendants were known to be unusually strong – she had seen the Phantom lift Leeroy right off the ground using only one hand. Enid didn't look as if she planned to attack her but Jude wasn't prepared to take any chances.

She pulled back the drapes. Moonlight spilled in through the dirty glass and Jude looked out on to the grounds of the house and the cajou tree below. When she tried to open the window she found it locked, but the magic word solved that and Jude pushed it open. She was glad to breathe in the fresh air herself and she'd only been in the room a few minutes. She couldn't even imagine what it must be like for the girl.

"There," she said, turning round. "How's that?"

Enid's lips parted in a smile. The moonlight gleamed off her white teeth. "Just what I need," she said.

Her hands wandered down to her waist and Jude

frowned at the sight of a big bunch of keys hanging there, all different sizes, all glowing with a soft silver light.

"Where did they come from?" she asked.

"What, these?" Enid ran her fingers over the keys but they didn't make a jangling sound like ordinary keys. Instead they made a ringing sort of noise, a cold music that was like glass wind chimes knocking together on a frozen morning. "I made them," Enid said. Her smile widened. "From moonlight."

That was when Jude knew something was very wrong. That she had made a mistake somewhere. Before she could think about what to do, or how to fix it, she felt Ivory take control of her body. She'd been half expecting something like this and was already braced to stop her from running over to free the girl from her chains. But Ivory didn't do that. Instead she reached into the pockets of Jude's dungarees with both hands, grabbed items from inside and threw them. Jude watched as both the bone flower and the devil's coin sailed across the room to land at Enid's feet.

The girl snatched them up immediately, as if she'd been waiting for them all along. Then she lifted the roof of the Ghost Station and the whole façade came away in her hands, revealing the cajou altar hidden underneath. Jude saw the candle, the bowl of water, a bottle of graveyard dirt and the incense just like her own altar. In the centre was a jar filled with some kind of liquid and, floating in the middle, was a poppet that Jude realized, to her dismay, was supposed to represent her. It wore a pair of dungarees and had a small trumpet clutched in its hand.

"I've had it ready and waiting," Enid said, taking a matchbook from her pocket and lighting the candle. "Just like you said."

"What the—?" Jude began.

But that was as far as she got before Enid threw the devil's coin and the bone flower into the jar, screwed the lid on top and then shook it up and down. And all of a sudden Jude couldn't speak because it felt as if the contents of her stomach were sloshing around inside her in time with every shake of that goddamned jar.

"Don't shake it so hard!" Ivory snapped, using Jude's throat to speak out loud. "It's working, I can feel it!"

And Jude realized she was right. Something *was* happening. She could feel a weird tugging sensation deep in her guts. The next second she felt a wet, slithering, dragging feeling making its way up her throat and right into her mouth, and then there was a bonfire-flavoured smoke rushing out through her lips.

It was over as quickly as it had begun and Jude felt suddenly lighter, lighter than she'd felt in a long while. She gasped for breath, just about managing to stay on her feet as the hazy cloud of smoke raced across the room to Enid, who tipped back her head and opened her mouth, allowing the thing to rush in down her throat with such force that the girl gagged slightly. Then it was finished and Enid was wiping her mouth and smiling across the room at Jude. And when she spoke, it wasn't her voice that came out, but Ivory's:

"I'm sorry about that, Jude," the cajou queen said. "But your stubborn human body was right on the verge of dispelling me."

"Dispelling you?" Jude frowned. Her mind was reeling and she still felt an unpleasant queasiness in the pit of her stomach. "What do you mean dispel you? I thought your spirit would stay put until it killed me?"

She looked down at her wrist and saw that the Royalty charm there no longer glowed red.

"You will see the necessity of the lie, I am sure," Ivory replied through Enid. The girl's eyes were shining with some deep joy that Jude didn't like the look of one bit.

"You told me that so I'd think I had no choice but to help you," Jude said, as the truth dawned on her. "So what's your intention now?" she asked. "Do you really think you can use this child to go into the Black Bayou and track down the devil's wishing well?"

Enid bent forward slightly and Jude thought she was going to be sick. But then she realized the girl was laughing. A weird, silent laugh that made her shoulders shake and brought tears to her eyes.

"I have no intention of hunting for the devil's wishing well," she said.

"But ... I don't understand. Isn't that what all this has been about? Wasn't that the entire point of going into the bayou and facing Sheba and—"

"I'm afraid you've only had half the story," Ivory said.

"You mean you *don't* want to find out who killed you?"

"My dear, I already know full well who killed me. I've known all along. I knew before it even happened."

Jude gaped at her. Enid's dark eyes gleamed back and it felt as if everything was starting to unravel. "What do you mean?"

Enid stood up a little straighter, raised her chin and just for a moment Jude thought she could almost see

310

Ivory gazing out at her from behind the descendant's eyes.

"I am the cajou queen of Baton Noir," she said in a cold, proud voice. "The only reason someone managed to murder me is because I wished it to be so."

"But why the hell would you *want* to be murdered?"

Jude recalled the grisly scene in the bathroom of the Blue Lady. The unseen blade. The feeling of skin tearing and warm blood soaking her sleeves. She recalled that sense of wrongness she'd felt at the bar afterwards and finally understood what it was. She'd felt the cajou queen's emotions at the memory, and there'd been hurt there, anger, yes, and even fear. But there had been no surprise whatsoever and Jude realized Ivory was telling the truth. She'd known the attack was coming.

"My body was growing weaker and frailer by the day," Ivory said. "I was nearing the end of my life, I could feel it. I knew there was nothing I could do to stop it. But there are other ways for a cajou queen to cheat death. So when Charity took it into her head to murder me, I decided to let her go ahead. I ordered Beau to stay home and not try to help. There's more power in murder, you see, more passion and wickedness, which are both excellent things for cajou."

311

"So why the heck did you have me running all over town?" Jude demanded. "Why did we go to Etienne's club, and the bayou, and—"

"Isn't it obvious? I needed the devil's coin and the bone flower for the spell you've just seen. I hoped if we found some of Etienne's hair then I could perform a spell that would compel him to hand back the coin. He should never have had it in the first place. If he hadn't been there then the coin would have been given to Charity and it would have been far simpler getting it from her. But at least it gave me an excuse to draw you into the bayou."

"You knew we were never going to find the devil's wishing well," Jude said. "You knew that we'd run into Sheba instead."

"Of course. I had to get the flower and the coin in order to finish the spell that would transfer my soul from your body to Enid's."

"How did you know I'd end up in the water?" Jude asked. "If Sheba hadn't pushed me—"

"Then I would have found some other way," Ivory replied. "But I was pretty sure Sheba would dunk you at some point. She's done it before. And once you were in the water I knew I'd be able to grab a flower."

That goddamned flower, Jude thought, furious at

herself. She'd known that something wasn't right about it.

"I knew your spirit wouldn't be able to contain me forever," Ivory went on, "and I wouldn't want it to either. But I also knew you were my best hope of ever getting up here to Enid. A descendant is far stronger than a human, you see, and can house me indefinitely. Not only that, but Enid *wants* me. She wants to do great things with me. She wants to be cajou queen and she wants to be free of Moonfleet and André. So everybody's happy."

"What about our bargain?" Jude said in a low voice. She was terribly afraid that she already knew the answer, and her voice trembled slightly as she said, "You promised to help my pa."

Enid slowly shook her head. "You were a means to an end, Jude," Ivory said. "Even if I wanted to, cajou can't help your father. Some wounds run too deep—" An odd little spasm flashed across Enid's face and when she spoke it was the girl's voice rather than Ivory's. "We must go," she said. "Before my brother returns."

She leaned down and used one of the silver keys to unlock the metal cuff round her ankle, giving a little hiss of satisfaction as it fell to the floor with a clatter. When she looked back up and spoke again, it was Ivory's voice that came out.

"Come on, Beau," she said. "It's time to go."

But the great snake remained draped round Jude's shoulders, making no move to stir.

Ivory made an impatient sound at the back of her throat. "Beau!" she said, more sharply. "Come here."

The snake moved a little, but only to tuck his flat head into Jude's collarbone.

"I don't think he wants to go with you," Jude said.

For a moment, Enid simply gaped at her. Jude could almost feel the cajou queen's hurt and betrayal coming across the room to her in waves.

"So be it," she finally said.

And with that she turned and walked out of the attic without another word to Jude, as if she was completely insignificant, as if she hadn't spent the last few days risking life and limb to help her. Jude felt a rising sense of rage bubbling up inside her as she began to comprehend how completely she'd been conned right from the very beginning. She should have realized from the moment Sofia left her that note about the poppet and she'd seen her own name stitched into the doll's back.

"Wait!" Jude said, hurrying to the doorway.

She knew that she'd made a huge mistake by coming into Moonfleet. She knew that Ivory had made use of her time inside Jude's head to pray on her thirst for justice and her desire to help the downtrodden in Baton Noir. But she still didn't really understand who Enid was or why she'd been locked up in the attic in the first place. Still, it was obvious to her now that her first instinct had been right and that the Phantom must have had some important reason for doing such a thing. André had said he wouldn't be long. The only thing Jude could think to do now was to try to prevent the girl from leaving, to delay her until the Phantom returned.

It was a vague, desperate plan, but it was all she had. As she reached the doorway, she saw Enid disappearing down the servants' staircase in a swirl of blue petticoats.

"Hold up!" she called, but to her dismay this only made Enid speed up. She could hear the child clattering away at a run. She was small and faster than Jude on the narrow stairs. By the time they reached the kitchen, Enid was several yards ahead. She threw a glance over her shoulder and giggled at the sight of Jude pursuing her as she ran into the corridor. But Jude had anger to fuel her steps and managed to catch up with the girl just as she reached the front hall.

"I said *wait!*" she said, gripping Enid's arm roughly, forcing her to stop.

The girl went suddenly very still, staring up at Jude with a strange look in her indigo eyes.

"Ivory, we had a bargain." Jude choked out the words, almost crying. "You know what this means to me, and to my pa. You've got to help."

"You'd better let me go," Enid said quietly.

"Or what?" Jude said, trying for a bravado she didn't feel. "You might be a cajou queen, but you're still trapped in the body of a kid."

Enid stared up at her, unblinking. "You stupid Scrap," she whispered. "You have no idea what I can do. Or what I've already done. I'd show you, only I don't have time. The Cajou Night inauguration ceremony will be taking place soon and I need to claim my crown." She touched the keys at her waist with her free hand and they made that odd, icy music once again. Now that she was closer, Jude could see that they really were made from moonlight, shining strange, unnatural and beautiful in the gloom.

"What are those for?" she asked, instinctively wary of them.

But Enid only smiled at her. "I like to understand how things work," she said. "To take things apart and put them back together again. That's why I performed those experiments in the attic. Yes, it was me, not my useless sister. So believe me when I say I'll do the same to you if you don't get out of my way. How would you like to have your brains stirred round and round with a stick? It causes the most interesting things to happen."

Jude stared at her. "But … I thought that Violetta—"

"Violetta!" Enid sneered. "Violetta was mad and that made it easy for people to believe she was responsible. When André discovered what was happening in the attic I had to blame her. There was no other choice. Now, let me go." Her voice lowered, soft and dangerous. "I won't ask you again."

But before Jude could reply there came an awful sound from the double staircase looming above them. It started soft and quiet, like wood settling, before transforming into something shrill, shrieking and high-pitched.

And livid.

Enid tugged her hand free from Jude's grip and turned, frowning, peering into the shadows at the top of the staircase. Jude found her eyes straining too, and the next second a shiny dark shoe came into sight, but at a weird, unnatural angle. Jude realized the thing inside the shoe wasn't a foot at all.

It was a root.

"Violetta?" Enid said, suddenly uncertain, taking a step back towards the front door.

The root continued to creep further down the staircase as the entire monstrous form came into view. Jude's gasp stuck in her throat at the sight, Beau hissed and Enid gave a squeak of alarm.

The thing on the stairs was Violetta.

And yet it wasn't her.

She was, quite clearly, a ghost. There was no substance to her and Jude could see right through her to the staircase behind. But she was now only partly human. It seemed that after her death, her spirit had somehow warped and moulded itself together with the cajou tree. From the waist down she was more tree roots than flesh, although Jude could see the tattered remains of the green skirt she still wore. The roots came spilling out from beneath her petticoat like octopus legs. There was an unbearable insectile precision and a spider-like grace to the way she scuttled down the stairs, getting closer and closer.

From the waist up she looked more human than tree, but she was quite changed from the sixteen-year-old girl she'd once been. There were buttons of different sizes and colours embedded in her skin, along with pins and needles sticking out as if she was some kind of life-size cajou poppet. Trails of red and black wax ran down her face like blood and her hair was a matted bird's nest of leaves and feathers and ivy. When she moved, shards of bark came crumbling out from beneath her clothes and there was moss growing over the ends of her fingers.

"Fascinating," Enid breathed. "I suppose it must have been … yes, perhaps the blood running down the tree, soaking into the soil, feeding the roots—"

"I *died*!" the ghost hissed, drawing her lips back in a snarl, revealing a fat, shiny beetle skittering over her tongue. "I died," Violetta said again. "For something *you* did!"

She flew the rest of the way down the stairs, roots snapping and clothes tearing, stopping barely an inch away from Enid. From this new angle, Jude saw that one of Violetta's eyes had been almost entirely eaten away. Only a small jellied lump remained in the socket, along with dozens of writhing woodlice that spilled down her cheek like tears. The ghost opened her mouth wide, wider than any human would be able to manage without breaking their jaw, and wailed another inhuman shriek that felt as if it would peel the wallpaper from the walls and crack the windows in their frames. As if appalled by the noise, beetles came pouring up out of her throat, spilling from her mouth to land on the floor with wet splats as their shiny carapaces split open and white goo seeped out on to the floorboards.

To Jude's amazement Enid didn't so much as flinch at this dreadful display. As soon as her sister ran out of breath, Enid gave a delighted grin then opened her own mouth wide and screamed right back at the ghost with such volume that the crystals in the chandelier above actually trembled.

Violetta recoiled, staring at her sister, aghast.

"You don't scare me!" Enid snarled. "You're just a wraith." To demonstrate the point she waved her hand through Violetta's body, watching it go straight through like smoke. "You can't touch me. You're just as useless as you were when you were alive."

Recalling the blood she'd seen on the Phantom's collar and the scratches on his hands, Jude knew that this couldn't be the case. The next second, Violetta blinked away the red wax tears that had pooled in her eyes and spoke so quietly that her words were almost lost in the large room.

"You're wrong, Enid. I may not be able to touch you. But the cajou tree can."

There was the groan of wood twisting and stretching and Jude's eyes went to the double staircase. It was changing shape right in front of her, the banisters warping into something that suddenly looked like a hand – misshapen and deformed, fingers broken and grotesque, reaching out towards them with a sort of awful hunger.

Jude pressed her back up against the wall as Beau protectively coiled himself round her a little tighter. Enid fled for the front door. But before she could get there, it flew open. Silhouetted in the doorway stood the Phantom, who took in the scene with one glance then turned his masked face towards Jude. She half expected him to shout in anger but when he spoke his voice was low and hoarse.

"Gracious gods," he said. "What have you done?"

CHAPTER
TWENTY-SIX

Before anyone could say another word, the long tree fingers shot out to wrap round Enid's throat, lifting her right off the ground, both feet kicking.

"It should have been you!" Violetta's ghost screamed as she glared up at her sister. "You're the one who should have hung from the tree by their neck! You're the one who should have turned into this ... this..." She looked down at her own transformed body in despair. "This *monster*!"

Enid croaked for breath as both her hands scrabbled in vain against the wooden fingers.

"Hurts, doesn't it?" Violetta said sweetly, a fierce pleasure burning in her eyes. "Oh yes, I was surprised too. I never imagined how painful hanging could be. Never dreamed there could be such agony to it."

"Violetta!" the Phantom said, walking further into

the room. His voice was a harsh whisper. "Stop it. Put her down."

The ghost turned her eyes towards her brother and a fresh flash of hatred passed over her features. "You told the police it was me! You're as much to blame as she is! You stood and watched as they hanged me!"

The other side of the staircase groaned as it morphed into another hand that whipped out for the Phantom, but he raised his arm and there was a white flash of moonlight that seemed to take on the shape of a hawk owl. Silver talons wrapped round the wood and snapped the tree's arm at the wrist before dropping it to the floor with a thud.

The Phantom strode forward and stopped before Violetta.

"You know I tried to stop it," he said softly. "But it was taken out of my hands. I was wrong to accuse you and for that I am sorry, Violetta, and will go on being sorry until the end of my days. I did you a great wrong I can never put right."

The ghost gave a little sob, and perhaps sorrow weakened her concentration for a moment because she loosened the cajou tree's grip on Enid's throat just enough for Ivory's voice to rasp out a single magic word that caused a small spark of flame to leap from her lips and on to the wood. It was only a tiny spark but it caused the wood to scorch and smoke and the hand recoiled, dropping Enid to the floor. Without a moment's hesitation, she scrambled to her feet and raced across the hall and out of the front door. Violetta barely seemed to notice. All her attention was fixed on the Phantom.

"I loved you," she whispered. "Of the whole wretched, rotten lot, you were the only one I loved."

"I know," the Phantom returned. "Gods help me, Violetta, I know I can never make amends for what I allowed to happen to you."

The girl-tree buried her face in her hands, which suddenly seemed to be made from twigs and leaves more than fingers and skin. When she spoke, her muffled voice had suddenly taken on a subdued, hostile edge.

"The cajou tree," she muttered, "is eating my soul. I can feel it, but I can't stop it. I can't control it. I don't know if I want to any more. It won't be happy until it's gobbled up everything. Consumed Moonfleet. It feeds on evil. Grows fat from our family's wickedness." She dropped her hands and raised her eyes to the Phantom's. "Maybe that would be for the best? Maybe I should just let it?"

He shook his head. "Violetta," he began. "Listen to me—"

"I'm done listening to you!" she said. "I'm done with all of you."

And then she spat in the Phantom's face.

The staircase reared up from the floor fast and hard, branches shooting out, straight through the windows, which burst outwards in an explosion of glass. Roots rippled out across the floor, ripping up the green tiles, breaking them into jagged shards. Thick ropes of ivy twisted up towards the chandelier, cutting through the wire holding it there.

Seeing what was about to happen, Jude raced across the hall and hauled the Phantom to his feet, seconds before the chandelier fell to the floor, glass flying out in every direction.

"Come on." The Phantom gripped Jude's hand and they both sprinted towards the front door, shoes crunching on glass and tiles and twigs.

Jude threw a glance over her shoulder as they tumbled through the door and got a brief glimpse of Violetta, still crouched in the middle of the hall. Wax tears were dripping down her face as red as blood, as the black cajou staircase sprouted more and more branches that criss-crossed in front of her, like a great dark web.

♛

From the front gates, Jude and the Phantom stood and watched the cajou tree destroy the house from the inside. Cursed and haunted as the mansion undoubtedly was, there was still something dreadful about seeing it overrun in such a way. The noise quickly brought other Fountain District residents out from their neighbouring mansions to gawk at the devastation. One portly gentleman expressed concern that the out-of-control tree might come after the other houses once it was done with Moonfleet, but the Phantom shook his head and said curtly, "It's just Moonfleet she wants."

Before long, branches had broken through every one of the manor's windows, cajou ivy covered every stone inch of the façade, as well as the roof. Great thick roots crept out from beneath the floors and there was something belligerent about the way they lay in front of the house, like a hound guarding its master.

Even the cajou tree in the garden reacted to what was happening and leaned over to the Owlery, smothering the building in sewn leaves and strings of beads.

They saw all the owls that had been inside take flight through the open windows, their wings spread wide against the backdrop of the swollen moon overhead.

Finally all was quiet, the cajou trees were still and the two buildings sat like captured prey within giant spider webs. The spectators went back to their own homes, shooting dark looks at the Phantom as they left. And then, at last, Jude and André were alone. Even Beau had vanished, melted away back into the spirit world.

"I'm sorry," Jude said, cringing at the uselessness of the words. "I ... I know I shouldn't have gone into Moonfleet. Ivory tricked me. She told me there was a child locked away in the attic. I didn't mean to free her. I only meant to open the window to give her some air but as soon as I did she had this bunch of keys and—"

"You let the moonlight in," the Phantom said sharply. "We can do things with moonlight sometimes. We're descendants of Krag, after all. Legba of the moon and the night spirits."

Jude hurried to explain how Ivory had always known who her killer was and how she had planned to possess Enid right from the start. As she stumbled over her words, the Phantom gazed through the gates at the ruins of Moonfleet and was silent.

"Well?" Jude said. "Aren't you going to say anything?"

"What is there left to say?" he returned. "It's not your fault that this has happened. If the blame belongs anywhere, it is with me. Violetta is my great sin. And if there is any justice in the world then one day I will burn in one of the hells for her. For Enid too, I suppose."

"How did … how did everything get like this?" Jude asked.

The Phantom turned his red mask towards her, grey eyes glittering behind it in the gloom.

"You know of the horrors that took place in our attic. For too long I was blind to them, chose not to wonder about the number of servants who would mysteriously go missing. I suppose it was a simple enough matter for Enid to lure them up there under some pretext or other. When I finally realized what was going on I informed the police. At first I thought it was my father who was responsible, you see. And I thought that, cajou Royalty though he was, even he would have to be imprisoned for something as depraved as this. But then Enid managed to convince me that Violetta was the perpetrator. And I believed her. I was taken in by her – just as you were by Ivory. Still, I never thought they would hang her the way they did…" He trailed off for a moment.

"A couple of months after she died, it started happening again – this time with homeless people lured in from the street. It seemed like a nightmare I couldn't escape. When we realized that Enid was the one responsible it was too late to undo what had been done to Violetta. My father was all for killing Enid ourselves. I was the one who stopped him. Enid became my responsibility and the attic was … well, it was the only solution I could think of. We overpowered her between us and chained her up in there." His hand went to his face. "She was more powerful than we could ever have imagined and it was not easy. She managed to hurl her reserves of cajou acid at me before we contained her."

"That's why you wear the mask," Jude said. "And how you hurt your arm."

He nodded. "It could have been worse. She went for my face because it seemed the most vicious attack to her but if she had burned my hands then I would no longer have been able to play the violin, or any other instrument, and that would have been far worse to me."

"And she's just been locked away up there for the last fifty years?" Jude asked.

"Yes. Once my father died, I knew that if something were to happen to me, then there'd be

no one to care for Enid. She would starve to death
– a torture I did not want for her, even though she
has inflicted far worse horrors on others. What were
the alternatives? Kill her myself or put her in the
asylum, which amounts to the same thing. In fact,
the asylum is…"

His hand shook slightly as he ran it through his
hair. "I would not wish that place on anyone. It is …
inhuman. But I did not want to murder my sister in
cold blood either. That was why I asked Ivory to come
to Moonfleet, in the hope that she'd find some magical
solution to keeping Enid calm. I tried to persuade
Paris to move into Moonfleet after I was gone and act
as jailer, but that was never going to work. There just
didn't seem to be any solution to it. It was exhausting,
trying to work out which evil was the least bad choice.
And now here we are. Enid roams free and if she
becomes the next cajou queen then who knows what
wickedness she will unleash upon Baton Noir."

"We have to stop her," Jude said. "Her and Ivory."

The Phantom glanced up at the sky. "But what is
the point of it all?" he asked, with a sort of desperate
hopelessness. "What's the use in trying to prevent
dreadful things from happening when they happen
anyway. It only seems to make things worse."

"That's … no way to think," Jude said, a little dismayed, although some small part of her agreed with every word he'd said. It *was* exhausting sometimes. "The world pushes you but you push back harder," she forced out the words. "That's the only way."

"Well," the Phantom replied. "You are very young. By the time you're my age, you may find you have had your fill of pushing back."

"We've got to do something," Jude insisted. "We have to at least try. We know where she's gone. The Cajou Night celebrations will be properly under way now. She'll be there on Moonshine Boulevard when they hand out the Queen Cakes. We need to be there too."

"And then what?"

"Then … then I don't know, OK?" Jude threw up her hands. "Perhaps if we tell everyone what's going on, they won't allow her to be crowned and the title will pass to Charity like it was supposed to."

And what then? a small voice said inside her head. *The crown goes to a wicked young woman rather than a wicked old woman. A girl who happily murdered her own grandmother, and the rotten cycle just goes on and on…*

"Let's just get there," Jude said, suddenly feeling weary. "And we'll figure it out."

CHAPTER
TWENTY-SEVEN

The city was packed for Cajou Night. It was always Baton Noir's biggest event of the year, but tonight there was an air of excitement and anticipation, a sense of history in the making. It was, after all, the first time in almost fifty years that the city was to have a new cajou queen and it seemed that everyone had turned out to see it. It was a warm night, made even hotter by the number of people, and a haze of smoke hung in the air from the many street-food vendors. There were hot dogs, crawfish stew and Stompin' Zombie Jambalaya, dirty rice, sweet pancakes drizzled in maple syrup, and of course there were Queen Cakes. Queen Cakes everywhere, in various forms, sizes and shapes.

The cake itself was a simple cinnamon doughnut, topped with multi-coloured icing to represent all the city's colours — the red of the vampires, the green of the Subjects, the blue of the witches. The multi-coloured cakes were supposed to symbolize the fact that anyone could become the next queen on Cajou Night. Inside one of the cakes would be a small plastic crown, put there by the legba themselves, to show the world who they had chosen. But it was a formality more than anything. Because every year the legba had chosen Ivory. And now no one knew for sure what would happen next. Most people thought that Charity Monette would be crowned, but it was common knowledge that she hadn't been speaking to the legba and that created doubt and made people whisper that perhaps someone else would become queen instead.

No one ever tried to trick the system by producing a fake crown. For a start, such a crime was punishable by execution, and secondly, there was only one way to prove to the world that you were the rightful queen of Baton Noir, and that was for the famous cajou python to appear on your shoulders at midnight. Jude hadn't seen Beau since he'd disappeared at Moonfleet and she felt a little pang at the thought that he would soon belong to someone else, followed by a small flare of hope as she recalled how he had refused to go to Ivory when she'd called him from Enid.

The streets were packed and for once the Phantom's mask didn't mark him out because everyone else wore one too. It was one of the rules of Cajou Night. Many of the masks were beautiful bejewelled creations, while others were fearsome and frightening. Several vendors stood at the end of the street selling plain black paper eye masks for a few pennies, mostly to Scraps who couldn't afford anything better.

Jude hurriedly bought one and slipped it over her face in order to be allowed on to the street, and then she and the Phantom wove their way through the crowds. The parade was in full swing and Jude spotted the Done and Dusted Brass Band, along with several others, all playing different tunes that merged and swelled together into one great cacophony of jazz. Jude could feel the pounding of the drums coming up through the soles of her feet from the cobbles. It was the one night of the year when even poor Scraps could listen to some of the best jazz bands in the world for free. And then there were the parades. Many of Baton Noir's societies, organizations and churches had floats, elaborate and striking, from which they threw Cajou Night beads and other trinkets into the waiting crowd.

Jude and the Phantom were forced to stop at the junction between Barbershop Alley and Moonshine Boulevard as the last bit of the parade passed by. First came a float created by the Jazzman's Jumbo Club, which had a quartet of life-size sponge musicians who moved their arms and heads in time with the music. Members on the float threw plastic trumpets out into the crowd as they went by.

Next came the Alligator Appreciation Society, with a huge wooden alligator that opened and closed its great jaws to reveal glittering teeth within. Jude thought of how her pa had taken her and Daryl to see the Cajou Night parade during happier times and how the alligators had been Daryl's favourite. One year, Pa had put him up on his shoulders to help him try to catch one of the plastic alligators tossed from the float or, even better, a real gator fang. The old sense of loss pressed down on her shoulders, heavier than any cajou snake, but Jude was used to its weight by now and would not allow herself to crumble beneath it.

Finally there came a float created by the church of Amelia. Several scantily clad Pearls posed on top of it and threw tiny bottles of perfume into the crowd, along with stings of plastic pearls and pink chocolate hearts.

Coming up behind the float was a gaggle of Amelia's fans, and briefly Jude caught sight of Sofia and Belle in the crowd. Sofia had removed her mask and was gazing around, a troubled expression on her face, as though she was searching for someone. Jude wondered whether she was looking for her but Belle tugged impatiently on Sofia's arm and the two witches were swallowed up by the masses.

Once the parade had passed by, Jude and the Phantom crossed the road and made their way to Cadence Square, where the crowning ceremony was to take place. The full moon shone fat and bright over the scene; twinkling fairy lights were wrapped round the trunks of the banana trees, and paper lanterns hung from the branches of the old oaks. More street-food sellers had crowded into the space along with the usual array of jugglers, magicians, acrobats and illusionists. The smell of fried onions from the hot-dog carts and powdered sugar from the Queen Cakes, mingled with the ever-present swampy smell that blew in from the bayou, the spilled moonshine and the sweet-olive trees in the park. Jude breathed it all in and, even in a moment such as this, felt a wave of love for the city, imperfect and corrupt though it unquestionably was.

There was a platform erected in the centre of the square beneath a great oak tree and Jude saw the two glass jars there from the vote that had been counted up earlier, to find out which of the legba brothers would rule for another year. Ollin's glass jar contained plastic dogs to represent votes cast for him; Krag's contained owls. Unsurprisingly, Krag's vase was almost full, while Ollin's contained hardly any votes at all. Each province sent in their vote beforehand but Jude had her doubts as to how clean the system was. It wouldn't surprise her at all to discover that the vote was always fixed in favour of Krag by those in power. It really wasn't a fair fight at all.

At the front of the stage, Charity sat white-faced alongside Rufus Seething, the Mayor, a plate of Queen Cakes at her elbow ready to be bitten into at midnight. She looked different from the way she had in Ivory's memory at the Blue Lady. Although still blond, petite and pretty, with a heart-shaped face and pale blue eyes, there was now a gaunt, haunted look about her too.

"They say her boyfriend died just last night," someone in the crowd nearby said. "The poor thing."

That explained why she looked so terrible then. All that plotting and wickedness and it hadn't got her what she wanted in the end anyway.

Jude noticed a roped-off VIP area near the stage and was dismayed to see Etienne's ice-blond head among the group, his eyes back to their normal blue.

She didn't have time to worry about him just then, however. They had arrived at Cadence Square along with the final float, which signalled the time for the music to end. Jude couldn't see Enid anywhere, but then how would she have been able to see a child in this throng anyway?

The crowd was a sea of masks, all turned expectantly towards the stage. Everyone wanted to get a good view and it was almost impossible for Jude and the Phantom to make their way to the front. Some of these people had staked out their places hours beforehand and they didn't take lightly to newcomers shoving their way through. Nevertheless, they persevered as the Mayor began his speech.

And then, through the crowd, Jude saw him. Only for a moment, and it was only a glimpse, but she clearly saw a man in a top hat and tails, gazing down at an open pocket watch. Somehow, impossibly, Jude could hear its rapid little *tick-tick-tick*, even above the Mayor's voice and the murmuring crowd. Suddenly the man snapped the watch shut, slipped it into his pocket and raised his head. The light from the lanterns reflected off his smoked glasses as he looked Jude's way, smiled, and slowly and deliberately tipped his hat, before melting away into the crowds.

"André!" Jude said, tapping him on the shoulder. "Did you see…? I think … I think I just saw Baron Lukah over there."

"What?" The Phantom glanced over his shoulder at her. "You couldn't have. Only the cajou queen can see the legba. It was probably someone dressed up."

People *did* sometimes dress up as the legba on Cajou Night, but they picked ones like Kai, the legba of rain, or Astra, the legba of charity. Nobody would come as Baron Lukah. No one would dare…

"*STOP!*"

Everyone looked up at the sudden outburst and any remaining whispering or chatting died away. Charity Monette was on her feet, shoving the Mayor away from the microphone and staring out across the crowd with a wild expression on her face.

"I don't want to be queen! I never wanted it! All I wanted was to speak to Baron Lukah, to make a deal to save Wade. And now he's dead and it was all for nothing." She heaved a dry sob. "I killed my grandmother. I sold a piece of my soul to the devil for it and it still wasn't enough."

A gasp went up from the crowd and everyone leaned forward slightly, thrilled at the direction things had taken.

"Baton Noir is a rotten, awful place," Charity went on, making Jude feel immediately, ridiculously offended on the city's behalf. "My mother was right about that. I never would have stayed here at all if it hadn't been for my grandmother. That *bitch*!" There was such venom in the word that it made Jude's skin crawl. "If she hadn't been so stubborn," Charity went on. "If she'd only helped Wade when I asked her to, then none of this need ever have happened—"

"You stupid child!" a familiar voice rang out. "Do you still not understand that there are some things so broken that even cajou can't fix them? Even if I'd wanted to, I couldn't have saved him."

Jude wasn't the only person who recognized the voice. Suddenly the crowd was parting, stepping hastily back to allow a small, dark-haired child to walk through to the stage. It was Enid, speaking in Ivory's ancient voice.

Charity stared down at the girl, aghast. "G-Grandmother?" she said. The remaining colour drained from her face so fast that Jude thought she might actually faint. "No. It's not possible."

No one made any move to stop her as Enid, head held high like she was queen again already, walked up the steps on to the stage.

"I wasn't ready to die, my dear," she said. "So I came back and possessed this descendant, with her blessing. Allow me to present my new partner: Enid Majstro of Moonfleet Manor."

The crowd muttered at the name, unsure what to make of this turn of events. Everyone knew that the Majstros were a wicked bunch and nobody liked the idea of one being crowned queen, even if it was in partnership with Ivory Monette.

"And look," Ivory went on, still using Enid to speak. "To show that there are no hard feelings, Enid has a gift for you."

Jude strained to see over the heads of other people, everyone standing on tiptoe to see what was happening. Enid put a hand to her waist and that cold, soulless chiming drifted over the square as the keys jangled. Then she pulled one free and held it out to Charity, the key shining silver and beautiful in her hand.

"No!" the Phantom said, the word coming out as a gasp. "No, don't!" he shouted, louder this time. But other people were talking too and his voice was lost in the crowd.

Charity frowned, suspicious, already starting to back away, but Enid grabbed her and used her descendant strength to effortlessly drag the girl down to her knees on the stage before her. In one smooth movement, Enid lifted the key and pressed it to Charity's temple. The end slipped straight into the skin, as if sliding through a keyhole, and Enid gave it a good hard twist to the right.

Charity's eyes rolled back in her head and she let out a shriek, a scream of such agony that several other people in the crowd groaned along with her. Enid turned it a second time and all the blood vessels in Charity's eyes burst, leaving them as red as a vampire's when the blood lust was upon them. Her mouth hung open slightly and a thin line of drool dribbled out. Enid's grip seemed to be the only thing that was holding her up.

The crowd began to make disapproving sounds but Ivory said, "An eye for an eye. I'd have every right to take her life if I chose. So far, all I've done is to unlock her mind and free her from her inner torments. All her worries and concerns gone. Just like that!"

Someone tapped Jude on the shoulder and a mellow voice said, "You dropped this."

Jude turned and saw an elderly black man just behind her. Everything else seemed to fall away suddenly. The sound of Enid talking, the crowd, the confusion and the fear – leaving a little bubble of quiet.

The man was dressed in a tatty suit and a wide-brimmed straw hat, with a rather sickly looking owl perched on his shoulder. In his hand he held out a paper plate with a slice of Queen Cake on it, the multi-coloured icing shining and enticing in the flickering glow of the lanterns. Jude looked up into his face and his eyes crinkled at the corners as he smiled gently at her. It was a good face, full of knowing, wisdom and even sympathy. It was not at all the way Jude had thought it would be.

"That's … not my cake," she said.

He raised his eyebrows. "You sure? It's got your name on it."

He thrust the plate into Jude's hand. She looked down and saw he was right. The icing had formed itself into elegant letters that spelled out her name: *Jude Olivia Lomax*.

"Tastes mighty good too," the man said, reaching out to break a piece off the end. He popped half of it into his mouth. The rest of it he offered to the little owl on his shoulder but the bird only sniffed at it before hunching further down in its mass of bedraggled feathers.

"I think there's something wrong with your owl," Jude said.

He shrugged. "She's just sick and tired, that's all. Don't you ever get sick and tired of the way things are, Jude?"

"Yes," she whispered. "Sometimes."

She couldn't seem to take her eyes off the cake. It was as if her name in the icing called out to her.

"Wouldn't you like a chance to change all that? To do things different?"

Jude's hands began to tremble. "Are you who I think you are?" she asked.

"Only one way to find out," he said.

Jude looked down at the cake and now that a piece had been broken off, she could see that there was something in there – something small, shining and golden. Something powerful and forbidden. And dangerous.

Almost against her own will, Jude tugged the object free. The tiny crown lay in the palm of her hand, solid and heavy. She could already tell it was no plastic fake.

"Go on!" Enid cried, pulling Jude's attention back to the stage for a moment. "Tell them you're happier this way!"

Charity was on her feet, swaying slightly. Her eyes

were still bloodshot and drool hung from her mouth in strings, but she nodded and said, "Yes, ma'am."

"You see?" Enid grinned.

Jude glanced behind her but the man with the owl was gone.

"She's turned her into a zombie," the Phantom muttered beside her, his gaze still fixed on the stage.

Jude stuffed the crown charm into her pocket and turned her attention back to André.

"What can we do?" she asked.

He glanced at her, then did a sort of double take and said in an incredulous voice, "Did you stop to buy cake?"

"Of course not! Someone just gave it to me."

She passed it to a nearby spectator who grabbed it from her greedily.

"It took me many years to create these keys," Enid went on, beckoning Charity to her side. "They can do great and terrible things. You've seen what two twists will do. Now let me show you the third – and let it be a lesson to anyone else who thinks they'll have a go at assassinating the cajou queen!"

The Phantom reached up and it was as if he snatched moonlight straight from the sky. Then he threw out his arm and the hawk owl seemed to take flight from the ends of his fingers, all gleaming talons and wild, ferocious eyes. Enid was so intent on the key she was inserting into Charity's head that she didn't see it coming.

The hawk owl went straight for her face, clawing at her eyes with a terrible screeching sound. Enid released Charity and fell back with a scream. The next moment, the bird took off, melting away into the night sky, leaving Enid hunched over on her knees, both hands clasped to her face. Lines of what seemed to be moonlight flowed down through her fingers. The Phantom was hurrying towards the stage, finding it easier now that people were drawing back. Suddenly no one really wanted to be at the front of the stage any more, no matter how much they were enjoying the gory spectacle. Even the Mayor had disappeared into the crowd.

Jude hurried after André. Enid had lowered her hands and Jude saw that one of her eyes had turned a blind milky-white, her lips were drawn back in a snarl and it was Enid's own voice that came out as she shrieked at her brother.

"You devil! It isn't enough that you've kept me locked up, a prisoner in Moonfleet for decades, now you take my eye as well?"

"You leave me no choice, Enid," André replied as he reached the front of the stage. "You *never* give me a choice. You box me in at every turn and compel me do unspeakable things, force crimes upon my soul until I must be more and more monstrous in order to keep up with you!"

"Keep up with *me*?" Enid stared at him and then a chilling laugh burst from her lips, even as moonlight ran from her ruined eye. "You must be joking! You could *never* keep up with me! You don't have the ambition, the drive or the vision that I have! You've got nothing but your ruined nightmare of a face and your tortured soul, and your self-righteous bullshit. You're a freak and you belong in a pit with the other freaks. And once I'm queen, that's exactly where I'm going to put you. Then we'll see how much *you* enjoy being the animal in the cage!"

Enid's nostrils flared and she looked up at the crowd. Ivory's voice came out loud and strong. "There are many rumours about the Phantom of Moonfleet Manor," she said. "And I can confirm that many of them are true. This despicable creature locked up his own little sister, imprisoning her for many years in the attic, and all because she knew his secret. Violetta Majstro was not responsible for the atrocities that took place fifty years ago. It was André. You hanged the wrong person."

She threw out her hand and a rope beam of moonlight looped itself round his wrists, tying them together behind his back, while a second rope reached down from the thick branch of the oak tree above to form a noose round his neck.

"She's lying!" Jude yelled. "It wasn't André, it was her!"

But her voice was lost in the crowd and no one was listening to her anyway. She grabbed hold of the Phantom's jacket and tried to hang on to him, but when Enid stretched over the side of the stage, her descendant strength was no match for Jude and she easily hauled her brother up on to his knees beside her.

"Just take a look at his face if you don't believe me!" she cried. "Look upon the monster for what he truly is!"

And before anyone could stop her, she reached up and ripped away the Phantom's mask.

CHAPTER
TWENTY-EIGHT

Jude had known that it must be bad. Why else would he always wear a mask? And yet somehow she hadn't expected it to be quite so awful as it was. Perhaps it was the softness of his voice, the beauty of his music or the kindness that he'd tried to show her that made her think his appearance couldn't really be that terrible. She realized then that she had almost expected there to be a handsome face beneath the mask, some trace of the man she had seen in the portrait back at Moonfleet, perhaps marked with a dreadful scar or something of that kind – and yet still attractive in a dark, mysterious kind of way.

The reality was nothing like that.

When Enid first ripped his mask away and threw it into the crowd, the Phantom tried to lower his face, but she gripped his hair. "Don't be shy!" she hissed in his ear, before forcing his head up to face the crowd.

Some people gasped. Some groaned aloud. They said later that one person near the front actually vomited and that another woman fainted.

It was, without a doubt, a horror of a face. In fact, some might say it was barely a face at all.

In that first moment, Jude couldn't help recoiling along with everyone else. She wanted to push down her disgust, hide it away, pretend she'd never felt it, and yet it was impossible to deny the crawling sensation that crept over her skin. The Phantom's chest rose and fell rapidly as he gasped for breath and his grey eyes, the only thing that remained the same, sought hers in the crowd. For an endless moment they just stared at each other and Jude could see the sick shame in his eyes before they slid away from her.

Then someone in the crowd threw their paper cup of moonshine at him. It hit the side of his face, cutting the raw skin there and drenching him in alcohol that plastered his hair to his head and ran down the side of his neck to his collar.

It didn't take long before everyone was doing it, throwing whatever they had to hand – cups of moonshine and bowls of dirty rice, cajou beads and trinkets. Some in the front row even managed to spit on him. Then the crowd was surging forward, ripping at his clothes and tearing out pieces of his hair with their bare hands, everyone wanting a gory memento.

"Stop it!" Jude screamed, but no one paid her any heed and she found herself elbowed aside.

Enid was laughing and Ivory was laughing too, and Jude thought it must be one of the most terrible sounds she'd ever heard – two laughs coming from the same throat like that. And then Enid cut away the noose and pushed the Phantom off the stage, into the crowd. They immediately swarmed round him, like piranha suddenly scenting blood in the water.

Jude was terribly afraid that they might not be content with tearing his clothes and might start beating him as well. She fought against the crowds to get there but only found herself pulled further and further away from the stage. As always, she was just a tiny, insignificant Scrap with no chance of making any difference at all, and the anger and rage boiled up inside her until she thought she would explode...

And then the clock tower at the edge of the square chimed out the hours for midnight. A wave of silence spilled out across the square as everyone turned towards the stage, watching Enid as she eagerly snatched up the Queen Cake and pulled it apart with her bare hands, looking for the crown charm she fully expected to find there.

But the cake fell apart into crumbs that ran through her fingers and there was no sign of any crown charm. The crowd began to mutter, casting concerned looks at one another as their anticipation turned to confusion. Sensing this was her moment, Jude pulled the crown charm from her pocket, held it high above her head and yelled, "It's here. I've got it."

Everyone turned to look at her, and at long last the crowd parted for her and she was able to march straight down to the stage.

"Impossible!" Enid cried. "How … how did you…? That's *mine*! Hand it over!"

But Jude wasn't listening to her. She was only interested in the Phantom. He was sprawled on the ground with his fine suit ripped into shreds, but to her relief he didn't seem to be hurt apart from a few scrapes and cuts, although his breath came in short, hard gasps.

Jude reached down her hand and helped him to his feet. She wanted to ask if he was OK, but such a foolish question stuck in her throat.

This close, his face looked even more hideous and Jude had to force herself to look at him, all the while hating herself for being affected, to some extent, by his appearance, along with everyone else. He took a shuddering breath and said, "My mask."

Jude stood up, raised her voice and said, "Who has the mask? Give it back now."

There was a long, drawn-out moment of silence. Nobody moved and Jude clenched her fists by her side as she realized that whoever had the mask wasn't going to give it up. It was too impressive a souvenir.

"You don't give orders here," Enid said. "That's my job. Give me that crown charm or I will take it from you."

Jude looked up at her. "It doesn't work like that," she said. "You can't *take* the crown. It has to be given to you."

Enid frowned and for the first time she looked unsure. "It's just a charm," she said. "And you're just a Scrap. I don't see any cajou python on your shoulders."

Jude was about to reply when a warm, wet muzzle pressed into her hand. She looked down and saw a bony old dog with loyal, warm eyes, gazing straight up at her and wagging its tail. And beyond it stood two men, brothers. Identical twins.

Sound fell away again and time slowed down, and Jude could tell that she was the only one who could see the twin legba standing in front of her. There was the old man with the sickly owl on his shoulder, only now he held a great white snake in his hands as well.

"Beau," Jude breathed. She was glad in her soul to see the python again but he wasn't the only snake this time.

The second man also held a snake in his hands – a huge black serpent.

"And Betty," Jude said.

The old dog returned to Ollin's side and sat down beside him, panting gently. The man reached down to scratch him behind the ears.

"So how 'bout it, Jude?" he asked. "Beau has taken quite the shine to you. And I guess he'd like to have his sister back. The crown is yours if you want it."

"I'd get both snakes?" Jude asked.

"Sure you would," Krag said. "We weren't giving Betty back to Ivory. You only get to kill your snakes once, see? But every cajou queen starts off with two."

"I'd never kill either of them," Jude said.

Ollin shrugged. "Well," he said. "Most people say that in the beginning, but folks soon change their tune if there's something they want bad enough."

"I'd never do it," Jude said again.

"You're accepting the crown then?" Krag asked, eyebrow raised.

"Why are you offering it to me?" Jude replied.

"Why not?" the legba replied. "Beau likes you. That means the Snake-God himself likes you. And it's time for a change, maybe."

Jude paused for a moment. Beyond the brothers she could still see the rest of the square, but it was frozen and silent. Her eyes swept over the masked crowd, the Phantom bleeding in the dust and Enid baring her teeth on the podium.

"Course, if you don't want it," Ollin went on. "Then we can give the crown to the girl instead. It's your choice."

Jude looked at Enid and she couldn't help thinking that perhaps it wasn't really all that much of a choice at all. Her eyes fell on a small, sad little object at the base of the great oak tree. It was a rooster, nailed to the trunk, thirteen pins sticking from its chest – the grisly remnants of some cajou ritual or other, of the kind that commonly took place throughout the city every single day.

Then she looked at the Phantom, mistreated and beaten for his freakish face, and she felt how cruel and corrupt Baton Noir had become, like a chill deep in her bones, and she knew that the city was better than that. It could be better – it could go back to the beautiful place it had once been. Of course, tonight's vote had already been cast in Krag's favour, but if Jude became queen then she could use the year before the next Cajou Night to campaign in favour of Ollin. And she could see to it that the vote was carried out fairly when the time came.

Here she was being offered the chance to change things, and suddenly it didn't seem to matter why or how it had happened. It was as if her whole life had always been leading up to this very moment and this decision. Jude didn't want to cool down her temper any more. She wanted to throw gasoline on it and *burn*. She wanted to blaze bright enough to light up the entire night sky. She wanted to be the next cajou queen of Baton Noir and make the city into something wonderful once again.

"OK." The word slipped softly from her mouth.

The snakes immediately slithered down to the ground from the hands of the twin legba, heading straight towards Jude. Ollin and Krag each took a pipe from their jacket pockets and lit up. The vanilla scent of their smoke filled the air.

"Good luck then," Krag said.

Then they were gone, leaving only the echo of tobacco in their wake. Sound and movement burst in on Jude once again as the world came back to life. Everything was the same and yet everything was different because now the Royalty charm at Jude's wrist glowed bloody, and there were two heavy cajou pythons coiled round her shoulders. She looked up at Enid and said, "You mean *these* snakes?"

CHAPTER
TWENTY-NINE

Enid's face contorted into a frozen mask of outrage.

"No!" she hissed. Jude realized she was talking to Ivory when she said, "You promised the crown would be mine!"

She reached out towards Jude, as if half thinking of simply taking the snakes from her shoulders, but both pythons immediately reared up, hissing ferociously, exposing their fangs, which were dripping with cajou venom.

Enid snatched her hand back and an object soared through the sky from the crowd, landing at Jude's feet. She looked down and saw it was the Phantom's mask, and a thrill of excitement raced through her. She hadn't even had to ask this time. She scooped it up from the floor and passed it wordlessly to the Phantom, who pressed it back to his face with trembling hands.

"You lying bitch!" Enid exclaimed up on the stage,

still having some kind of argument with Ivory that they could only hear one side of.

Jude looked up and saw that she'd been joined by another person on the stage, someone that only she could see. It was Baron Lukah, leaning against the podium in a casual position, one hand in his pocket and the other holding the stopwatch in front of him.

"Any minute now, I'd say," he murmured.

"I don't care if you meant to trick me or not!" Enid exclaimed. "You've broken our agreement. The only reason I agreed to have you in the first place was for the crown. Without that you're worth nothing to me!"

And then, before everyone's eyes, Enid pushed Ivory's spirit right out of her body. From the gasps around her, Jude realized that everyone else could see Ivory's ghost too. She looked just as she had whenever Jude had glimpsed her in a mirror – an old woman, dressed in her finery, with blood running down her face in lines from her sliced scalp and gaping throat. To think that she had willingly allowed this to happen to herself made the sight even more horrible and Jude shuddered.

"*You!*" the cajou queen snarled, glaring at Jude with such a look of hatred that she had to force herself not to take a step back. "You stupid girl! You don't know what you've done!"

Through Ivory's transparent form, Jude saw Enid scramble from the stage and disappear into the crowd. The Phantom must have noticed too, because he took a step in her direction but then paused, seeming to hesitate.

"You think being queen is easy?" Ivory went on. Her ghost already seemed a little paler and thinner than it had before. "You think it'll make you happy and solve your problems? Just you wait!" She let out a cruel laugh. "Just you *wait!*"

"Excuse me, madam."

Ivory whirled round to see Baron Lukah standing behind her. The legba smiled at her. "You are late for our appointment," he said in a soft voice.

Ivory recoiled from him. "No!" she cried. "I'm not… I'm not ready to go with you!"

"And yet you must," Baron Lukah replied. "Just the same. No one escapes from me a second time."

He wrapped his hand round Ivory's wrist and although she struggled in his grip she didn't seem to have any effect on the legba, and the effort only made her ghost fade even faster.

Finally she gave a dry sob, then her head snapped up and there was venom in her eyes as she looked at Jude.

"Very well," she gasped. "If I must go then so be it. But with my last dead breath, I curse you, Jude Lomax!"

Her hand disappeared inside her own chest and when it came back out it was filled with a sticky black mass that seemed to writhe and wriggle in her hand like a pile of snakes. Before Jude could take in what was happening, Ivory threw this straight at her.

A large body curled round her as the Phantom yanked her back, putting himself between her and the dead cajou queen. The wriggling black mass hit him right between the shoulder blades and Jude felt his body shudder with the impact.

Icy air rushed past them and there was a noise, close by and yet out of sight, a *clip-clop* that sounded a bit like the sound of goat's hooves on the cobbles as cajou priestesses shepherded them off for sacrifice. Only it was a bigger, louder sound than that, like the noise Jude expected a horse's shoes might make. Then there was a warm snort of exhaled air on the back of her neck and she whipped her head round, fully expecting to see a horse standing right behind her. But there was nothing.

"Enough," Baron Lukah said. "Time to go."

He dragged Ivory Monette into the spirit world, impervious to the fact that she screamed the entire way, leaving the stage empty and everything quiet. Jude wriggled free of the Phantom's grip and twisted him round on the spot, thinking there would be a bloody wound in his back, but there wasn't a mark on him.

"What what was that?" she said. The snakes shifted restlessly on her shoulders. Jude could sense their disquiet and suddenly had a very bad feeling about what had just happened. She came back round to face the Phantom. "What did she do? Are you hurt?"

"I am fine," he said, but his voice came out in a gasp.

"You're lying," Jude said.

And then she heard it – the soft, shivering *beat-beat-beat* of a heart that shouldn't be there. The Phantom tried to draw his hands away but Jude tightened her grip and pulled off his gloves, and the cold shock of seeing what she had known all along she would see hit her like a blow.

The little black heart on the Phantom's palm was misshapen, twisted and toxic, and they both knew what it meant: this was a fright hex, destined to one day bring about the victim's greatest fear. Others in the nearby crowd saw it too, and there was more murmuring and whispering, an air of thrilled excitement and horrified fascination from the people around them. Jude hated them, absolutely hated them all for enjoying watching their lives get smashed into pieces.

She looked up as the Phantom yanked his gloves back on and she found herself suddenly meeting Etienne's gaze across the crowd. There was an odd look in his blue eyes – something strange that she couldn't quite place as he gazed at them. Then he was turning away from her, putting his top hat on his head and walking out of the square with his head down.

She realized that the Mayor was back on the stage, now that it was safe and Enid and Ivory had both gone. He was saying something about continuing with the celebrations of Cajou Night, but Jude had no interest in any of that.

"Let's go," she said to the Phantom.

"Your highness!" the Mayor's voice rang after them. "Forgive me but you must stay for the celebration. It's the custom—"

"I don't care!" Jude cut him off. "Party all night if you want, but know that tomorrow a whole load of things are going to change around here."

CHAPTER
THIRTY

The next day Jude stood in her pa's kitchen trying to calm herself down, but she could feel her temper fraying and unravelling inside her. She'd returned home with a sense of excitement. After all, even if Ivory had said she couldn't help her pa, Jude knew that cajou included healing magic and she was already making plans to use this to ease some of his physical pain. Somehow, she had thought he might be pleased she was queen. It would mean a freedom from bills, respect from people and a mansion in the Fountain District – the chance of a better life. But he didn't see it that way. He didn't see it that way at all.

"You're the enemy now!" he hissed at her. "Worthless cajou scum!"

Jude had spent so much time worrying about her pa, missing him or trying to work out what else she might possibly do to help him. Now, though, she didn't feel any of that. She just felt furious right down to her bones.

"Do you have any IDEA what I've been through the last few days?" she shouted at him, her anger bursting its banks like a flooded dam. "I've been to hell and back! And it was all for you, you ungrateful bastard!"

"Don't you DARE blame me for your wickedness!" he roared straight back at her. "You're no daughter of mine. Get out of this goddamn house, and don't you ever come back!"

"YOU WON'T LAST A WEEK!" Jude screamed at him as loud as she could, revelling in the vicious horribleness of it all. After so long of trying to keep everything together, it was almost a relief to have it unravel around her. "You need me!"

"Get! Out!" He snatched up a mug and threw it at her. Jude ducked and it smashed harmlessly against the wall above her head.

With a great effort, Jude finally bit down on her tongue. She suddenly sensed that they would destroy each other if they could and she really didn't want that, despite all the things she was saying. She realized she should go before any further harm was done, so she turned and marched towards the door.

She grabbed the handle and hesitated. Even through her rage, some other part of her was aching to turn round and tell her pa that she loved him, that he was all she had left and that all of this had been for him. Only what was the point? It wouldn't change anything. It wouldn't make her into the daughter he wanted.

She was still hesitating when her pa snatched up a plate and threw this at her too. His aim was off and it hit the wall beside her but Jude could see he was in no mood for talking right now, and that no possible good could come of her staying. So she left, promising herself she would be back once they'd both had a chance to calm down. Surely he'd see reason eventually? Life would be better for both of them.

She knew she could go to the cajou queen's mansion in the Fountain District where she was now supposed to live. It had already been cleared out and made ready for her, and Charity had been taken away to an asylum, which seemed to be the only place for her now that Enid's key had broken her mind. Of Enid herself, there was no sign, though the police were still searching for her. But Jude didn't want to go to the mansion just yet so she made for Praline Street, where the Phantom's townhouse was.

As Moonfleet had been taken over by the cajou tree, Jude and the Phantom had stayed at the Majstro's townhouse on Cajou Night, collapsing into exhausted heaps on the beds almost as soon as they arrived.

But when Jude returned to the house after the disastrous meeting with her pa, she was hit by another blow.

"I'm leaving," the Phantom told her.

"This house?" Jude asked, trying to understand.

"No. Baton Noir."

"You can't," Jude said. She told him what had happened with her pa. "I need you," she said. "And we have to find some way of undoing the fright hex."

The Phantom shook his head and Jude realized that there were packed bags by the front door. He must have been out buying the things he needed while she was gone.

"I'm sorry," he said. "But I can't stay. It wouldn't be safe. For you or for anyone. My boat leaves in twenty minutes."

"I'll walk to the pier with you," Jude said quickly. That would give her a bit more time to think. To work out how to stop him from leaving.

A few minutes later they were on the sunny street outside, making their way towards Paradise Pier.

"What is it?" Jude asked again, falling into step beside the Phantom. "Your greatest fear? If you'd just tell me then perhaps we can find some way of avoiding it."

"There is no way of avoiding it," the Phantom replied.

"So you're not even going to try?" She felt suddenly furious. "You're really just going to go off and leave me?"

"You don't understand." He gazed at the sidewalk in front of him rather than at her. "I have to go."

They carried on walking in silence for a while and soon enough they reached the salt-stained planks of the pier. There was a paddle steamer moored nearby loading passengers and their luggage, and Jude guessed this was the one the Phantom meant to board as he stopped beside the gangplank.

"All those things you said outside the hospital," she said. "Did you mean any of them?"

He paused then said, "Every word."

"Then you won't leave me like this."

It was the wrong thing to say. The Phantom's reply came out hard and sharp. "You've seen what happens to those I love."

Unbidden, an image of Violetta flashed into Jude's mind – the anguished half girl, half tree spirit she had become. She shook her head impatiently.

"I don't know how to be a cajou queen," she tried. "I could use a friend in the city."

"You have friends," the Phantom replied. "That boy Sharkey sent a congratulations telegram from the hospital. It went to the mansion but someone brought it round here this morning. I almost forgot." He took it from his jacket and handed it to her, but Jude stuffed it straight in her dungarees pocket without looking at it. "Then there's the witch doctor you told me about, Sofia," the Phantom went on. "Besides, no one knows how to be a cajou queen to begin with. You just have to find your own way. Which I'm sure you will."

Jude caught hold of his wrist. Although his glove covered the mark, she could feel the *boom-boom* of the black heart beneath.

"That fright hex was meant for me," she said. "You should never have taken it for yourself like you did. I will *not* let you leave with it."

"You don't have a choice," the Phantom returned. "I don't regret taking the hex in the slightest. I would do it again in a moment." He looked out at the water. "It is the one purely good thing I have ever done."

"But … but where will you go?"

"I can't tell you."

Jude swore. She knew her emotions were in danger of getting away from her, like runaway horses, and she took a couple of deep breaths in an attempt to steady herself. She could feel a terrible sense of frustration tangling itself up into knots in the pit of her stomach. She wasn't saying the right words, wasn't communicating what she wanted to, wasn't even sure herself what it was she needed to say or how she was feeling.

"Please listen to me," she finally said. "It … it isn't just because I don't know how to be a cajou queen. I'm also … I'm trying to say that I care about you."

She felt the Phantom stiffen. "Do not be absurd," he said in a dismissive tone that made Jude bristle.

"Don't tell me how to feel," she shot back. "Look, I'm not saying I'm in love with you. How can I be? I don't really know you. And you don't really know me either. But … I like you. And … I think something in your soul calls out to something in mine. And I would like to have the chance to know you better."

"You've been through a lot," the Phantom said. "You're not thinking straight. You've seen my face. After that, how can you possibly want to… How can you even think of… We both know there can never be anything between us."

Jude flinched. She felt as if he'd struck her, and to her dismay she felt tears prickle the back of her eyes. "You don't know me at all if you honestly believe that."

"It is not a question of knowing you," he replied impatiently. Then, a little more quietly, "It is simply that no one ever chooses the monster."

The word hung in the air between them. It had been all over the headlines of the papers this morning – that ugly word printed over and over again alongside photos of the Phantom from last night.

"How dare you call yourself that?" Jude said. She thought of the food parcels, the music and the silver owl that had chased away Leeroy, and said, "All my life, you've been like an angel to me."

"I already told you," the Phantom returned. "There are no angels in Baton Noir. Only devils. Perhaps you can change that, in time. But Jude, I meant what I said before. I am tired. This isn't my fight any more. I'm done with this city."

The paddle steamer gave two loud blasts on its whistle, signalling that it was the last chance to board.

"I have to go. Goodbye, Jude. Good luck to you. I am glad I had the chance to—"

But that was as far as he got before Jude gripped him by the front of his shirt, pulled him towards her and without thinking or hesitating pressed her lips to his. He gasped and she thought he might push her away. But then his hand curled round to the small of her back, his lips responded to hers and he was kissing her back.

Electricity seemed to spark and tingle between them and Jude wasn't sure whether he was trembling or she was, but she could almost feel part of her soul, that part she had just spoken of, reaching out to the Phantom, yearning for him with a longing she couldn't really understand.

Finally the Phantom broke the kiss and pulled back, staggering slightly on the boards.

"I am leaving," he gasped. "I'm leaving right now."

It occurred to Jude that she could find some way on board the boat. That she could follow the Phantom in secret, not allow him to run away like this. But that would mean leaving her pa. She had to believe that he would forgive her eventually, and she wouldn't give up on finding a way to help him. And if she left with the Phantom then it would also mean leaving Baton Noir, which was something she couldn't do. The city was in her soul. It was the whole point of becoming cajou queen in the first place – to fix things. She had a year to reign before the next Cajou Night, a year to try to convince everyone that they should bring Ollin back into power next time. She couldn't give up everyone and everything she loved simply because her treacherous heart was making her feel some flickering start of something for the Phantom. She had to stay in Baton Noir and make things right.

André picked up his case. "There's just one final thing I must say to you," he said, turning back to her. "You were wrong. I *do* know you. I've watched you grow up from a small, scared, stubborn little girl into an extraordinary woman. I know who you truly are when you're all alone and think no one is watching. You will be a far greater cajou queen than this city deserves but … don't forget to carve out some corner of happiness for yourself along the way. And if another Leeroy ever slithers into your life I hope you will crush him like the cowardly, despicable, *worthless* piece of shit that he is." He reached out to lightly touch her arm. "Will you please do that for me, Jude?"

She took a deep breath and nodded. Over the last weeks and months, she had felt some new core of strength she had never known she possessed hardening inside her. And when the two cajou snakes rested on her shoulders she felt more alive, more herself and more able to face all the daily struggles of life than she ever had before. She knew she wouldn't fall into the trap of allowing anyone else to treat her the way Leeroy had – to get inside her soul and make her love them, only to unravel her sense of self in the cruellest way possible. It was good to feel strong for a change.

"I'll find you again one day, if I can," she said, looking up at the Phantom.

"You won't," he replied with a small smile, already turning away. "You'll never see me again."

He walked down the gangplank and there was nothing Jude could think to say or do to prevent him from leaving. He paused at the top and raised his hand in a wave, but Jude didn't even have time to wave back before he'd disappeared on to the boat.

And shortly after that it was gone.

It was an easy enough matter for Jude to find out that the paddle steamer was heading to a port town upriver, but this was used as a stopping point en route to countless other destinations. And even if she could leave the city, even if she did somehow track down the Phantom, she couldn't think what she could possibly be able to do to help him.

She made her way back to the cajou queen's mansion. As soon as she arrived she sent all the servants home before going straight to the library and collecting together all the books she could find that contained mention of fright hexes, determined to learn all she could without delay.

Not long after the sun went down there was a knock on her door and hope bloomed painfully inside her chest. In her mind she imagined answering the knock to find André on her doorstep. He would say that he had changed his mind. He would say that he had decided to stay after all.

But when she threw open the door, it wasn't the Phantom of Moonfleet Manor standing on the other side.

It was Etienne Malloy.

Jude recoiled, feeling once again the snap of breaking bone, the hot agony of skin tearing and blood running down her wrist, hearing the cries of the waiter as Etienne knocked his teeth out, seeing the teenage girl sprawled on the train tracks…

He must have worked out that it was she who had summoned the Thief and stolen his devil's coin. And now surely he had come here to punish her. Sensing her distress, both snakes immediately appeared on her shoulders, hissing aggressively as Jude staggered back from the door. "You can't come in!" she gasped. "I haven't invited you."

"I'm not here to hurt you," the vampire replied. "I swear it. Look."

He held up both hands and Jude saw the purple glow of a humanity charm dangling from the bracelet on his wrist. He looked different from the other times she had seen him. His shirt was crumpled, there were grey hollows beneath his eyes and his blond hair was messy rather than neatly brushed.

"I don't understand," Jude said slowly. "Why are you here?"

"I'm here because you need my help," Etienne said.

"*Your* help?" Jude stared at him. "What could I possibly need your help for?"

"Everyone knows that Ivory Monette cursed the Phantom with a fright hex last night and that he left Baton Noir earlier."

"So?"

"So André was my dearest friend once," Etienne replied. "I know the demon that's chasing him because I know what his greatest fear is. I also know where he's gone. If you want to help him, I'm the best chance you have."

Jude narrowed her eyes at him. "You attacked me," she said. "You broke my finger and—"

"Ah, yes. So I did." The vampire shrugged and offered

her a crooked smile. "Sorry about that. I've done far worse to others, if it makes you feel any better."

"It doesn't," Jude said shortly. "How can I trust you?"

The vampire slipped both hands into his pocket with a sigh. "I don't know," he said. "I guess you probably shouldn't. I haven't worn a humanity charm in a long time. I'm not sure I know who I am myself any more."

"Why did you put it back on?"

"For André," he said. His blue eyes turned suddenly cold. "What happened on Cajou Night... The way they treated him... Well, I suppose it woke something up inside me. Something André had been trying to wake up for a long time. Besides, I know what's coming for him if no one does anything." He shuddered. "He's a good man. Far better than I ever was, even before I became a vampire."

Jude thought of Ivory and how badly she'd been burned the last time she had decided to trust a member of the cajou Royalty. But she couldn't do this by herself and sometimes you had to take chances. Right now Etienne was the best, and only, chance she had of helping the Phantom.

"All right," she said slowly. "I'm not saying that I trust you, or that I like you. But you can come in."

The vampire grinned and to Jude's surprise a glint of warmth flashed in his eyes. It transformed his face, making him look quite different from the cold-faced man who'd beaten the waiter so mercilessly back at the Fang.

He stepped over the threshold into the hall, standing directly in front of Jude. This close she could see that there was a greyish tinge to his skin and he did not look at all well, but there was still a spark in his eyes as he said, "We haven't been properly introduced. Who are you, exactly?"

"My name is Jude Lomax."

"And what would you have me call you? Is it 'Your Highness', 'Majesty', 'Madge?'"

"Jude will do," she replied.

"Well, Jude," he said. "I'm Etienne Malloy. It's a pleasure to meet you."

He offered his hand and Jude took it reluctantly. "We've already met," she said.

The vampire's grip tightened slightly on her hand. "Actually, we haven't," he said. "That other man is … he isn't me. Not really."

"That's convenient," Jude said, withdrawing her hand. "When it comes to disowning any crimes he may have committed."

A muscle twitched in the vampire's jaw. "It is not as convenient as you might imagine," he replied, his voice a little cooler. "But we have bigger problems to talk about. No one's ever heard of a fright hex being successfully broken. You are aware of that, I suppose?"

"Yes, I know. I don't have any ideas about that yet either," Jude replied. Her hands clenched into fists and she felt the weight of the two snakes, heavy and reassuring on her shoulders as she gazed at the vampire. "But if there is a way, any way at all, to undo what's been done, then I intend to find it. So let's get started."

Alex Bell is the best-selling author of *Frozen Charlotte*, *Charlotte Says* and *The Haunting* in Stripes' YA horror series, RED EYE. Alex lives in Hampshire and also writes middle-grade fantasy books, including *The Polar Bear Explorers' Club*. Her favourite things include Siamese cats, Old Crow Medicine Show music, vegetarian tapas and visiting New Orleans.

www.alex-bell.co.uk
@Alex_Bell86